THE RECKONING

BEVERLY LEWIS
THE
RECKONING

BETHANY HOUSE PUBLISHERS
MINNEAPOLIS, MINNESOTA 55438

The Reckoning
Copyright © 1998
Beverly Lewis

Cover by Dan Thornberg

Published by Bethany House Publishers
A Ministry of Bethany Fellowship International
11400 Hampshire Avenue South
Minneapolis, Minnesota 55438
www.bethanyhouse.com

Printed in the United States of America by
Bethany Press International, Minneapolis, Minnesota 55438

ISBN 1-55661-868-9 (Trade Paper)
ISBN 0-7642-2475-1 (Mass Market)

DEDICATION

❖ ❖ ❖

To Sandi Heisler,
childhood friend and confidante . . .
ever dear to me.

By Beverly Lewis

THE HERITAGE OF LANCASTER COUNTY

The Shunning
The Confession
The Reckoning

❖ ❖ ❖

ABRAM'S DAUGHTERS

The Covenant

❖ ❖ ❖

The Postcard
The Crossroad

❖ ❖ ❖

October Song
The Redemption of Sarah Cain
Sanctuary*
The Sunroom

www.BeverlyLewis.com

*with David Lewis

ABOUT THE AUTHOR

❖　　❖　　❖

BEVERLY LEWIS is a former schoolteacher and the author of over fifty books. She is a member of The National League of American Pen Women—the Pikes Peak branch—and the Society of Children's Book Writers and Illustrators. Her books are among the C. S. Lewis Noteworthy List Books. Bev and her husband have three teenagers and make their home in Colorado.

The truth shall make you free.

—John 8:32

The Lord will bless his people with peace.

—Psalm 29:11

PROLOGUE:
THE MISTRESS OF MAYFIELD MANOR

❖ ❖ ❖

Years ago, as a young Amish girl, I decided that I would age *very* gradually. Cheerfully, too. I'd become the kind of old grandmother who finds contentment in sowing simple, straight rows in her vegetable garden, whispering proverbs to her rutabagas.

After the untimely death of my first and only love, I feared I would grow old thinking only of Daniel Fisher. I would hoe my garden, weed my tomato plants, all the while missing Dan and wishing he'd never drowned on his nineteenth birthday.

Ach, I'm still a young woman, only twenty-two. My adult years stretch out before me. Yet I find myself thinking back to carefree childhood days in Hickory Hollow—giving my Plain past the once-over, so to speak. At the same time, I know that I am a shunned woman, an outcast from the People, my adoptive parents and brothers—excommunicated from those who loved and raised me. A sobering thought, true, but I have come to terms with what has been done to me and the necessity of *die Meinding*, at least from the Amish viewpoint. The pain of rejection gnaws at me

11

each and every day. Yet in contrast, I cherish the memories of my birth mother's words of love—*for me!*—spoken as she lay dying.

"I wish I had kept you for my own."

Revealing and bold, Laura's loving expression has begun to mend my broken heart. Daily I continue my search for her journal, the one she wrote before I was born.

I've begun to nestle down for the winter in my sumptuous new setting in Canandaigua, New York, truly celebrating the remarkable turn my life has taken. How very surprising it is, for often through my growing-up years, I had fantasized about the ways of *Englischers*—non-Amish folk— secretly wishing I could taste just a sip of what I might be missing. And here I am: *Mistress of Mayfield Manor.*

A right dignified name, I suppose, yet the implications of such a title have me all but befuddled at times. The sprawling estate, every square inch of the rolling grounds and magnificent old-English mansion—one hundred percent—belongs to Laura Mayfield-Bennett's flesh-and-blood daughter.

And all this has come about because of an unexpected encounter with Dylan Bennett and his smooth-talking attorney. In just a single meeting with Mr. Cranston—Laura's own attorney—the idea that any part of the estate might rightfully belong to Mr. Bennett proved indeed to be laughable. Not only could he not gain Laura's wealth through deceptive means, but he might well have lost his own resources in an ensuing court battle had he continued to contest Laura's revised last will and testament.

No, the *Schwindler* left the state and his business affairs behind, including papers found in his personal effects proving that he'd employed and encouraged an impostor, a false daughter for Laura.

So the scoundrel is gone, and Katie Lapp—the former me—has also departed. No more holding fast to the rigid rules, the restrictive dress code, the do's and don'ts of my past.

Still, if there is anything I might've done differently, it would've been to soften the blow somehow for Rebecca, my adoptive Amish mamma. I cannot stop thinking of her, missing her, wondering what Cousin Lydia *really* meant when she said "Rebecca's not herself" last time we spoke. Surely my leaving wasn't the only cause for Mamma's pain. The shunning decree—Bishop John's bitter pronouncement—had to have been the more grievous.

I have thought of writing her a long letter, telling her that I am safe; that little by little I am growing accustomed to the strange, modern world around me. And that I am, for the most part, happy. I fear, though, such an honest letter might stir up false hope of my return, and I would never want to put such a notion in her head. Not for the world. So when all is said and done, it's best for me to keep still, hoping that Rebecca and all the others will simply forget me. Though I am not so sure the People *can* forget.

For sure and for certain, they'll remember me as having been romantically linked to Dan Fisher. Our names will be eternally sealed in the cement of history, in the chronicles of the Amish community I once called home. The People— Bishop John, too—will long remember the stubborn auburn-haired woman they so cruelly shunned and the young man with blueberry eyes who loved her. So . . . both Dan and Katie are lost to the Old Ways. One to death, the other to life.

Truth be told, had it not been for my artist friend, Justin Wirth, and my renewed hope of marriage, I might've gone ahead and lived out my morbid plan of growing old. Old, without the pleasant laughter of grandchildren. Forever puzzling over long-ago memory pieces, wondering what might have been. . . .

CHAPTER ONE

❖   ❖   ❖

Daniel Fisher was roused from slumber by the song of morning birds. Sitting up, he imagined himself awakening in his own bed.

Upon further investigation, he realized that this room was not the upstairs bedroom of his New Jersey bungalow. Rather, it was a well-appointed suite of rooms in a Canandaigua bed-and-breakfast establishment.

He stretched and yawned, shaking himself back from his dream, a dream as vibrant as any real day. In it he had seen Katie, his sweetheart girl, gathering daisies in a wide green meadow. She wore a blue Amish dress without the apron and no devotional covering on her head. Her auburn hair fell in waves, long and lovely, over her slender shoulders.

The sun stood high in the treetops, its intense rays blinding him, momentarily blocking his vision. When the light parted, he saw her look his way, smiling slightly. Then, unheeding, she turned and skipped barefoot away into a thin gray mist.

"Katie, wait . . . *wait!*" He called to her again and again.

Dan groaned, recalling the summerlike dream. Such visions had taunted him on many a night, but this portrayal of a young, seemingly reckless Katie gripped him anew.

His eyes fell on his Bible, near him on the bedside table. Reaching for it, he eased himself off the bed, sitting on the edge as he shuffled through its pages till he found the letter to Katie—one she would never receive. A confession from his heart to hers, it was a way to spur himself on to do what he must do this very day.

My dearest Katie,

I'm writing this to you in a bed-and-breakfast here in Canandaigua. I know from the map I purchased days ago that the mansion you now live in is only a few short miles from where I sit tonight. Lately, it seems that I am likely to lose my focus on the important things if I do not put my thoughts down on paper. And though I do not expect that we will ever really be able to talk the way we used to, I'm hoping that my visit with you might turn out to be a positive, good thing for us both.

Just last week, I went to Hickory Hollow to visit with my parents—the first time in over five years. I met with my sister, too. It was from Annie that I first heard of your shunning and your subsequent leaving. There was pain in her eyes as she spoke of your yearning to find the mother who gave you birth.

If only God will allow me to see you for even a few moments and you would hear me out. Believe me when I say that I let you down, dear Katie, that I should have done something to right this wrong between us a long time ago. All these years, trying to fit in with the English world around me, I longed to know if you were all right—if you were safely settled in the Amish church—yet constantly wished for a gentle, perhaps divine, way to say that I loved you in spite of my "death." And I always prayed that you might find the truth of God's grace through His Son, Jesus Christ.

Nothing matters now but meeting you face-to-face, hoping you will not be too startled at my return from the "grave."

Please forgive me for not making things known to you sooner. For running away from my religious disputes with my father and the People. For letting you think I'd drowned on that boat so many years ago. Please . . .

Sighing, he held the letter in his hands, glancing over at a pastoral scene in a gilded antique frame across the room. "You may never believe that what I did, I did for us," he whispered. "For our love . . ."

He slipped the handwritten letter back into the leather Bible, closing it thoughtfully. *The matter is in God's hands*, he decided and stood to walk the few steps to the washbasin, leaning hard against its porcelain surface.

Staring into the mirror over the sink, he ran his fingers through a scraggly beard. Though in no way a vain man, he turned sideways, surveying his profile. Which should it be—with the beard or without?

He opened his shaving kit and pulled out his electric razor and a small pair of scissors he kept there. Leaning closer to the mirror, he picked up the scissors and thoughtfully opened and closed the blades a few times while he studied his face. The absence of a beard would clearly indicate his singleness—in the eyes of the Amish community, at least. Yet he'd come to realize that facial hair tended to make him look older—even, perhaps, wiser. *Believable* was the thought that came to mind as he stood there, scissors ready.

How will *Katie react to seeing me alive?* he wondered. He tried but couldn't begin to imagine the personal impact his appearance on her doorstep might make. She would be shocked, at best.

Never mind the beard, would she be happy to see him after so long a time, after thinking he was dead and gone? More than that, would she understand? Would she forgive him upon hearing his story—the truth, at last?

He vacillated between trimming the beard and shaving the whole thing completely off. In the end it remained, neatly clipped and quite bold, marking the outline of his jaw. He dressed in his finest clothes: a dark business suit and his favorite maroon-and-blue striped tie. Stomach rumbling, he proceeded out the door and down carpeted steps to enjoy breakfast with the other B&B guests.

"A good Saturday morning to you, Mr. Fisher," the lady of the house greeted him. "How do you take your coffee?"

"Black, thank you."

She led him through a sitting room where tufted antique chairs and cherrywood lamp tables were scattered about on a large area rug. An inviting fire crackled in the fireplace, warming the room and the intimate breakfast nook just beyond.

Through the expanse of windows, he glimpsed patches of a January sky, sapphire and bright off to the southeast, with brooding clouds gathering in the north. Wide-trunked beech trees stood ancient and stark against the snow-covered terrain. A shaft of sunlight teased the tip of a squirrel's tail as it scampered across the yard.

"Looks like we're in for an afternoon storm," said one of the guests, a stout, bejeweled woman, as Daniel took his seat at the table.

Her husband craned his neck to peer out the window. "Certainly does."

The guests introduced themselves all around, a total of six seated at the round, candlelit table. Daniel was politely curious and inquired about their homes and destinations. Two women—mother and teenaged daughter—had come up from Jersey for the weekend; another guest hailed from Kansas; and the only married couple present was from Florida, on their way up the coast to Maine on vacation.

Daniel spent most of his breakfast time chatting with the mother and daughter who were seated next to him. They were in town visiting an elderly uncle who lived in a nursing home a few blocks away.

"Nursing home? There are some folks who don't ever need such places for their elderly." The comment slipped out before he realized what he'd said.

The girl, about fifteen, looked startled. "Are you talking about Amish people?"

He did not wish to reveal his ties to the Plain community but felt the need to explain. "*Both* the Amish and Mennonites often look after their aging relatives."

She studied him curiously. "You seem, uh . . . you must be . . . Plain yourself."

So the girl had guessed it, in spite of his tailored suit and colorful tie. Perhaps it was because of the lingering Pennsylvania Dutch accent, beard, and the absence of a mustache. "Well, not anymore," he replied.

She seemed rather excited about this admission. "Is it true that the Amish never buy medical insurance?"

"We . . . uh, *they* don't need insurance. Their people grow old at home, surrounded by the extended family." He explained how it was commonplace for families to build on additions to their houses, making space for aging parents and grandparents.

"One *big* happy family?" She laughed good-naturedly.

"You could say that."

Her mother spoke up. "Did you ever ride in a horse-drawn buggy?"

He chuckled. "Always."

"Why not cars?" asked the man from Kansas.

"We could ride in them, just as long as someone else did the driving—someone English."

"English?" the girl's mother said.

"Amish refer to outsiders that way. You're either Amish or English."

A frown appeared on the girl's face. "What's so terrible about owning a car?"

He sighed, remembering the *Ordnung* and its grip on his former life. "Cars offer too much freedom . . . makes it too easy to abandon one's important family life."

The topic drew the rest of the folk like a magnet. "What was it *really* like growing up without cars or electricity?" asked one.

Dan was taken aback by their eagerness, their curiosity, having nearly forgotten the many years of answering similar questions from tourists who flocked to Pennsylvania, their cameras poised for sneak shots of the "horse-and-buggy people."

"Well, my *Dat* used to say 'Yer never gonna miss whatcha never had,' so I guess that's how it was."

They chuckled at the dialect. "Do you speak Dutch?" the teenager asked.

"*Jah*, but not so much anymore. That part of my life is all but over for me now." He paused, reaching for his napkin and wiping his mouth. "I've come to know a better way. Some of the People back home tend to disagree with me, though I know a good many Plain folk who've experienced God's gift of salvation through grace, same as I have."

The girl's eyes lit up with recognition. "Mom and I are Christians, too." She turned to nod at her mother.

Dan smiled, continuing the conversation and enjoying the opportunity to share and witness at the same table. Later, when asked again about his childhood, he replied, "Unless you've grown up Amish, it's hard to explain. The life, in general, is quite simple, yet mighty hard all the same, and there's often a price to be paid."

The girl was about to speak, but the man from Kansas said, "We have Amish and Mennonite settlements scattered in different parts of our state. What's confusing to me is the way they dress—they all look a little bit different."

Dan agreed. "Like Heinz—fifty-seven varieties, right?" That got them laughing, though he hadn't intended to poke fun.

"What about shunning?" the girl asked. "Do Amish actually kick their people out of church for disobeying rules?"

Dan felt a twinge. Though he hadn't actually suffered the sting of excommunication directly, he figured Bishop John Beiler and the Hickory Hollow membership had most likely started his initial six weeks of shunning probation. "Some groups still ban unrepentant members, but there are large church districts in Ohio, for instance, that have split away from the stricter groups, because they couldn't see eye to eye on shunning practices."

She shook her head. "A heartless thing, seems to me."

"Cruel, in many cases, but its legitimate origins are found in the New Testament, nevertheless." He paused, choosing his words carefully. "I'd have to say, though, that too often folks are shunned for mighty petty transgressions." At their urging he mentioned one instance: a man's hat brim—just one quarter inch too wide. " 'Worldly,' the bishop called it. And because the fellow was too stubborn to confess and buy another hat, he was cast out of the church and the community, severely shunned." That brought a few muffled snickers and even more ardent discussion. Dan, however, was especially grateful that no one pressed him for answers as to why he'd left Hickory Hollow.

Moments later the hostess came in to clear the table, an unspoken cue for her guests to wind things up. Dan observed the hasty brushing off of crumbs and the removal of water glasses and took the hint.

"Very nice chatting with you," he said to the group.

The girl followed her mother out of the room but stopped to say, "Have a nice day!"

"Thank you, and God bless you, young lady."

A nice day, indeed! Come rain or come shine, he was off to see his Katie girl!

He headed upstairs to wash his face and brush his teeth once again. Eager for the day, this first encounter after years of separation, he knelt at the desk chair and prayed for divine guidance. "Assist me, Father, as I speak the words of truth . . . surprising as they will sound to Katie's tender ears. I pray that she may receive me with an understanding heart, that I might be a witness of your saving grace and love." He hesitated for a moment. "And if it be your will, I ask that in due time, I may woo her back to the love we once knew. In Christ's name. Amen."

He left by way of the front walk, glancing upward through bare tree branches. The sky had grown dark, now an ominous charcoal gray. The air was brittle and cold, sharp against the throat. He was glad for his fur-trimmed overcoat and leather gloves as he walked briskly to his rental car, city map in hand.

❖ ❖ ❖

Katherine scoured each of the closets on the main level of the mansion, looking for her mother's journal. One after another, she discovered well-organized linen closets—tidy stacks of velvety monogrammed towels, satin bed sheets, and plush blankets—and now *this* closet not far from her own suite of rooms.

She removed folded sheets from the bottom, then moved on to the next shelf, inspecting each piece of linen, including doilies and crocheted dresser runners on the middle shelf and the one above, stacked clear to the ceiling. There were numerous seasonal items—damask tablecloths and napkins in every hue imaginable, matching napkin rings, and floral table accessories.

When she had completed her rummaging, Katherine

closed the door and headed upstairs to the spacious sunroom. Her ailing birth mother had spent many hours soaking up warm, healing rays in this room, praying for a reprieve from her pain.

With a sigh, she settled on the chaise lounge nearest the south exposure. *Where did Laura keep her diary?* she wondered. *Where?*

Katherine thought of Lydia Miller, her Mennonite relative, who—right this instant—would doubtless be encouraging her to seek divine assistance in this frustrating matter; that is, if Lydia lived close enough to be aware of the problem. The woman prayed about everything, no matter how incidental.

In like fashion, Laura Mayfield had often prayed, beseeching the Lord in conversational tones. Rosie Taylor— her birth mother's longtime personal maid and now Katherine's—had recounted the prayers she and Laura had shared during the weeks before Laura's passing.

"Your dear mother prayed in earnest for you," Rosie told her one evening as they sat by the fire in the library.

"That I'd be found?"

"Indeed, yes. She prayed faithfully that you would come to her before the MS made her mind hazy or confused. With all of her heart, she wanted to get to know you before she died. But in spite of her pain, in spite of her longing to see her daughter again, she was deeply grateful for life. Each new day was another opportunity to rejoice in her Savior."

Her Savior. Rosie had mentioned the name with such reverence and joy. It was obvious to Katherine that the devoted housemaid and her husband—Fulton, the butler— had found salvation, same as Laura.

So Katherine had been surrounded by prayer. "All these years," she whispered, leaning back with her head against the soft chaise pillow. She wondered if it had been Laura's prayers that ultimately had brought her here to Mayfield

Manor. If so, what of Rebecca Lapp's? Surely *she*, too, was pleading with the Lord God heavenly Father for her adopted daughter's return. How, then, could *both* women's requests be heard and answered?

She didn't rightly know but pondered the question. Her eyes took in the lush green ferns and other plants in matching terra-cotta pottery, and she tried to relax in the luxurious room, far removed from the hustle and bustle of modern-day life. It provided all the conveniences she'd always longed for.

Suddenly thirsty, she noticed the pitcher of ice water and several clean glasses facedown on a tray next to her. Pouring herself a glassful of water, she began to hum softly. The song was one of the many she had made up over the years. Forbidden, according to the Ordnung of the People.

Crossing her legs in front of her on the chaise, she sang her song, taking occasional sips. Something about the clear, cool taste of the water or the way the ice cubes clinked against the sides brought to mind an Ascension Day picnic she had attended with her parents and brothers when she was only eight years old. . . .

It was at Uncle Moses Lapp's farmhouse situated on a broad bend of Weaver's Creek, several miles from Hickory Hollow, that the sun beat down hard on little Katie's back as she stood on the front porch step, gulping down a tall glass of ice-cold lemonade.

"You'll have yourself a headache if ya drink too fast," Mamma called from the shadows, rocking and fanning herself to beat the band.

"Ach, Mamma, it's so awful hot," she complained, holding out her glass. "Please, mayn't I have more?"

Mam obliged cheerfully, getting up and going inside to bring out the entire pitcher. "Here's just for my little girl." She poured the sweetened lemonade into Katie's glass.

"Ach, young Katie's spoilt, I'd say," whispered *Mammi* Essie. "Ain't so?"

The other women—her mamma's married sisters, Nancy Yoder and Naomi Zook; feisty Cousin Mattie Beiler, the midwife; and three aunts, including Ella Mae, the Wise Woman—*all* of them, just kept a-rockin' and a-fannin', the strings from their prayer veils floating forward and back, forward and back. Katie couldn't rightly tell if the womenfolk were agreeing with her mamma's mother or trying to ignore Essie, the way they were known to on occasion.

Never mind them, she decided and poured herself a third glass and guzzled it right down in front of them. Satisfied, she went to sit *under* the porch in a sort of nesting spot where the shade was cool and damp, the breeze sweet, *and* the listening-in right fine. Happy to have chosen this private place away from the critical eye of Mammi Essie, she folded her long dress tightly around her legs so no *es Mickevieh*—pest of flies—might go a-soaring up her skirt. She sighed, pushing stray wisps of hair back into the braids that wound around her sweaty head.

She stared out across the yard and over to the barn. On past the newly plowed corn and potato fields to the ridge of trees in the distance. The landscape was as familiar to her as the seams that ran up and down the inside of her long dress and apron. This land was her home, her world.

Above her, the gossips and storytellers of the homeland took turns talking in their native tongue. The rolling *thump-a-thump* of hickory rockers overhead lulled her for a time, and she was comforted by the sounds of the familiar.

Leaning back on her hands, the dirt dug into her palms, making prickly indentations. Uncaring, she whispered to herself, feeling terribly pleased about it, "I'm spoilt because Mamma loves me."

At that moment, nothing else much mattered.

Katherine stretched her arms up behind her head as she lay on the chaise, wondering what *Grossmutter* Essie would think of her now. Would she say Rebecca's spoiled daughter was much too pampered, living like a princess in a New York mansion far from home? What would she think of the gourmet cooks and sumptuous meals, the staff of servants . . . the housemaids? And the rayon trousers, silk blouses, and angora sweaters Katherine now loved to wear?

She took another long drink from her glass. What Essie King, or anybody else, might think about her now was irrelevant. This was the fancy sort of English life she'd longed for as long as she could remember.

The sun had disappeared, devoured by a slate gray bank of clouds that seemed to spread its vastness from the horizon directly toward her. She felt the cold of the glass begin to seep into her, making her feel chilly, and without a second thought, she got up and turned on the space heater fixed in the wall. Returning to the chaise, she felt gleeful at having flicked a switch, producing warmth at will.

Music filtered through the intercom on the far wall, and she silently congratulated herself on recognizing the composer—Johann Sebastian Bach—who, had he been Amish, would have fit right in, what with the twenty children he helped produce. But then again, the prolific side of Bach's *musical* creativity would have posed a problem for the People. A source of contention, they might have decided.

Thinking on this, she tried to hum along a passage here and there, not in defiance of her past—no need—but merely enjoying the moment.

When she was fully rested, she got up, turned off the wall heater and headed downstairs to her private quarters. There she began to play her guitar, thinking of Mary Stoltzfus.

Mary.

Such a beautiful, perfect name for a woman. One who

had always tried to do the right thing before God. To think that Mary had secretly written her a note back before Christmas was right surprising, to say the least. Yet Katherine couldn't blame her friend for doing such a disobedient thing. Cords of sisterly love were mighty strong between the two.

Had it not been for the fact that Katherine was adopted, the intermarrying and crisscrossed bloodlines deep in the Hollow might've made them cousins, if not a mite closer.

What are you doing today, Mary? wondered Katherine. *Do you have any idea just how much I miss you?*

CHAPTER TWO

❖   ❖   ❖

What if somethin' could be done to lift the Ban off Katie just a bit?" Mary Stoltzfus asked her mother. "It's much too harsh, seems to me, not bein' able to communicate with her and all." She didn't mention anything about not being able to write letters to her friend, of course. Still, she would've liked to be able to do so, without going behind the bishop's back about it, the way she'd up and done once already.

Her mother turned from the woodstove, where she was steaming carrots. "If we ease up on Katie Lapp, where will that put Daniel Fisher?"

"Jah, 'tis a knotty problem, I 'spect." Mary thought of her best friend; missed her more than words could tell. Yet she was anxious, today more than any other, to hear Mam's feeling on the matter. Mostly because she was supposed to spend the afternoon with Katie's former *Beau*—the man her wayward girlfriend had stood up on their wedding day back in November.

John Beiler had invited Mary to accompany him on a ride into town. Just where they were headed, she did not know. But, to her thinking, it wasn't so much the place the horse and carriage would be taking them as the fact that they were going *anywhere* together that was a godsend.

"Daniel's gonna be under the Ban in a bit . . . soon as the six-week probation's up," Rachel was saying. "Unless he hightails it back here and offers a kneeling confession. Not so likely, I 'spect, what with him having five years to think on his sinful ways."

"Prob'ly so."

"No prob'lys about it," retorted her mother. "Word has it, that boy's as rebellious as ever. Believin' he's saved and all. Why, it'sa out-n'-out manifestation of pride . . . nothin' less."

Mary sighed. "Dan's not a boy anymore, Mamma. He's a grown man with ideas and opinions. Can't go blamin' him for wanting to follow his heart." She'd almost said his *Bible* but knew that sort of talk would get her in more than just hot water. No, for a girl who'd grown up with a consuming desire to do the right thing, this was a startling notion. She would voice it to no one. Not to Mamma, and never to the bishop.

Bishop John Beiler was the divine answer to her prayers, widower or no. She had more sense than to risk losing her chance to be courted and married, not with her twenty-first birthday fast approaching. Besides, she'd fallen in love with John's ruddy-faced grin, his twinkling gray-blue eyes, and all five of his children. Even Levi, that eight-year-old rascal of a boy.

Thing was, she was worried sick what Katie might think if she ever got wind of Bishop John's growing interest in her. Would she just assume that Mary thought the widower was fair game, having been spurned as he was?

Mary shuddered to think what it might do to their friendship if Katie ever did return to Hickory Hollow to make amends. *What then?* she wondered. Surely, Katie— who had adamantly insisted on being called Katherine Mayfield before she ran off in search of her *real* mother—surely she'd overlook her best friend's relationship with John

Beiler. If she understood anything about forgiveness and love, she would.

Besides, now that Dan Fisher was out searching for Katie, who knew what still might happen between the two? Mary brushed away the romantic notion with a sigh. Ach, what she would give to be a little mouse in the same room as the unfortunate lovers, when and *if* they found each other again.

Mary went about setting the table, even though the men wouldn't be coming in for lunch just yet. Dat and her married brothers had gone over to the Gordonville Print Shop to see about picking up some curriculum for the Amish school. They'd planned to return around noon—another *gut* hour or so away.

"Do ya think I oughta bring it up with Bishop John?" Mary ventured.

"About Katie's Meinding?" Rachel looked up from the stove, a curious expression on her face. "*Puh*, ya must be jokin', daughter. Besides, it would do no good spoilin' your chances—"

"Mamma, please . . ." Mary felt her pulse race. The afternoon's buggy ride was a secret and must be kept so. John Beiler had promised to pull his carriage off to the side of the road and wait for her.

Just past the wooden bridge, near the clump of fir trees, he'd told her two days ago when she'd bumped into him quite by accident at Preacher Yoder's General Store.

Her mother went back to stirring the carrots. "Don'tcha worry none. I won't breathe a word. Wouldn't do any gut for somethin' to leak out 'bout you and the bishop."

Mary agreed, and her face grew warm with the romantic thoughts tumbling through her head.

❖ ❖ ❖

Rebecca Lapp was so weak in the legs, she wished off and on all morning that she were a fattened sow left to lie in the sun, wallowing in the muddy grief of her life. But she headed down to the cold cellar beneath the house, where hundreds of quarts of vegetables and other foodstuffs were stored for the winter.

Standing there in the dark, damp place, she momentarily forgot what vegetable she'd had in mind for the noon meal. "Oh, what'sa matter with me?" she mumbled, fighting back tears. "Will I never stop thinking of my Katie?"

Locating her flashlight in the pantry cupboard, Rebecca allowed her eyes to roam over the cellar, coming to rest on the handcrafted pine cupboard in the corner—a constant reminder of the weeks before Katie's shunning and the ultimate hiding place for the satin baby gown.

Ach, how she longed for the soft, perty thing. Missed it so. If she could just hold it next to her heart again. Hold her daughter, too. If she could only be near the girl, her precious Katie . . .

How long had it been since she'd heard the forbidden guitar music creeping through the walls of the *Dawdi Haus* next door? How long since she'd kissed Katie's tear-streaked face?

Shivering, she turned back to the task at hand and chose some green beans and corn from the orderly pantry shelves. Samuel, Eli, and Benjamin would be mighty hungry, wondering why a hot, hearty meal wasn't awaiting them, hardworking men that they were.

She turned and trudged upstairs, one foot in front of the other, till at last she stood at the top, winded and tired. Leaning against the door momentarily, she sighed and caught her breath a bit before letting herself into the warm, savory kitchen. Oh, she wished for a day when she might search out and find the entrance to a place of wholeness in her mind. How far off was such a day? How long before she'd start adjusting to life without her little girl?

Sadly, she pried open the canning lids and dumped *both* the corn and the beans into a large pot, completely by accident, before realizing what she'd done.

❖   ❖   ❖

Ella Mae Zook sat at her daughter Mattie's kitchen table, surrounded by quilting squares stacked in groups of nine. She was making ready to teach Sally Beiler, one of her younger great-granddaughters, the arrangement of a "Ninepatch"—the simplest quilting pattern. "You'll catch on in no time," she promised. "Watch me once."

The girl paid close attention, and when it was her turn to try, the Wise Woman jumbled up all the squares again, handing them over to Sally. Carefully, the youngster positioned the fabric on the long wooden table so that one dark square lay next to a lighter square, in the familiar tic-tac-toe pattern.

Across the room, Mattie stood at the cookstove, seasoning a pot of creamed potato soup. Every few minutes, she came over to check on Sally's progress.

Without ever glancing up, Sally asked, "It wonders me . . . when do ya think Bishop John and Mary Stoltzfus'll end up tying the knot?"

Ella Mae harrumphed, feeling the need to set the conversation on course. "No need to be speculatin' on such things. If it's God's will, they'll get together in all good time. Won't matter just when, I should say."

"*If* they do," Mattie added. "You know the poor man is probably still heartsick over Katie Lapp, what with the way she jilted him . . . on their wedding day, no less. Why, if it was me, I'd be laying low on the subject of marriage, I 'spect."

"Well, it ain't you, so just let it be," Ella Mae advised.

"The man needs a good mother for his children, and he's smart enough to make up his own mind. Mary, well . . . bless her heart, John Beiler's the man of her dreams."

"Ach, ya mean it?" Sally spoke up, blushing slightly. "You think she's been dreaming 'bout the bishop?"

Mattie shook her head, muttering as she walked back to the simmering potato soup. But Ella Mae kept on, attempting to smooth things over, without divulging any secrets. "You know, sometimes it just seems that one person fits right fine with another. Belongin' is what it's all about, I do believe."

Right then, the old woman thought of Daniel, wondering how the dear boy was doing. He'd come to visit here lately, knocked hard on the door of her side of the house— come straight back from the dead—inquiring as to Katie's whereabouts. Ella Mae had filled him in as best she could. 'Course, she didn't have much hope of his ever finding the shunned girl, not as awful crowded as New York was. But true love sometimes wins out over great odds, she thought. Lord willin', that would be the case.

Sally silently worked at her grid of nine patches while Ella Mae observed, still struggling with unsettled feelings over the whole notion of Daniel's being alive and all. Where had he been all that time? And how was it that Bishop John had up and slapped the Ban on him, almost the minute the People found out Daniel had not drowned in that sailing mishap years ago?

Oh, and they'd faulted him for "finding salvation, full and free," Dan had told her as he sat sipping tea in her little kitchen. A body could see he was telling the truth, too. His face purely shown with a radiance, and when he asked to see her Bible, she gave it to him gladly, listening with eagerness as he read one verse after another.

One passage stirred her very soul. "He that believeth on the Son of God hath the witness in himself . . . and this is

the record, that God hath given to us eternal life, and this
life is in his Son."

The promise of salvation right there in the Scriptures! It
was ever so clear. Daniel *knew* he was saved.

By the time he'd said his good-byes, she was altogether
convinced that Dan was telling the truth about his finding
eternal life in Jesus Christ. *Himmel!* The more she thought
about this Meinding business, the less it made any sense.

❖   ❖   ❖

Daniel parked the rental car out some distance from the
entrance to the Mayfield mansion. The circular drive was
configured in such a way as to allow for several parking spots
along the side before the grand bend led up to the paved
walkway, now dusted with a layer of snow.

Refolding the map, he placed it on the seat next to him
and stared through the windshield at the fine English-style
country estate. To think that his Katie had come *here* to find
her birth mother! What a grand and beautiful place it was.
The startling information was still in the process of seeping
through to his brain, thanks to his sister Annie and beloved
old Ella Mae. It gave him no insight, however, into the girl
he'd once known and loved. Her parents were and always
would be Samuel and Rebecca Lapp, the kind and generous
folk who'd raised Katie as their own. What could have happened to make their adopted daughter want to abandon
them and go on such a search?

The answers, he knew, were bound up inside the ram-
bling, vine-covered dwelling. Inside Katie's heart, as well. If
only he might unlock those secret rooms and find his sweetheart girl waiting there.

Yet the Wise Woman had warned him, "She's not the
girl you grew up with. Katie's suffered great pain; is more
headstrong than I've ever seen her. If you find her, best go

gentle on her . . . let her take her time tellin' you her side of things."

Oh, he'd gladly give Katie all the time in the world. Beginning right now.

Prayerfully, he opened the car door and walked the long drive. Up past lantern-shaped lights that lined the walkway on either side, to the portal. "Dear God in heaven, help me. Help *Katie* and me," he whispered, running his fingers through his beard, still wondering if he'd made the right decision by keeping it intact.

Without further delay, he reached for the brass door knocker.

CHAPTER THREE

❖   ❖   ❖

Katherine sat with her back to the blazing fire. She had spent the morning playing her guitar and singing freely, allowing her voice to fill the sitting room, one of the several comfortable places to relax in her private suite. She had kept the arrangement of furnishings the same as when Laura was alive: overstuffed chairs and a cherry sofa table placed so as to accentuate the Tibetan area rug, a favorite of her birth mother.

Flitting from one song to another, Katherine let her mind roam back to Pennsylvania, settling on the letter Mary had written in mid-December. She had read it so many times now, she had it nearly memorized.

It's all I can do to keep myself from sneaking off down the lane for a visit. . . .

She knew just what her friend must've been feeling as Mary penned those words. They *both* had missed out on friendship by losing touch with each other.

Katherine curled her toes inside her house shoes, despising the bishop—that wretched man who might've become her husband if she hadn't had the gumption to walk out on their wedding service. She stopped singing, stopped strumming her guitar. John Beiler had cut her off from her

37

loved ones, *her* People. A typical shunning was one thing, but declaring that none of them could speak to her or she to them! The memory stung like a hundred angry wasps.

Getting up, she strolled to the windows, still carrying her guitar as she looked out at the snow-covered lawn and formal gardens. Hundreds of barren trees—beech, fir, and maple—stood at graceful attention over the rolling acres as far as the eye could see.

A light snow had begun to fall. The enormous flakes seemed to suspend themselves momentarily, high in the air, as if holding their breath before consenting to drift to earth. The overcast sky and the mood of the day reminded her of midwinter days in the Hollow, when snow-encrusted country roads were sliced deep by narrow carriage wheels and trampled over by one trotting horse after another.

Then and there, she decided to make contact with Mary. She wouldn't put her friend in jeopardy by writing the letter herself. No, she had a better idea. Rosie, her trusted maid, might be the ideal person to take dictation.

Katherine turned slightly, ready to put her guitar away and call for Rosie Taylor with her plan, when her eyes fell on a bright blue sedan parked off to the side of the circular driveway. Looking more closely, she noticed a single set of footprints, their indentation breaking through to the pavement beneath.

It was then she heard the muffled sound of the door knocker, followed by Fulton's hurried steps. She knelt to place the guitar in its case, a flicker of a memory surfacing as she did. Tired of his share of run-ins with his father, Dan had insisted on giving the beloved instrument to her years ago. "Will you hide it for me?" he'd asked, smiling down on her that sunshiny day.

How could she have refused? " 'Course I will."

"You'll take good care of it, won't you, Katie girl?"

And care for it, she did. Marched right off to the barn

and hid it away from eyes that would misunderstand her need—*their need*—to create the prohibited music.

She might've lingered, taking pleasure in the endearing scene from years gone by, had it not been for the sound of her loyal butler, his voice rising to an ever higher pitch. Goodness' sake, the man sounded ruffled. Who on earth could be at the door?

She went to the window but saw nothing out of the ordinary. *Must be a traveling salesman*, she assumed, seeing only the back of a man's overcoat. *Fulton will get rid of him.*

How secluded and safe she felt. Sighing, she wondered what it might've been like having servants to wait on you hand and foot your whole life, people responsible for making your existence as sweet as cherry pie. Had Laura kept her infant daughter, she, Katherine, would have experienced such a life. This estate was the home of Laura's parents long before her birth mother had ever conceived and borne her first and only child.

Dismissing the clamor, Katherine went to sit at the petite writing table across the room and searched for her prettiest stationery.

Daniel stepped back, away from the door. "Are you saying . . . that Katie Lapp no longer lives here?" His breathing was coming fast.

"Lest I repeat myself, young man—she is gone like so much rubbish," the butler said, his nostrils flaring like an irritated horse. "The no-good woman left on her own accord weeks ago, though I rather regretted not having thrown her out myself."

Daniel shook his head, pained by the man's words. "Is it possible that we're talking about the same woman? You see, it's *Katie* I wish to see—the Amish girl from Lancaster County. We grew up together, we were sweethearts. . . ." Daniel made an attempt to demonstrate just how tall Katie might be, then mentioned the color of her hair, physical traits—all to no avail.

"Sounds as if the woman's got you fooled, too."

"But I was *told* she'd come here."

"Come she did . . . caused absolute mayhem, too." The butler's face grew red. "Over the holidays, no less."

Dan grimaced at the stranger's disparaging remarks. How could this be? Where *was* his precious Katie?

Quickly, he had the presence of mind to inquire, "Do you have any idea where she might've gone? The slightest tip—anything—would be appreciated."

"I would expect she returned to New York City, from whence she came."

"Who in the world does she know there?" he said, more to himself than to the distinguished-looking gentleman before him.

"Contacts at a talent agency, I was told." The tall man reached for the door handle. "I don't mean to be rude, but the woman was a phony, through and through. Now, if you'll excuse me. . . ."

"Uh, I'm very sorry to have bothered you." His hopes were dashed. "Thank you for the information."

"Good day," said the butler.

Turning, Daniel made his way across the wide snow-dusted driveway to the car. He thought of the Wise Woman, her words of warning. *Katie's not the girl you grew up with.*

Well, certainly, she would've changed some since their teen years—their blissful courting days. Given the circumstances of the imposed shunning, she may have seemed somewhat rebellious in her coming here, but understandably so.

Despite what he thought he knew about his former girlfriend, this encounter with a stranger—a butler—at the door of Katie's birth mother's estate troubled him greatly. And the information offered made no sense. None whatever.

The noise from the front door disturbed Katherine. She'd gone to stand just outside the wide French doors leading from her suite to the main hallway. She listened, though no matter how hard she strained to hear, it was impossible to make out the nature of the exchange taking place on her doorstep.

Unexpectedly, two housemaids rounded the corner, nearly bumping into her. Stepping back, she decided against eavesdropping and closed the glass doors behind her.

Preoccupied with her plan to have Rosie write a cordial letter to Mary, she slid open the narrow drawer in the center of the desk. There she found several plain white pages, just right for taking a few notes, making something of a rough draft.

Picking up a pen from the drawer, she began to write an example for Rosie:

Saturday, January 17

Dear Mary,
    You do not know me. However, I know something of you.

Stopping to read, to see how the English words looked on the page, Katherine wondered if they sounded affected. Stilted.

"I'll ask Rosie," she said aloud. Mrs. Taylor would know. After all, she was of British descent. In fact, her writing style might seem even more formal than the forced, sophisticated way Katherine was attempting to word her initial thoughts.

She sighed, not sure if she should begin by owning up to the fact that the ultimate writer—Rosie—knew only of Mary through Katherine. That the Amish girls had been dear friends all their lives, but because of the physical separation caused by the Ban and the many miles between them, they'd lost touch with each other.

She wrote several more first lines before crumpling those pages, too, into the wastebasket. Clearly, she needed help. Going to the wall, she pulled a velvet rope, the bell that would summon her favorite housemaid.

Rosie arrived quickly, appearing rather puzzled about Katherine's idea once the explanation was offered. "Here, I'll give you an idea of what I mean." She showed Rosie a newly written single-line greeting.

Wide-eyed, the maid read the beginnings of a letter. Sliding her reading glasses down off her nose, she shook her head. "Won't it seem rather peculiar for your friend to receive a letter from a perfect stranger?"

"Maybe, at first." Katherine hurried to her writing desk. "But it's the best way, I think. Wouldn't want Mary getting in trouble. The bishop would never hear of it . . . her receiving mail from me. Never . . . *never.*"

"Well, if you say so." Rosie, looking a bit stumped, sat down and picked up a pen.

"This might seem a bit awkward, but I think we—you and I—will make a great team," Katherine said. "You see, I really miss talking to my friend. We grew up sharing everything."

Rosie, wearing her prim white apron and maid's cap, nodded. An understanding smile played across her lips. "I fear you've been through too much for one so young."

"I've brought a lot of it on myself." Katherine pulled up a chair next to the desk, staring into Rosie's kind face.

Leaning back in her chair, Rosie sighed, laying the pen on the table in front of her. "Why don't we begin by *you* telling *me* about your girlfriend. I would like to know more about Mary." She chuckled. "After all, she and I are soon to become pen pals, right?"

Katherine had to laugh. Then she and Rosie spent the rest of the afternoon talking about her fondest memories of Hickory Hollow and her bosom buddy. She was careful, however, not to speak a word about either Bishop John or her long-deceased love, Daniel.

When they finished their letter-writing collaboration, Rosie addressed the envelope to Mary Stoltzfus in her own hand, and the two headed down the long hallway to the kitchen.

At Rosie's insistence, Katherine joined the staff—Selig, the assistant cook, and the other domestic help, including Garrett Smith, head steward and nephew of the grandfatherly chauffeur, Theodore Williams—for lunch. The tasty meal consisted of a fruit and nut salad, tuna casserole, homemade rolls, and a warm mug of cocoa.

This was not the first such occasion. After several days of eating alone in the grand dining room—not much fun at all—Katherine had decided she much preferred the company of her new friends. After all, she'd grown accustomed to sharing meals with family and friends after house church meetings and quilting frolics. Breaking bread and fellowship went hand in hand with community living.

Selig hadn't forgotten Katherine's weakness for sweets, she soon discovered. The noontime dessert was a delicious, moist German chocolate cake. While enjoying a slice, she thought of Mary once again. Her friend's birthday would be coming up in a couple of months. Lifting a forkful, Katherine stared at her plate—Mary's all-time favorite cake. She knew it sure as the day, desperately missing her friend and hoping the unusual letter might not offend or cause trouble.

"Will you drive me to town this afternoon?" she asked Theodore, who was sitting in his usual spot next to the spacious kitchen window.

"Just state the time, Miss Katherine."

"Theodore's got cabin fever, I suspect, what with the weather being so dreary," Fulton spoke up, glancing down the table at the older gentleman.

"I wouldn't be surprised if we got snowed in," Rosie

observed, at which they all turned their heads toward the window.

"I see what you mean," Katherine said, peering at the overcast sky. "So we'd better plan to leave right after lunch."

"Very well, miss," Theodore replied.

She shook her head. "I wish you'd call me Katherine—just plain Katherine. I wouldn't mind it one bit if you never addressed me as 'miss' again."

"Consider it done," Theodore replied with a grin.

"Better mark it down," Fulton teased, and Rosie elbowed him playfully.

They continued to eat amidst chatter and laughter.

Garrett, at one point, leaned up against the table, looking now at Fulton. "Excuse me, but what was all that racket this morning?"

The butler adjusted his glasses. "Quite odd, I must say. The fellow showed up at the door asking for Katie Lapp. Of all the gall."

"Did you tell him we sent her packing?" Katherine said, glad of it.

"Absolutely, but the man seemed intent on tracking her down. He persisted with an inquiry as to her destination upon leaving here."

"Did he say who he was?" Rosie asked, no longer smiling.

Fulton was thoughtful, frowning as he placed his dessert fork next to a few chocolate crumbs on his plate. "The fellow never stated his name. But he assured me that Katie and he went a long way back . . . to Pennsylvania Amish country, no less."

That brought a volley of laughter from them all, including Katherine, who couldn't help but wonder if the poor fellow had been duped by the impostor, or if he was in fact an actor himself, seeking unlawful employment as the fake Katie Lapp had. "You got rid of him, then?"

Fulton nodded. "And if I'm not mistaken, the young man seemed quite upset by the end of our conversation."

Katherine didn't feel one bit sorry for whoever had come to call this morning. In truth, she hoped she'd never have to see hide nor hair of that woman . . . that obnoxious "Katie"!

❖   ❖   ❖

A brisk breeze blew as Mary hurried down Hickory Lane, careful not to stumble on icy patches of snow along the roadside. The sky was a vast cloak of gray hanging in heavy folds overhead, nearly close enough to touch. Two crows flew across the road, their black wings flapping hard against the impending sky.

The Hollow seemed deserted this afternoon. Maybe *everyone* had gone to Gordonville to shop—plenty of stores to buy such things as fabric and sewing supplies. On Saturdays, Amish folk often hired Mennonite van drivers to take them places, shopping, and such. Folks liked to get out and about, even in the middle of winter, especially if the roads were fairly clear of snow. And they were this afternoon, although the darkening clouds held the threat of a winter storm. Best to get out before the weather turned nasty.

Not a quarter of a mile away, the bishop's enclosed gray carriage was parked off to the side, by the grove of trees, just as he'd promised.

"Glory be," Mary whispered as she quickened her pace, willing her heart to resume its normal pace, but to no avail.

Several yards away, as she approached the buggy, she slowed to a proper walk, not wanting to give the bishop the notion that she was too eager.

John surprised her by jumping out of the carriage. "*Wie geht's*, Mary?"

"*Hullo*, John."

They fell silent straightaway, Mary keeping her head down, wondering what to say next.

He coughed a little. "Trouble gettin' out today?"

She knew he was asking if anybody might be privy to their planned rendezvous. "Dat has no idea." Careful not to mention Mamma's womanly intuition, she changed the subject. "A *wunderbaar schee* day, jah?"

"Nice, it is, though a bit nippy and gray." He offered his gloved hand, helping her into the carriage, then hurried around to the other side to get in.

More than anything she wanted this—her first time alone with John—to go real smooth. Without a hitch in conversation, deed, and thought. The lovely moments must pass perfectly. Yet her heart thumped hard against her woolen shawl.

The bishop flapped the reins, and the horse moved out onto the road, into plain view. They rode for miles and miles without saying a word, the sleek bay mare steaming in the cold, clip-clopping along at a comfortable trot.

At last John broke the silence, speaking of his eldest son, young Hickory John. "The boy's leanin' hard toward learning a trade instead of farming. Said it just this mornin' . . . wants to be a blacksmith like his old *Daed*."

"Ach, but you ain't old," she said cautiously, lest he think she was debating him. "Really, you ain't."

He turned to her and gave her a broad smile. "S'right kind of ya, Mary."

"Well, it's not just *my* opinion." Her voice felt fragile, as if it might give out on her.

"*Your* opinion matters more than ya know."

She was thankful to be sitting down just now, for she felt the strength drain clean out of her legs—downright weak-kneed as always whenever she was around this man of God. "The smithy's a good callin' for a boy, I'd say," she managed.

"Jah, I tend to agree."

She was aware of the wind against her bonnet as they neared the town of Bird-in-Hand. It was ever so much like riding through a dream, floating through a familiar yet somewhat hazy world. She found herself holding her breath, lest the ride come to an end and she awaken.

John halted the horse, bringing the carriage to a smooth stop, then excused himself to run into the bank. Watching a man of his years scamper across a parking lot like a colt was a sight to see, to be sure. She thought she might laugh out loud. Oh, joy! Was John feeling the first stirrings of love for her? Did he feel half as giddy as she?

The horse puffed out plumes of warm air from bulging nostrils as Mary waited. Then lickety-split John was back, pushing a bank receipt into his coat pocket. Mary was amused by his rushing to and fro. Whatever the reason, she dared not surmise . . . or question. She must be careful lest she jump to conclusions.

"Do ya care for some ice cream?" he asked, almost shyly.

"Sounds gut." She couldn't imagine anything colder on such a chilly day, though, and had to keep her face muscles in check so as not to let a chuckle loose.

Up the road a bit, they pulled into a roadside stand. John drove the carriage right up to the order-out window. "Would ya like a chocolate sundae?" He smiled as he asked.

"Jah, with plenty whipped cream and nuts, please." She was awful surprised that he seemed to know her taste in desserts.

He turned to the window and ordered the chocolate sundae for her and a banana split for himself.

The return trip to Hickory Hollow was pleasant enough, but terribly cold by now—what with the ice cream settling in her stomach, frosty and sweet, and a sizable case of nerves—sitting next to the bishop thisaway. Her teeth began to chatter uncontrollably.

"Feelin' a bit chilly, are ya?" Before she could answer, he

reached back and pulled up another heavy lap robe from the backseat, letting go of the reins in order to place it gently over her legs.

"*D-denk-ki,*" she stuttered, ashamed of herself for not being able to conceal it, yet glad for another layer of warmth.

"I best be gettin' you home."

It was the last thing on earth she wanted to hear. She'd much rather freeze to death than have the ride come to an abrupt end. Still, in spite of her disappointment, she nodded submissively. She thought for sure he'd let her out somewhere away from the house, the way they'd arranged the meeting in the first place. But when nothing was said, even when they passed the familiar shoulder and the grove of trees, her pulse quickened. It looked as though he was really going to drive all the way into the barnyard before letting her out.

Mary folded her mittened hands as the horse made the turn into her father's long lane. Her heart felt ever so soft toward the widower. And when he turned to bid her good-bye, his eyes were filled with tenderness toward her as well.

"I'll be seein' ya, Mary, at the meeting tomorrow," he said, tipping his black felt hat like a real gentleman.

"Jah" was what came out. Oh, but she wanted to say so awful much more to the kind and gentle widower. Things such as were not becoming to a quiet, submissive young Amishwoman on the verge of being passed over for marriage. She was smarter than to say anything except, "Denki for the ride . . . and the ice cream."

"I hope we might ride again." His eyes brightened as he said, "God be with ya, Mary Stoltzfus."

"And with you." By now, she couldn't even whisper his name at the end. But it was strong in her mind all the same. *John Beiler . . .*

Despite dark clouds and the lack of sunshine, she believed this to be the most beautiful day the good Lord had likely ever made.

Mary's legs held her up just long enough to push open the back door and rush into the utility room off the kitchen, collapsing on the old cane chair. Giggling under her breath—trying for all the world to keep from bursting out— she struggled to remove her shawl and outer bonnet.

Certain that the family would be waiting by the kitchen stove, she took several deep breaths to calm her flutterings. And when her composure was restored, she marched into her mamma's scrumptious, warm kitchen.

Much to her surprise, nobody was around. "Gut," she said to herself, going to the sink and running water over her cold hands to warm them gradually. In many ways, she was delighted to have the house all to herself. With no one to dampen her spirits by probing too much, she could day-dream to her heart's content, reliving every single second of the afternoon's ride.

Strangely enough, her tryst with the bishop had been truly a secret one in every way. Perhaps by Divine Providence.

CHAPTER FOUR

❖ ❖ ❖

After lunch the phone rang at Mayfield Manor. Katherine unconsciously heard the ringing but ignored it, her ears unaccustomed to the newfangled device. She checked the address on the envelope once more. Seeing the words *Hickory Hollow Lane*, a tiny burst of air flew past her lips. *How odd— kariyos*, she thought, Pennsylvania Dutch invading her thought freely.

Many weeks had come and gone since she'd spoken much of the Old German dialect. It would be impossible to forget her first-ever language, she figured, yet with no other Amish around, she wondered if her native tongue would lie dormant in her brain. Not that she was worried about it. No, she was more concerned these days with learning how to put words and phrases together in a more sophisticated manner. Especially now that she was seeing the likes of Justin Wirth and wanted—for his sake, if for no other—to become a refined English lady.

One of the young maids came to her French doors, standing between them, giving a quick curtsy. "Miss Katherine, a Mister Wirth is on the line . . . for you."

"I'll take it in here, thank you." She hurried to the phone, surprised that he was calling her so soon. My goodness, she'd

51

just seen him last night! "Hello?"

"Katherine, how are you today?"

"Fine, thank you. How are *you*?"

"Never better." His voice held a hint of intrigue. "I wonder if you might join me for dinner Sunday evening. I know of an elegant, quiet place not far from Canandaigua. An old castle."

She could hardly believe he was asking her *again*. "It sounds lovely."

"Shall I come for you about five-thirty?" he asked politely.

"Five-thirty is fine with me." She felt so terribly unsure of herself. "Good-bye" came out a mite too quickly she feared, yet Justin's farewell sounded altogether pleasant . . . almost sweet. The sound of his lilting voice rang in her memory as she set about gathering her coat and a stamp for Mary's letter.

❖   ❖   ❖

When Theodore pulled the car up for her, he was wearing a mischievous grin. "Your wish is my command," he said as he opened the back door.

"The post office, please."

"Right away, miss." He closed the door and walked around to the driver's side.

All the way downtown they talked—chatted, really. At one point she asked, "Why are *you* so happy today?"

"Can't a chauffeur be jolly now and again?"

"Why, of course!"

He glanced over his shoulder. "I must say, it's quite delightful seeing *you* so chipper, Miss Katherine."

She wondered about his comment. "Do you think I should be more sober . . . in mourning for Laura?"

"Oh my, no. I didn't mean that at all."

She didn't dare mention Justin and their dinner plans. Theodore, being the older gentleman he was, might not think it proper for such gaiety so soon after Laura's funeral. Sighing, she settled back for the short ride to town. The limousine was pure luxury and the drive as smooth as vanilla pudding.

"Warm enough for you, Miss Katherine?" asked Theodore at a red light.

Pointing her finger, she wagged it at him. "I'm plenty warm, but remember, don't call me 'miss' again, or I'll . . ." She paused. "Let's see, how could I possibly threaten you?"

He chuckled, tilting his head and glancing through the windshield at the falling snow. "Well now, you could taunt me with a norther on top of this white stuff. In fact, that just might be what's in store for us. Take a look at that sky."

She did as he said, surprised that the snow was descending on them at such a fast rate—a cloudburst of flakes. "Suppose we *do* get snowbound like Rosie said?"

"What of it?"

"Well, are there plenty of candles in the mansion?"

"Always."

"And the pantry. Is it well stocked?"

"That's been taken care of," he assured her.

"What about firewood? Anyone thought of chopping a pile just in case the electricity goes off?"

He shrugged his shoulders. "If I remember correctly, more than two cords of wood were delivered back in early fall."

She couldn't help chuckling. "Just might be you fancy folk could take a lesson or two from an Amish girl. A *former* Amish girl, that is."

Theodore seemed to ignore her mistake. "Well, you may be right about that." He turned the car into the post office parking lot. "Here we are, Katherine . . . without the 'miss.' "

"Thank you, Theodore, minus the 'sir.' "

He grinned, tipping his chauffeur's hat. "Let's keep it that way, shall we?"

She agreed, handing the letter to him to be mailed, mighty glad that she could stay snug and warm inside the beautiful car. She thought of her brothers—Elam, Eli, and Benjamin. Wouldn't they be flabbergasted to see her riding in such a fancy automobile? Why, she even wondered if such a vehicle might not tempt one of them to have a ride. Or worse.

"Probably not Elam, though," she whispered to herself, thinking better of it. Her married brother was much too straight-laced to think of straying from the Ordnung. His young wife, too. Puh, there'd be no getting either Elam or Annie and their new baby inside a car like this.

She watched for Theodore's return, thinking that if she ever did go back for a visit to Hickory Hollow, it would be to see her mamma—shunning or no—and she'd take Theodore along to drive her around. Oh, she wouldn't be flaunting her new station in life, nothing like that. But she'd show the People, especially that bishop of theirs, that no matter how badly they'd treated her, they could never squelch her adventuresome spirit.

❖   ❖   ❖

Back in his room at the B&B, Dan Fisher dialed the long-distance number, using his calling card. The receptionist for the New Jersey drafting office answered.

"Hello? May I speak to Owen Hess, please?" he asked.

The secretary patched him through without hesitation.

"Dan, good to hear from you" came the familiar voice. "How's everything up north?"

He smiled, relieved that he hadn't told his boss the specific nature of his trip. "Nothing more to be done here," he said. "I'll catch a flight the minute I check out."

"Glad you called, Dan. God bless you."

Owen's comment rang in his ears as they hung up. *"God bless you."* He needed to hear such words, especially on a day like today. Thankful that he had placed his faith and trust fully in the Lord Jesus years ago, he packed his personal belongings, scanning the suite for any stray items. Setting his suitcase by the door, he went to make one more phone call before checking out. He would have to arrange for a change in flight schedules before driving to the airport.

After making the call, he headed downstairs with his luggage. This was to have been an ecstatic moment in his life, a glorious reunion day with his sweetheart girl. He was leaving town without ever having seen Katie's sweet face— enduring the butler's horrendous slurs instead.

The owner's wife looked surprised to see him. "Oh, Mr. Fisher, you're leaving us so soon?"

"Yes, well, I hope this won't be an inconvenience for you. My stay has been shortened considerably, but I appreciate your kind hospitality and will offer to pay for an additional night if it means that I might return in good standing—if ever the need may arise, that is." He had no idea why he'd said such a thing. There would be no returning to this place. His Katie girl was gone—flown the coop.

The woman dismissed his offer with a nod of her head. "You mustn't pay a cent more than is due. But be sure to sign our guest book before you leave."

With that, Dan paid for a night's lodging, said his fare-wells, and rolled his luggage outside to the rental car, his heart as heavy as the snow clouds.

As he pulled out, he noticed the young girl and her mother making the turn into the parking area. They smiled and waved back, setting his mind on course for a replay of the morning's events, beginning with breakfast and the curiosity over his Amish background.

Once his luggage was checked in at the airport, Dan was free to sit and rest a bit. Emotionally exhausted, he found himself wishing he'd never made the trip. Not the way things had turned out for him—the closed doors, the overwhelming disappointment, the not knowing where Katie had gone in New York City, or why.

What's left to do? he wondered. It made no sense to pursue her, searching hundreds of talent agencies. The idea that she might be interested in such a lifestyle—that sort of vocation—had him truly perplexed.

Dear Lord, be with Katie, wherever she may be, he prayed silently. Then, to keep from dwelling on the most worrisome aspects of the butler's comments—that Katie was a phony and had caused such mayhem—Dan went to purchase a paper at the newsstand.

Forcing his attention to the minuscule newspaper in his hand, he studied the front page. Anything to keep his thoughts from wandering back to the disheartening encounter.

It was on the society page that he spotted a curious caption. *Young Amish Woman, Sole Heir of Local Estate*. Reading further, he began to mumble the words as he searched the page. "Katie," he said suddenly. "Katie is Katherine Mayfield!"

Slamming the paper shut, he rushed back to the flight counter and made arrangements to have his luggage retained. Without delay, he ran all the way to the front of the airport terminal, hailed a cab, and sped away to Mayfield Manor.

❖   ❖   ❖

After the brief stop at the post office, Katherine found herself daydreaming about her Sunday plans. An elegant dinner for two, Justin had said. A castle setting . . .

Such events required anything but Plain clothing: rather, fanciful, shimmering dresses of satin and lace or embroidered velvet. And an array of accessories. Rosie had been willing to assist her on a recent shopping expedition, offering her opinion of Katherine's purchases at a local department store.

Since her first real date in over five years, Katherine had pondered her attraction to the artist. Yesterday she'd indulged herself a bit, curling up by the fire at the coziest end of the library to think about the possibility of a future with the likable young man.

A short time had passed since their first meeting—Christmas Day. The handsome blue-eyed artist had come to the mansion, commissioned by Laura as a portrait painter. He was much more than good-looking. He was sensitive and kind—an honest man. She admired such wonderful-good qualities in a person. Perhaps because the same characteristics had been so evident in her dear Daniel. Dan . . . who'd shared her love for music and the guitar, who'd put up with her headstrong, impulsive ways, yet loved her still. If he hadn't drowned, she was sure they would be married by now. With several children, no doubt. As sure as the sun. Sure as the moon, too.

Dan Fisher, forever adored by the People. Forever missed by his Katie girl, the woman who'd mourned his passing far longer than need be. Longer, because she believed the two of them had really and truly belonged together, had found utter joy in discovering each other's heart.

Now there was someone else. Someone who was alive. Two social events in two days. Ach, Rebecca Lapp would say such a fella had courtship on his mind. Snuggling against the backseat, Katherine grinned, hugging herself.

"Looks like you may have some company," Theodore said, his voice startling her out of her reverie. He nodded his head at a taxicab parked in front of the main entrance.

Katherine could see just the back of a tall blond man wearing a dark overcoat as he stood at the doorway. She also noticed Fulton, his arms crossed at his chest as if annoyed. "I wonder if it's the same fellow who was here earlier looking for that horrible woman, that actress who—"

"Allow me to spare you a run-in with such a man," Theodore said, pulling the limousine around the side of the house. He turned, looking over his shoulder, his eyes kindly searching hers. "You won't mind going in through the east doorway, will you?"

Nodding, she gave her consent. "It's not like I haven't used this entrance before." She remembered the unnerving time when she'd slipped into the mansion, sight unseen, hoping to find her birth mother still alive.

"Very well, miss . . . uh, excuse me, *Katherine*. I'll let you out here." He parked the limo and got out, hurrying around the car to open her door for her. The snow was piling up quickly and because of it, the chauffeur accompanied her, his hand supporting her elbow, right up to the entrance.

"Thank you, Theodore. You're so very kind." She offered him a warm smile and quickly entered the house, stomping the snow off her feet before heading into the main hallway, still wearing her coat and hat.

Approaching the grand staircase, she heard voices—the measured, low tones of men arguing but doing it politely. Curious, she peered down the long hallway and saw Fulton standing like a sentry in the doorway, a human barrier. If she wasn't mistaken, he was doing most of the talking, quizzing the stranger with many questions.

She stopped to listen. Studying what she could see of the caller and making note of his overcoat, she was fairly certain it was the same man she had seen earlier that morning. Inching closer, she focused on his thick hair—just visible over Fulton's head. It was striking, like a thousand dandelions in summer. Something about its golden color reminded her of someone back in Pennsylvania. A schoolmate? One of her cousins? She couldn't be sure, probably because she had so many relatives, distant and otherwise.

Beyond the two men, the snow was falling fast and heavy. Like someone had cut open a feather pillow and was shaking it hard, creating an intermittent curtain of white.

She heard her name and a sharp response from her butler. "I cannot allow you to see the mistress if you refuse to state who you are or the nature of your visit," came the curt reply.

By now Katherine had crept close enough to make out the stranger's words. "Miss Mayfield is a dear friend of mine."

"I'd be surprised at that," Fulton shot back. "You said the same thing about Katie Lapp earlier today."

"But . . . I plead with you, let me speak with Katherine. Let her decide for herself."

Katherine fell against the wall, stunned by an impossible thought. The soft-spoken voice seemed as familiar to her as her own. Yet it could not be.

Fulton began to push the door closed. "I'm sorry, sir. Once again, I'll have to ask you to leave."

"Wait!" Katherine called, taking a step forward. "Please . . . won't you let the man in, just for a moment?"

Fulton's eyebrows arched in a pinnacle of astonishment. "Miss? Are you quite certain of this?"

"He says he knows me . . . and it's all right," she assured him, barely breathing. "I'll meet with the gentleman in the parlor."

The butler was blinking his eyes rapid fire, but nonetheless he opened the door wider and showed the man inside.

Katherine stepped back and turned toward the hallway mirror, not looking at the young man as Fulton showed him into the formal sitting room. Rosie hastened down the hall to her, offering to take Katherine's coat and hat. "Oh, thank you, Rosie. I nearly forgot." Her mouth felt terribly dry, her lips stiff.

Turning back toward the mirror, she stared in it, straightening her sweater and fluffing her hair with trembling fingers, but seeing little. Stepping back, she took a deep breath and entered the parlor with a forced smile.

Fulton and the stranger remained standing as Katherine made her way across the room, past polished tables and numerous Victorian-style chairs and a cherrywood love seat upholstered in powder blue velvet.

"Sir," the butler said, turning to the stranger briefly, "may I present Miss Katherine Mayfield."

The man stepped forward to reach past Fulton, his hand extended. "Hello, Miss Mayfield."

Reluctantly, she accepted his hand, her mind reeling as she stared into his rich blue eyes. "And you are?" She waited, hardly daring to hear the reply.

"An old friend" was all he said.

Katherine nodded to Fulton. "Thank you. That will be all," she said, relieved to have remembered the proper words, the ones Rosie and the others had taught her. In that at least she found comfort.

"Please, be seated," she said, motioning stiffly toward the love seat. She clung to the security of the formalities, feeling as though she were in the middle of a terrible, confusing dream.

"Thank you . . . but I don't mean to take up much of your time." He seemed reticent to sit, awkward now that he was finally alone with her. He remained standing for a moment, then perching on the edge of the love seat, he examined her face. It was as if he might possibly be mistaken about ever really knowing her at all.

His voice dropped to a whisper. "I've been waiting for a long time to see you again, Katie." He studied her, a flicker of a frown crossing his brow again and again. "Perhaps it is too late," he added.

"Oh?" She, too, was staring at his face, his eyes, still unable to comprehend what she thought she was seeing.

"Perhaps you should sit down," she heard him say. Trembling, she lowered herself into a chair. The sensation was akin to floating through a muddled dream. A most outlandish dream.

Himmel, what was happening to her mind? Was she losing her sanity? This man reminded her of Daniel . . . but it *couldn't* be!

"I hesitate to go on," he said softly, gently, his words falling like raindrops on a rose petal. "I don't want to frighten you. I know you believe that I died five years ago."

She caught her breath, searching his face. "I don't understand. Who *are* you?"

He paused, his face intent on hers. "I'm Daniel . . . from Hickory Hollow."

A pain stabbed her. "Daniel? But Daniel Fisher drowned at sea." Her eyes searched his. She struggled to breathe, a hundred memories whirling in her mind. "I . . . I . . ." Her voice caught on a sob. "I don't know what to say."

"Please don't say anything, Katie. Let me explain."

She could hear him no longer, could feel the wrenching, black disbelief, the confusion. Looking away, a knot in her stomach twisted and churned.

Even so, her gaze was drawn back to his bearded face, his modern haircut. Most everything about him reminded her of Daniel. The blueberry eyes, the golden hair, the gentle voice. Especially the voice.

She held her breath for a moment, then spoke, barely able to utter the words. "How . . . can you be . . . alive?"

He paused, inhaling deeply, his eyes finding hers. "I never drowned, Katie. I made a terrible mistake."

She choked back tears, refusing to let them take over.

She found the courage to speak. "A mistake? You let me *think* you died?"

He bowed his head. "I don't blame you for being upset."

She clenched her fists in her lap. "How do I know you're really Daniel?"

Wincing, he looked up at her as if to recall times and dates . . . grasping for something, anything. It was then that a lightness came into his eyes. "Do you remember the day we sat on the boulder—*our* boulder—there in the middle of Weaver's Creek? I taught you to write music that day."

She folded her arms across the front of her, as if protecting herself from the reality of this unbelievable moment.

"I gave you my guitar. You hid it in your father's barn . . . in the hayloft."

Shaking uncontrollably, she glanced away, wishing she might hold herself together against the incredible truth, the torturing pain of remembered love, the mounting hurt and anger of having been deceived.

"Oh, Katie, I've missed you terribly . . . all these years."

She drew in a sharp breath. "I'm *Katherine* now. Katherine Mayfield."

He sighed, nodding his head slowly. "Annie told me about your adoption, that you'd left Hickory Hollow after the bishop imposed your shunning—that you'd gone in search of your birth mother. But it was old Ella Mae who was brave enough to tell me where to look for you."

She turned her face toward him. "So . . . you've been back to see the People?"

"Only to speak with my father and mother . . . and Annie." He stopped, as if there was much more to his story than he dared offer.

Her eyes found his, her heart breaking anew. "The Daniel I knew said he loved me. *He* said, 'No matter what happens . . .' " Her eyes filled with angry tears. "*That* Daniel would never have tricked me this way."

"That's why I came here. To ask your forgiveness." He stood up, rushing to her side. "I can explain everything."

"What's to tell?" she said, her voice rising without restraint. "You fooled me, Daniel . . . you broke my heart. I never thought I could live life without you. You let me grieve until I was so sick the People worried that I might never be well, and here you are—coming to me this way?"

He knelt before her. "I wish I could turn the clock back, Katie, truly I do. I should've taken you away with me."

She shook her head. "The past is done. *Should have*'s never solved anything."

His eyes glistened, but he was silent.

"I'm not the girl you once loved." She stood up abruptly, the pain of their past, the burning anger consuming her. "I wish you'd never come here."

He was on his feet. "Katie . . . I—"

"No more. Please, I can't talk about this." Her hands flew to her face, hiding her tears, muting her sobs.

She felt his hand on her shoulder. "Oh, Katie, I'm so very sorry."

"Please . . . will you go?" she whispered, stepping away. And with all the energy she could muster, she called for her butler. The click of Fulton's shoes on the floor brought her some relief. Fulton would handle things now. *He* would take care of her.

Daniel looked back at her once more as the butler stood in the wide doorway. "I never meant for this visit to cause you pain, Katie. God be with you."

Silently, helplessly, their eyes met and held.

Fulton wasted no time in leading the man to the door, and Katherine turned and fled to her suite.

CHAPTER FIVE

❖ ❖ ❖

Daniel's return from the "dead" was all Hickory Hollow could think about, and all Mattie Beiler could talk about following dinner, when dusk lingered about the old farmhouse deep in the Hollow. She'd gone so far as to say that the young man was "of the devil"—him and his deceitful ways—running off to New Jersey somewheres to rub shoulders with them Englischers.

Glancing at her mother, the elderly Ella Mae, Mattie spoke up again. "Goodness knows Dan Fisher broke his mamma's heart . . . letting her think he was dead and gone."

"Ach, don'tcha be judgin' him so," Ella Mae chided, looking up from her knitting with a stern gaze. "The poor fella knows what it means to suffer."

"Poor fella, my left foot!" Mattie scoffed, scooting her chair closer to the woodstove in the kitchen. "He brought his pain on himself, don'tcha know?" She bit her tongue, waiting for her Mam to strike out in defense of the likable lad. Rocking hard against the hand-hewn rocker, she gripped the thick-eyed needle and her handiwork, mumbling in disgust.

Her mother remained still, yet Mattie kept looking over at her, hoping the Wise Woman might size things up from her own perspective and add a little spice to the conversation.

Seconds passed, empty and unfulfilling. Mattie itched, nay *longed* to stoke the fires of discussion. Fidgeting, she could scarcely sit by and watch a perfectly good evening go to waste.

Finally, unable to withstand the silence any longer, Mattie huffed, "Seems to me, Daniel's folks been put through the wringer. And Bishop John's got every right to slap die Meinding on him—same as he did on Katie and anybody else who disobeys around here."

Ella Mae's knitting needles kept flying, clicking softly in a soothing, rhythmic pattern. Keeping mum, she never once looked up. The needle's song, gentle though it was, annoyed Mattie almost worse than if her Mam had stopped knitting altogether and lashed out about Daniel. About *anything*. Ella Mae was doing about as much talking tonight as a deaf mute, and Mattie figured she knew why. The old woman supposed she had a corner on things when it came to Daniel. Jacob Fisher's downright rebellious son had shown up clean out of nowhere to confess his past faults. "Word has it that Dan's not plannin' to stick around these parts. And he won't be making amends with the People or the church. He's got other things on his wicked mind—things like leaving Hickory Hollow all over again and going right back into the world to make money. He's a fancy draftsman now, you know—drawing up them blueprints for modern folk. Puh, if he had his head on straight, he'd know he could use the talents the Good Lord gave him right here in the Hollow. No need rushin' off to take a tainted paycheck from *sindhaft* men. No need a-tall!"

"Mattie, you're workin' yourself up over nothin'," her mother said at last, staring her down like she was so much bear bait.

"Well, what's a body to think?" she muttered, moving

her chair away from the fire a bit. "That boy's confession wasn't worth the air he breathes. And not staying around for the membership meeting, not bowing his knee in holy contrition—" She flapped her hand in the air. "Instead, he had to go and say he was saved—found grace in the sight of the Lord. Such pride! He'll rue the day, for sure and for certain."

The Wise Woman looked mighty disgusted, even though everything said just now had been honest-to-goodness truth. Mattie knew it was, 'cause she'd talked things over with a good half of the older female population in the Hollow. The consensus was that Dan and Katie probably *did* belong together in more ways than one, and if somebody didn't do something to bolster the Old Ways, and soon, they'd be losing even more young people to the world and the devil before long.

❖   ❖   ❖

Benjamin Lapp hauled several buckets of fresh well water from the pump, helping his older brother get the farm animals settled down for a bitter, cold night.

The young men exchanged a few heated remarks till Ben could stand it no longer. "I got eyes in my head, ain't I?" he shot back. "Mamma's gettin' worse, seems to me. Can't keep her mind on much of anything these days."

Eli pitched some hay for the mules. "Ya can't expect Mam to be gettin' over our sister's shortcomings all that quick."

"But what about Pop? He's strugglin', too."

Eli snorted. "*En wiedicher Hund*—a mad dog, he is."

Shaking his head, Ben walked toward the milk house. "It's all her fault, every bit," he muttered, stewing over the way things were around the house these days. Not a contented place no more. His Mam seemed upset and awful nervous most of the time, getting the jitters when a body'd least expect—leaning hard on Pop, of all things. The bishop had even come calling a time or two. But all for naught, so far as he could tell.

There was only one person who could calm Mamma down, and he'd witnessed it on several occasions. Most folk had quit referring to Ella Mae Beiler as the Wise Woman, what with the bishop putting the clamps on her lately. But from what he'd heard, the kindly woman had had herself a private chat with Dan Fisher, the boy who'd loved his sister way back when. The fella'd gotten himself shunned, too—comin' back here and strutting around, talkin' about finding forgiveness for his sins and all.

Why, he oughta have better sense than to be telling the People such things. Didn't he know what the Good Book said: "The fruit of righteousness is sown in peace of them that make peace"?

Ben spit a piece of straw out of his mouth and stood looking out the dirt-streaked window of the milk house, trying to think what it was he'd heard one of Bishop John's boys say the other Sunday after preaching service. Something about there oughta be a law about folk going around spreading such prideful talk. "We oughta put a stop to 'em when they boast that way."

Ben knew better than to flaunt any attempt at being holy. *Saved*, the Mennonites called it. He was raised up to be a right-gut Amishman, knew enough not to toot his horn about being washed and righteous. "Self-praise stinks," Dat had always said. From the time Ben was a little boy at his father's knee, he'd heard words like that; filled with goodness and truth, they were.

He turned to go to the house. The night was damp and cold, pushing its sting deep into his bones. High in the sky, stars peeped in and out of a wispy veil. Across the wide, open field to his right, the moon had risen, wearing a silken halo all around. "S'gonna snow to beat the band," he said to himself.

"Who're ya talkin' to?" his brother called, running across the barnyard to catch up.

"*Yuscht* myself."

They fell silent for a moment, walking toward the house. Then—"You miss her, don'tcha?" Eli said.

Ben pulled his coat collar up around his neck, holding it there with both hands.

"Well, don't you?"

"S'nobody's business if I do or don't."

Eli burst out laughing. "I could've sworn you'd say that!"

"We don't swear, brother. You oughta be ashamed." He wanted to slap Eli—him making a mockery of honest feelings and all. He really wanted to take his brother down on the miserably cold ground and pound him a good one. And he just might've, if it hadn't been for Mam poking her head out the back door, ringing her little bell like there was no tomorrow.

"Time for evening prayers," Eli spouted off, second cousin to a sneer.

"And a gut thing . . . for *your* sake."

Eli forced his breath out hard, and Ben saw it spiral up over his brother's worn-out work hat, toward a black sky. "Guess, if truth be told, all of us could benefit by a bit of prayin'. Lest we . . ." He paused. "Lest *all* of us end up shunned like Daniel Fisher and our sister."

Surprised at the forthright comment, especially coming from one so glib, Ben said nothing, and they hurried up the back steps and into the sandstone house.

❖   ❖   ❖

All five of the bishop's children knelt at the long bench in the kitchen, the warmest room in the big house. John

Beiler prayed a short prayer, thanking God for His many blessings and for leading and guiding them in His will and providence. Then he offered up to the Almighty the reins to his life and his family.

"*Gut Nacht*, Daed," said Hickory John, the oldest, when the prayer was through. The younger children—Susie, six, and Jacob, four—came to give their father a hug before following big sister Nancy, carrying a lantern, to the stairs.

"Sleep gut and fast," he called to them, hearing their feet pitter-pat up to the second floor and being comforted by the pleasant sound.

Ah, such a day it had been. Nippy . . . almost brittle cold with a dampness that chilled a body clean through. The brightest spot in the day had been his afternoon ride with Mary Stoltzfus. A right sweet girl, she was. And mighty happy to be invited to accompany him, it seemed. She hadn't succeeded in hiding the blush on her round cheeks or the hesitancy in her voice when she spoke to him. Still, Mary's qualities outshone her best friend by a country mile. He could kick himself for ever giving Katie Lapp a second glance. 'Course he hadn't known then what he knew now.

Tired from the day's work, he turned off the gas lamp and made his way to the stairs. It was no bother to climb them in the dark. He was accustomed to the slant of each one, the creaks on the third and the fifth, and the wood railing, rubbed smooth by so many hands, young and old alike.

He thought of his dear deceased wife. Miriam would chuckle to see him now, a middle-aged man trying to court but a *Maedel*—a twenty-year-old maiden. And he, with a houseful of children between the ages of twelve and four. Jah, she'd laugh, prob'ly.

Sighing, he sat on the bed, staring out at the darkness. For weeks now, Mary had been watching him hard during preaching services, especially on those Sundays when he was responsible for the Scripture readings.

Wondering just when his heart might begin to beat a little faster at the sight of her—the way it used to with Katie Lapp—he'd decided to take Mary along with him to the bank. As it turned out, not only was their time together surprisingly comfortable, he found that he really did enjoy having Mary sit beside him in the carriage . . . sharing sweets, too. Maybe, when all was said and done, it didn't matter so awful much if your heart was stirred up like a giddy schoolboy. Deep friendship was good enough to start things out—and the best thing about growing old together. Nobody would ever dispute that. After all, a man of his stature in the community needed a fine young woman to bear him more offspring and to help him raise the children he'd fathered with Miriam.

And Mary had the patience for such a task. Slipping into bed, he said his silent prayers and afterward decided that he wouldn't make *this* courtship a long and drawn-out matter. He'd go ahead and make Mary right happy by revealing his intentions in the next couple of weeks or so.

❖   ❖   ❖

Katherine propped herself up in her bed with as many plush pillows as she could gather. She'd brought with her a stack of books from the library just down the hallway, thanks to Rosie, who had shown great concern, even though Katherine had made every attempt to disguise her puffy eyes and splotchy face. She had even requested that the evening meal be brought to her in the privacy of her own sitting room.

It was Rosie who had assisted her in finding some of the old classics that Laura had enjoyed reading and rereading over the years. The nicest part of discovering the books was that some of them had Laura's childish handwriting in the front pages. This discovery delighted Katherine, and for all good reason.

In her present distraught state, she needed a reprieve, a moment of escape. Try as she might, the trauma lingered long after Fulton had shown Daniel to the door. She'd returned to her quarters weeping, and nothing Rosie or any of the other maids could do would console her. When asked about the stranger, she only shook her head and wept all the more.

Rosie sat with her now on a chair near Katherine's bed. "Perhaps if I read to you, the sound of my voice will lull you to sleep."

She turned to her maid, still suffering from having cried so hard and long. "Rosie, you're very kind, but why are you treating me this way . . . like a child?"

"You've had a trying day. No need to fret about it." Rosie got up to smooth the coverlet on the bed. "Not a thing wrong with pampering the mistress, now is there? One can certainly see you need someone to cheer you."

Nodding, Katherine searched through her pile of books, not wanting to discuss the tearful encounter. No one needed to know the story behind what had happened today in the parlor. Or anything else regarding Dan Fisher, for that matter. "This book looks interesting," she said, examining a well-worn edition. "*A Girl of the Limberlost.*" She handed it to Rosie.

"Oh my, yes. This was one of Laura's very favorites." Rosie opened the book to the first chapter. "Shall I begin?"

Katherine nodded, sighing deeply.

"Chapter one is titled, 'Wherein Elnora Goes to High School and Learns Many Lessons Not Found in Her Books.' "

"Such a long title for a chapter," Katherine said, getting cozy in her mountain of pillows. Listening intently, she wondered about the many life lessons she, too, had learned. *Most* of them difficult . . . not found in books.

Although the story began with Elnora arguing with her mother over her desire to attend high school, of all things, Katherine was not able to relate one iota. Amish schools provided for only eight grades; then came graduation. The boys went home to help their fathers farm or to learn carpentry skills; girls became their mothers' right hands in tending to younger siblings and keeping house, vegetable gardens, and canning and preserving food.

The sound of Rosie's voice, though she read with considerable expression and interest, served to make Katherine quite sleepy. She already understood from past experience—the weeks and months following Dan's supposed drowning—that continuous weeping brought with it great fatigue and an overwhelming sense of helplessness.

"I should've taken you away with me. . . ." His tender words followed her into the oblivion of sleep.

❖   ❖   ❖

She moaned and turned in her bed, realizing with a start that Rosie was nowhere about. The room was dark now, and a slice of muted light shone through the windows high above the headboard, casting dim shadows on the comforter near her feet.

"Daniel, was it really you?" she whispered against her pillow as tears involuntarily slid from her eyes. "Are you *really* alive?"

Falling again into tormented sleep, she dreamed she was a little girl, growing up Amish in Lancaster County, Pennsylvania.

CHAPTER SIX

❖   ❖   ❖

Smoke thickened the skies over New Jersey. Dan smelled its pungent tang as he hurried down the steps to his car parked at the curb. During his commute to church, this being the Lord's Day, he mistakenly pushed the fresh-air button on the dash instead of the heater, and the noxious odor filled the car.

He was tempted to go back home, to be reclusive, yet he knew he must not forsake the assembling of believers, regardless of his state of mind. The precious little sleep he'd had last night was fitful at best, squandered with snatches of troublesome dreams.

Stopping at a series of red lights, he felt hemmed in by the heavy weekend traffic. And the dismal gray sky. All of it reminded him of his brief visit to Canandaigua and the bleakness he'd felt upon driving to the airport for the second time. Desperately weary, he had fallen asleep during the flight to Newark, awakening to the hard impact of tires on the runway, the force of the landing thrusting him back against his seat.

"Daniel would never have tricked me. . . ."

Shifting gears, he kept his eyes on the lane in front of him, moving in and out of traffic only when necessary. How good it would be to see his Mennonite friends again, to sing praises to God, to hear the message by the Lord's anointed. Owen Hess and his wife, Eve, would be eager to see him, no doubt. But they would not inquire beyond courtesy as to Dan's trip to Canandaigua; thankfully, he could count on that.

If this had been Monday and he were headed for the office, his somber mood may have affected his work, distracting him beyond his ability to pull his thoughts away from Katie. Even with business typically slow this time of year, he'd have had to force himself to concentrate. He knew that. Yet ceaseless memories flooded his mind every waking minute. The past five years had been filled up with similar thoughts. In reality, nothing had changed.

"I wish you'd never come here. . . ."

He turned into the paved driveway that led to a parking lot behind the church building. Switching off the ignition, he pulled hard on the hand brake, then checked his watch. A few minutes to spare.

"Dear Lord," he prayed, "I ask for your strength today. Help me release Katie—Katherine, as she now calls herself—to your safekeeping and care. Yet help me win her to you. Open doors so that I may witness to her of your love and saving grace. I'm ready to do your will, no matter the cost. In Jesus' name. Amen."

Opening his eyes, he gazed through the windshield at the sun doing its best to pierce the gray pall of smoke and clouds. He scanned a stand of trees situated between crowded buildings, their spartan limbs like three- and four-pronged pitchforks thrust against the misery of the pollution-stained sky.

In spite of his prayer, Dan was smitten with gloom and might as well have worn mourning clothes to announce it to the world.

As he looked on, several other vehicles pulled in and

parked on either side. It was time to get out of the car and head into the white-columned Colonial-style church. Friends waved cheerful greetings, and though Dan might've given in to the urge to simply back out of the lot and drive home, he pressed on, eager to find solace in worship and the preaching of the Word. And especially today, he needed the fellowship of brothers and sisters in Christ.

❖   ❖   ❖

Katherine felt sorry about having to decline Rosie's thoughtful invitation to attend church services with her and her husband.

"Perhaps some other time," Rosie said with a smile. "Do take care of yourself, Katherine."

She hoped Rosie would understand. It wasn't that she had no interest in going to the church where Laura had been a member; there was so much more to it. Katherine felt terribly tired, emotionally exhausted from a night of tossing about in bed crying, even though she willed the tears to stop. Her world had tilted nearly off its axis yesterday. Everything . . . *everything* had changed. Even her dinner plans with Justin Wirth were now in question. And there was the letter to Mary, mailed just hours before Daniel's appearance.

Oh, if she'd only known, she might not have dictated the letter to Rosie at all, might not have started up such a preposterous correspondence. Her desire to reach out to her Amish girlfriend might've been hampered, truly, by her knowledge that Dan was alive.

She sighed deeply, deciding to spend the morning in her bedroom, taking her breakfast there. She preferred to stay put—alone, still wearing her nightgown and robe.

The weather played a role in her lethargy, she was nearly sure, and she sat near the window, watching the snow pile up, hoping her butler and maid had arrived at church safely.

After she'd eaten her breakfast of scrambled eggs, bacon, toast, and juice, she slipped back under the covers, desiring a reprieve from troubled thoughts. Trying her best to relax, she began to sing softly in German, an old song from her childhood. "What a friend we have in Jesus, all our sins and griefs to bear. . . ."

Griefs to bear.

The words filled up the hollow places in her heart, and she wondered about Laura's love for Jesus amidst the perplexing reality of her own life. It was hard to imagine the Son of God understanding her grief, leaning over the balconies of heaven to be intimately involved in one person's life. The idea seemed worldly, even heretical.

Turning on her side, she drew her knees up and wrapped her hands around her stomach, trying to get warm enough . . . secure enough to sleep again.

Several hours later, close to dinnertime, Justin Wirth phoned. Leoma, one of the several elder housemaids, came to the French doors leading to the secluded sitting room where Katherine was lounging. "Mister Wirth is on the line for you, Miss Katherine."

"Thank you," she said, reaching for the telephone on the small table next to her.

Justin's voice sounded edgy. "Hello, Katherine. I hope my calling this late won't upset your plans for the day, but the roads are becoming treacherous, according to news reports. I don't think it would be wise to risk taking you out on a night like this. I'm afraid the castle will have to wait."

Katherine was secretly relieved. She hadn't felt she could pull off such an event anyway—not the way she was suffering. "I understand."

"Would it be all right if I called again in a few days?" he asked. "Maybe then we can plan for another time."

"Yes . . . when the storm is past."

He paused. "Well, I trust this snow will end quickly."

They said good-bye without chatting further. She hoped she hadn't been too abrupt or aloof. Thinking back, she wondered if she might've mentioned something about looking forward to seeing him again. Something kind and gracious like that.

But she hadn't felt at all kindly toward him. Hadn't felt much of anything, really. Truth be told, she wished she were as young as her dreams last night. If so, she'd crawl right up in Dat's lap and let him rock her to her heart's content in his great big hickory rocker. And when she grew tired of it, she'd munch on one of Mamma's whoopie pies till she was that close to a stomachache. That's just what she'd do if she weren't all grown up and . . . English.

❖ ❖ ❖

After the morning worship service, Dan was invited to have dinner at a restaurant with Owen and Eve Hess. "Our treat," Owen said, wearing a broad grin. "We haven't seen much of you lately."

Politely, Dan asked for a rain check. "I'd like very much to eat with you, but—well, it won't suit this time. I hope you'll understand."

Eve linked her arm in her husband's, casting a curious gaze on Dan. "Are you feeling all right?" she asked as they moved down the church aisle toward the foyer.

"A bit under the weather, I suppose," he replied, not wanting to go into how he really felt.

"Very well, then, I'll see you tomorrow at the office." Owen gave a broad smile and turned to go.

It had begun to sleet during Sunday school, and as Dan made his way out of the church, he noticed that the parking lot had glazed over. Gingerly, he headed for his car and started it, letting the engine warm up while he scraped the ice off his windows.

Back in the car, he waited his turn, while church traffic snarled in the lot, tires spinning and vehicles lurching forward. Well, he was in no hurry. He reached over on the seat and picked up his Bible, thumbing through it till he found the letter he'd written to Katie the night before he visited Mayfield Manor. Holding it, he stared at the words, not seeing them but recalling Katie's demeanor, her modern dress . . . the changes her appearance had taken in the more than five years since he'd last seen her. Still as attractive as ever— same fiery hair, same bright brown eyes—yet her speech patterns, her choice of words, had thrown him somewhat as he sat in the well-furnished parlor. The lack of Amish attire, the absence of the head covering especially, and the stylish haircut had mystified him. Yet he assumed that she, too, must surely be grappling with the same unfamiliar images as she stared back at him.

In all the years he'd known her, Katie had never worn makeup. Never sought after or *needed* beauty aids. He wondered what had led her away from her Plain upbringing. The way she carried herself—her posture—spoke of a finishing school somewhere. But when would she have attended such a place? And why?

He was curious about her birth mother, the woman Katie had set out to find. Had Katie discovered and embraced qualities in her biological mother—traits she'd never known in Rebecca Lapp?

Dan turned on the windshield wipers. The snow was falling more heavily now, and inadvertently, he glanced in his rearview mirror and noticed a lady driver motioning for him to back out. He waved his thanks, chuckling softly to himself.

Ruth Stine. A sweet young lady, one that several of his single friends had mentioned on occasion. Owen and Eve, as well. He knew better than to think that any of them might arrange for a get-together with Ruth without his consent. Yet at the same time, he had never told those same friends of his sweetheart girl, now the mistress of an impressive estate. Though Owen had heard the story of Dan's long-ago love—at least some of it—he had no idea that Dan had met face-to-face with Katherine as recently as yesterday.

It would not do to try to explain things. Not since his encounter with the modern Katie had blown up in his face. And, really, what could he expect? Impulsive and headstrong, Katie had often exerted herself in a rather forceful way. Even during their courting years, she'd fired questions at him. Why was he going off to a Bible study, of all things? Why did he have so many friends outside the Amish church?

He was quite certain she'd suspected him of associating with Mennonites during those years. He hadn't gone out of his way to keep that part of his social life from her. And if it had seemed so, it was only out of concern for her, not wanting to stir up religious doubts in Katie, not wanting her to think that the Amish life might not have been right. . . .

The drive home was less stressful; traffic was sparse due to the snowstorm and icy roads. He thought of what he might cook for lunch, remembering the savory aroma and the mouth-watering taste of oven-fried chicken. Such a "plain-good" recipe! He'd copied it onto an index card years ago while living alone for the first time. The secret was in the amount of butter used. Planning this tasty treat occupied his mind as he turned cautiously onto the side street— *his* street—too narrow and deserted to be either plowed or sanded, even in a ferocious storm.

He parked the car by the curb and ducked his head against the stiff wind. Inside the house, Dan removed his coat and scarf, flinging it over the coatrack in the small entryway. Hurrying to the refrigerator, he opened the freezer, took out a package of frozen chicken and stuck it in the microwave, setting the control to automatic defrost. He went to the kitchen window and stood there, watching the snow—thick as goose down—fall through the gray fog. Thoughts of Katie filled his mind, his heart. He wondered now if perhaps she was right. Maybe he *should* have left well enough alone. Had he erred in locating her—going to the mansion unannounced, disturbing her life in such a manner?

Unable to think of much else, he felt the need to pray for her, pray that she might encounter someone—*something*—to lead her to faith in the Lord Jesus.

Turning back to the chore at hand, he gathered the ingredients to prepare the chicken—flour, salt, poultry seasoning, pepper, and butter—something to do to keep his hands busy. A man ought to allow himself a big meal in the middle of the day, if only to fortify himself against the pain of love lost . . . love wasted and betrayed.

CHAPTER SEVEN

◈ ◈ ◈

In Hickory Hollow the Amishwomen all looked alike, Katherine recalled while snowed in for the second day in a row. She sat snug by the fire in the enormous library, reading *A Girl of the Limberlost*, captivated by the similarities between herself and Elnora Comstock, a girl who caught moths to pay for her schooling. Elnora, a young woman growing up in Indiana during the 1860s, lived by the Golden Rule, loved nature, and longed to be loved by her mother.

Sighing, Katherine could almost feel the drab brown dress around her own ankles as she read the excruciating account of Elnora's first day of high school, entering the auditorium to taunts and jeers. She knew just how this dear girl from "the olden days" had felt. Katherine, too, had experienced the selfsame thing, usually while running errands in town at Central Market or at Roots, another gathering place where Amish farmers and other merchants sold their wares.

People, especially tourists, liked to gawk. She keenly remembered her feelings of resentment at being the object of ridicule, even if she never said anything about it. *All* the Plain women attracted attention—the way they pulled their hair into tight buns at the back of their heads, the severe clothing, the devotional head coverings. Looking the same as every other woman in Hickory Hollow had made her feel empty. Yet, at the age of thirteen, while her best friend had begun to fill out, growing rounder by the day, Katherine was still slender and underdeveloped. At times, she'd scrutinized Mary and the other girls in her grade at school, thankful for the differences between their bodies and hers. Even the shapes and sizes of their shadows at recess offered her reason to rejoice, for it was only in the dim reflections that she could sometimes see her own individuality.

❖   ❖   ❖

"Right nippy out, jah?" Mary's mother came in, carrying more wood for the cookstove.

Monday being washday, Mary had nearly frozen her fingers hanging the wash out front on the porch. "Don't think I ever remember a January this cold," she said, going over to the stove to help push pieces of wood into the fire below.

"Guess we come to that conclusion every winter. It near bruises the bones, I daresay," Rachel said, heading for the sink to wash her hands.

Mary set to work, making ready for bread baking and whatnot. "Come next Sunday, we'll have a houseful of folk," she remarked, thinking ahead to their turn for Preaching services. Bishop John would come with his five motherless children and stand in the front room of this very house, opening the Scriptures and reading aloud whole chapters at a time.

"Having church here doesn't come around for us all too much anymore," Rachel added. "The district's gotten so big, it's near burst its seams."

Mary laughed. "The seams are runnin' from Weaver's Creek all the way out to the highway."

"Jah, one of these days Preacher Yoder's gonna be callin'

for some of us to divide up, I 'spect. Make a new district of families."

Mary was surprised to hear it. "Ya mean it? We're *that* many Amish?"

Her mamma nodded, going to the pantry for some flour and sugar. "Ministers' council will be coming up here before long. Decisions will be made then."

Mary kept her thoughts to herself. In all truth, she was more than happy to hear of it. She could only hope that somehow or other, the People might be allowed to speak to Katie, if ever the shunned girl returned to Hickory Hollow. But if not . . . and if the Samuel Lapps were among the families chosen to move to another church district, well then maybe whoever became Preacher for that group—by the drawing of lots—might confer with the new bishop about the matter. 'Course, she had plans to speak to Bishop John about that very thing herself . . . someday. Even so, women were expected to keep their noses out of church affairs. And on top of that, she didn't want to take any chances with the budding romance. Nothing—well, hardly anything—was worth losing the interest of John Beiler.

❖   ❖   ❖

Katherine marked her spot in the book she was reading and placed it on the tea table in front of her chair. She walked the length of the library to the tall window and looked out. Snow was falling nearly slantwise and so thick with its steady motion that she felt momentarily dizzy. Leaning a knee against the low windowsill, she fixed in her mind the setting, taking in the expanse of meadow, the ridgeline of trees far to the east—the most beautiful place on earth. How all of this had come to belong to her, really and truly, she could scarcely comprehend. Yet it was so.

Here she was, settled in and quite snowbound, surrounded by shelves of intriguing books, flickering candles, and a roaring fire. At once, she realized that aside from the lovely furnishings, rugs, drapes, and wall hangings, she might well have been standing at the front room window in Samuel Lapp's home in Hickory Hollow, enjoying the afternoon without the luxury of electricity or indoor heating.

"What do you see when you look into your future?"

Daniel had asked her the question when they were yet young, back one summer while the two of them ran barefoot down a dusty lane, chasing after a stray pony in the squelching heat. Dog days, they'd always called the hottest weeks of July and August.

He'd asked the same question the following winter while they played outside during school recess. 'Course, she had no idea what he was really trying to say, and she went about patting the snow into a hard round ball.

She remembered the day as if it were yesterday—the way the snow had come down hard all around them, piling up steadily and erasing the footsteps that led away from the one-room schoolhouse in less time than it took to have recess. The first real blizzard of her life!

She recalled the heavy old boots she'd worn, the giant snowman she and Daniel had begun to make together. Still, they'd had so much help from their cousins and Plain friends that before they knew it, the snowman stood tall and finished, looking quite cheerful with eyes made of olives from somebody's sack lunch. The turned-up mouth was designed with broken bits of carrot sticks, as she recalled, and the black felt hat . . . young Daniel's.

He'd stepped back to survey the fat creature, laughing right out into the frosty air, laughing harder than she'd ever heard him. The sound rose from his belly, deep in the pit of him, and his face had turned peach red when she'd started chasing after him, yelling at him to please let her catch him.

And he had. He'd turned himself around without warning and stopped in the snow.

She'd plowed into him . . . hard, landing against his strong chest, but only because the snow was so deep and so slick she couldn't really help it at all.

Smiling now, she could see his eyes—blue as berries and all twinkly—like he was mighty glad she couldn't stop, glad she'd crunched into him like that, and probably glad she'd found herself all flustered up about it, too.

She moved back from the library window, wishing to let such childish memories fade, hoping that recollections from the past might not continue to confuse her, creating havoc with her recent decision to send Daniel away.

Garrett Smith came into the library just then, placing a round silver tray on the low table near the fireplace, a stately presentation. "Tea is served," he said, bowing. "Selig made your favorite cookies."

She knew without looking. "Please tell Selig thank you for me."

Garrett stood waiting for her dismissal as she strolled to the area where four matching wing chairs were situated around a wide oval table in the center of an expansive rug. "I was wondering," she began. "Could you . . . would you be willing to play a game with me?"

His eyes grew wide, followed by a peculiar grin. "Miss?"

"Checkers," she said. "Will you play a game of checkers with me?"

He nodded, bowing again. "At your service, Miss Katherine."

She shook her head, tiring of the proper conversational tone. "I won't call you 'sir,' if you'll promise not to call me 'miss.' How about that?"

He nodded, his cheeks turning red in the firelight.

"And furthermore, let's disband with such formal talk. It's starting to make my brain hurt . . . really 'tis."

"As you wish," he said, forgetting.

"Try saying 'gut idea.' " She watched him closely, his face not about to crack. "And make sure it sounds like 'goot' . . . jah?"

He shifted his weight from one foot to the other. Then nodding, he agreed. "Very well."

"Very *goot*," she prompted him.

"Goot" came the echo. And with that, the young steward poured a cup of tea, letting a few drops of milk drip into the china cup. "Sugar?"

"Always."

A game table was brought out, set up, and placed in front of the fire, so the blaze might light the checkerboard.

"You take the first move," she said as they sat opposite each other.

"As you wish."

"No . . . no." She wagged her finger at him, playfully.

"Ah, yes. Very gut."

She leaned forward, her eyes intent on him. "This is going to be a right-gut game. Ain't so?"

"Jah, right-*goot*," he said, surprising her.

❖   ❖   ❖

Katherine beat Garrett at checkers—three rounds worth—then called for Rosie. "Are there any lanterns around?"

"In the outbuildings, perhaps," Rosie replied. "Would you like one for your room?"

She rose and went to the fireplace. "Seems to me we could all gather here in the library for supper tonight. But it might be a bit dark without a lantern or two."

"Or at least a few candles," Rosie suggested. "Power lines are down all over the county. There may not be electricity yet tonight."

Katherine waved her hand. "I think we can adjust." She turned her back toward the fire. "It might be right fun, really."

Rosie cocked her head. "Perhaps you can teach us to enjoy it."

She knew the maid was referring to Katherine's childhood days—the absence of modern conveniences. "Oh, here's a thought. After supper, let's tell stories around the table."

Rosie chuckled and went to find someone to look for a lantern.

"Denki," she called after her friend and housemaid. Then, to herself Katherine whispered, hoping to make the words ring true, "A wonderful-gut night this will be."

She would try to enjoy herself while having supper in the library and sharing stories with her new friends around a crackling fire. Though, try as she might, it would be impossible to numb the sting of knowing that Daniel was alive . . . that he had been all along.

CHAPTER EIGHT

❖   ❖   ❖

The postman got his little white truck stuck in a snowdrift, smack-dab in front of the Stoltzfus mailbox. Mary's father ran out to help push as she observed the situation from her bedroom window.

The day had dawned bright, with the hope of much sunshine, but scudding clouds soon rolled over the Hollow, bringing with them heavy snow.

Mary had to laugh, watching her father huffing and pushing while the mailman revved up the engine of the tiny truck, spinning his tires to beat the band. Now, if he were Amish, the man could've hitched up a horse to a sleigh and gone about his duties, delivering the mail without any worry, just the way Dat used to take her and her older brothers to school back years ago on the worst days of winter. 'Course, there was no tellin' them Englischers how to carry the mail around to folks. She shook her head, thinking that there was nothing like right fancy tires for getting a body stuck in snow. Guaranteed.

She sat down at the window, entertaining thoughts of her next visit with John Beiler. When would he invite her to go with him somewhere again? Maybe he'd see her after church and speak to her about another ride in his family

Kutsch. Or maybe sooner. She could hope, because being around the bishop seemed so awful right . . . like the Divine Providence he often preached on. Spending time with John Beiler was just the way she'd always supposed it might be— back before he was ever really free to dream of. Back when he was engaged to marry Katie Lapp.

"Mail's here!" Abe Stoltzfus called up the steps to her. "There's a letter for ya, Mary."

For me? Hurrying to the steps, she ran down all the way. "Who's it from?"

"Hard to say. Looks like a New York postmark." His eyes squinted almost shut as he studied the return address. "Know anybody by the name of Taylor? Mrs. Rosie Taylor's the name."

She shook her head. "Never heard of such a person." But she was eager to read it anyway and headed for the kitchen, where she found a sharp knife and sliced the envelope open.

Sitting by the woodstove in her father's rocking chair, she began to read:

Saturday, January 17

Dear Mary,

Although I have never met you, I am told that you are a kind and devoted friend, and that you will understand fully the nature of this letter.

It has come to my attention that there is a young woman whom you know, but with whom you may no longer have contact. I am thinking of Katherine Mayfield, formerly Katie Lapp. I must confess to you that I do not understand such things as Amish shunnings, nor do I wish to pry. The reason I write today is for the sake of your friend Katherine, who does not want to cause trouble for you. Rather, she would like you to know that she misses you greatly and has not forgotten the many kindnesses you

*have shown her in the past. She is also concerned about
Rebecca Lapp, the woman who raised her, and hopes that
you might relay the message that Katherine loves and
misses her mother as well.*

*She would not think of writing to you directly, though
she would be pleased if such a thing were permitted. Katherine is not certain as to this way of corresponding—
whether or not your bishop would allow such a way of
"speaking" to her dear friend.*

*On behalf of Katherine Mayfield
(formerly Katie Lapp),
Mrs. Rosie Taylor*

Mary folded the letter and slipped it back into the envelope, hoping Dat would not come into the kitchen just
now and see that she was breathing hard, fingers trembling.
Pressing the letter to her heart, she held it there, desiring
with all her might that she could reply to the sender, to the
thoughtful woman, Rosie Taylor, who'd written this message with both Katie and Mary in mind. What a wonderful-
gut lady she must be.

Leaning back in the rocker, Mary was thankful that dear
Katie had met someone so kind, even though Rosie must
surely be English, for sure and for certain. Mary might've
spent the entire afternoon stewing over Katie, missing her
terribly, wishing she'd never left Hickory Hollow, but there
was work to be done. So she got busy with her mother and
Mammi Ruth—her father's Mam—patching Dat's work
trousers.

They sat around the kitchen table telling stories and
enjoying each other's company. After a bit, Mary took to
darning socks, thinking how she'd like to be doing the
same thing for Bishop John someday—for his children,
too. She felt that it wouldn't take much time at all before
she would be feeling true compassion for the whole
family.

"Abe mentioned a letter postmarked somewhere in New York," Mammi Ruth said, glancing up over her needlework.

Mary was silent for a moment. Wasn't sure what to say to her grandmother about it.

Rachel, however, didn't wait for Mary to speak up. "Isn't that where Samuel Lapp's daughter headed to? Seems to me Rebecca said it was."

Mary wouldn't go hiding the truth from her loved ones. Still, she wanted to keep the letter just for her own eyes, precious as it was. "The postmark was Canandaigua, a city up in New York somewheres," she managed.

"Jah, and who do ya know up there?" Mammi Ruth shot back.

Why the woman had to be so pointed, Mary didn't know. But she wished she might've kept the letter a secret, at least for a day or so. Then, if she *had* to say anything, it would be her idea alone.

"Mary?" Now Mamma was inquiring, and not about to let up on her, it seemed.

"Someone by the name of Rosie Taylor wrote to me," she replied with a sigh.

"Rosie?" Mammi Ruth stuck her needle in a spool of white thread and scratched her head through the prayer covering. "I don't know any Rosies in New York, do you, Rachel?"

Mary wondered if she should just go ahead and spill the beans on Katie . . . on herself, too. For if the People found out that Samuel's shunned daughter was using a stranger, an Englischer no less, to convey a message to one of the membership, well, there was no telling what an uproar might come of it.

Both women were looking over at her now, having abandoned their mending, just staring across the table.

"Ach, I don't know of any Rosies livin' up there, neither," she finally said.

"Well then . . ." Mammi Ruth picked up her needle and the loose knee patch, resuming her work.

"Jah, well . . ." Mamma did the same.

Mary sighed softly so as not to stir things up again. She was truly relieved that the matter had been dropped and quite abruptly at that.

❖   ❖   ❖

"You just have a bad case of cabin fever, that's all," Rosie said. "Which is quite easily remedied."

Katherine wasn't so sure. "Have you looked out the window lately? There's still plenty of snow everywhere. I don't know if it would be safe to go out just yet."

Rosie shook her head. "Street crews are out in full force. Have been all morning."

"So you think Theodore might be able to get around on the road all right?"

Rosie continued to dust and straighten up the sitting room adjacent to Katherine's bedroom. "I've never known a better chauffeur than Theodore Williams. You were very fortunate to have him stay on."

Katherine was curious. "What do you mean? Was he thinking of retiring?"

"Well, when Laura became so ill, he'd toyed with the possibility of ending his duties here—if and when she passed away."

"Really?"

Rosie nodded. "Yes, he'd thought of quitting, leaving the work to Rochester, the junior chauffeur, but you know what happened to *him*."

Circling the large room, Katherine wished she were the one cleaning up the place. It still seemed odd to have paid help working around her, always straightening things up, things *she'd* made messy. "I guess I don't miss Rochester much," she admitted. "But then again, I hardly knew him."

"The young man needed lessons in etiquette, among other things," Rosie said, lifting a vase to polish the sofa table. "It wouldn't surprise me if he changed vocations after Master Bennett dismissed him."

"Oh . . . why's that?"

"He just didn't seem to fit in around here. In my opinion, Rochester wasn't cut out to chauffeur high-society people."

Katherine felt suddenly self-conscious. "You mean fancy people like Dylan and Laura Bennett?"

Rosie stopped dusting. "Oh, dear me, no . . . I didn't mean what you must be thinking. *You're* one of them, too. A refined young lady. I see it in the way you enjoy fine things."

Rosie was overstating her case, it was clear to see. "But I was raised Plain . . . Amish," said Katherine. "I'm really not one of the elite, so to speak."

"Oh, but you *are*," Rosie insisted. "And you'll be surprised at how very quickly your backward ways . . . thoughts, too, probably, will begin to drop away. It's only a matter of time. You'll see."

Just now, the way her housemaid was going on about things, Katherine wasn't sure at all how she ought to view herself: English or just not quite.

Rosie began to explain further. "Look at the way your artist friend has taken to you. Certainly, Justin Wirth has noticed your aristocratic roots shining through—your *mother's* genteel background, of course."

Shivering at this awkward revelation, Katherine dismissed Rosie's comment, hoping that the interest Justin had shown her had more to do with Katherine herself than her fancy biological roots. Politely, she excused herself and went in search of Theodore Williams.

She found him outdoors, sweeping the back steps free of snow, the heavy shoveling already done. "Good afternoon," she called to him as she stood on the wide side porch.

Tipping his hat, he grinned. "What a nice change from such a storm." He paused to look up.

She followed his gaze, breathing in the crisp air and watching clouds skitter across a still-hazy sky. In the distance, the ridge was a gray-blue smear on the horizon.

"Is it safe out on the roads yet?" she asked hesitantly.

He nodded. "Where is it you'd like to go?"

She hadn't told a soul of her plans, but she was eager to find out about doing some volunteer work. "What about the hospice downtown . . . where Nurse Judah sometimes works?" she asked.

"Oh, the Canandaigua Hospice?"

"Yes, that's where I'd like to go." She said it with all confidence, hoping to see again the cheerful nurse who had personally tended to Laura during the most critical phase of her illness.

Theodore leaned on the broom. "When would you like to leave?"

She checked her watch, still unaccustomed to wearing jewelry, and—of all things—a right fancy jeweled timepiece. "Is one hour from now too soon?"

"Absolutely not. I'll bring the car around the front entrance promptly at three o'clock."

"Thank you, Theodore. I'll be ready." She turned to go inside, nearly bumping into Rosie, who was waiting just outside the kitchen, near the butler's pantry.

"May I have a word with you?" Rosie asked, her face drawn, eyes anxious.

"What is it?"

"I'm afraid I may have offended you, Katherine. I may have spoken out of turn—talking about your . . . past, that is."

"Please, don't think a thing of it." Katherine understood what the maid was attempting to make right between them. She had wondered, upon further reflection, if Rosie might not come to this conclusion regarding her comments made in the sitting room earlier. "You've done nothing but good for me since I came here. You owe me no apology."

Rosie's face broke into a smile. "It's a pleasure to serve you, Miss—"

"Just *Katherine*."

Rosie's eyes met hers. "That's what I like about you. You're so easy to be around . . . no airs. None of the elitist manner of thinking."

She agreed. "Let's keep it that way, jah?"

Rosie had to chuckle. "Very well."

Without further discussion, Katherine excused herself once again and hurried past the main kitchen by way of the narrow hallway, then to the main corridor of the house and to her suite.

❖   ❖   ❖

Downtown, the streets were well plowed and adequately sanded, according to Theodore, who sat squarely in the driver's seat while Katherine occupied the back, off to the right side.

She watched several people, wearing heavy coats, hats or scarves, boots, and either mittens or gloves. Peering out from behind the tinted limousine window, she contemplated each of the folk, some waiting at stoplights to cross the street.

In those faces she saw purpose. Some were headed to

make deposits of money at the bank, no doubt, others, to visit the post office. Still others were out for a bit of fresh air after having been cooped up for two solid days. Store lights twinkled in shop windows, and she thought of the Englischers having to suffer without electricity indefinitely. Why, their world would surely crumble over such a hardship. Yet, if truth be told, she'd enjoyed the lack of electrical lights, an excuse to use firewood for heating and cooking at Mayfield Manor. And just now, thinking about it, she wondered how the staff might feel if, on occasion, they outened the lights and used candles and lanterns in the mansion. Something to consider. . . .

❖   ❖   ❖

Natalie Judah's face lit up when Katherine first spotted her. "Well, hello again."

She smiled at the nurse. "It's good to see you."

"You're looking well," Natalie said, extending her hand.

"Thank you." Katherine glanced around the common room. Its walls were bordered with lush and leafy greenery, and at one end an aviary was filled with many colorful birds flying about. Such a tranquil setting for a terminally ill patient. "I can feel the peace in this room," she said.

Natalie, dressed in a soft blue sweater and cream-colored trousers, looked so natural and relaxed that it dawned on Katherine she'd never seen Laura's nurse in street clothes. Nurse Judah must've noticed Katherine glancing at her nonprofessional attire. "The charge nurse and all the staff wear casual clothing here at the hospice," she explained. "One of the ways we can connect more closely with our patients."

"How many are there?"

"We have a twelve-bed unit here presently but could

care for ten more if we had the space." Natalie went on to say that the hospice was highly regarded in the community. "We've been here for many years and have literally outgrown the building."

Katherine paid close attention, concerned that she not miss a single word of the nurse's comments. "Do you have a music program?" she asked, thinking of her guitar.

"We have a traveling unit that can be rolled from room to room, and once a week we have a flutist and harpist duo who come to entertain. It's quite therapeutic, even for the staff," said Natalie, smiling. "So, yes, we do encourage volunteers who are musically inclined. Would you like to have a tour?"

"I'd love one, thanks."

Although she didn't ask to see any of the private rooms, where hospital beds and personal belongings were located, Katherine did enjoy touring the dining area. Long family-style tables encouraged conversation and fellowship for those who were able. Most of all, she was taken with the enormous aquarium filled with numerous colorful fish.

She decided toward the end of the tour that a hospice such as this was a lovely, peaceful place to spend one's final days on earth.

Farther down the hall, Katherine was surprised to see a young boy, gaunt and pale, sitting in a wheelchair. He couldn't have been more than eight or nine, and something about him reminded her of Levi Beiler, Bishop John's son in Hickory Hollow. Her heart went out to the child . . . to all the patients, and she was glad to offer her time and her services.

At the end of the quick tour, she asked if she could discuss the process involved in becoming a volunteer. "I'm very interested."

"Sure. Come with me." Nurse Judah led her to a small

room where several nurses' aides sat, having coffee. "Would you care for something to drink?"

"Water's fine."

Natalie let the water run before holding a clean glass under the spigot. "How have you been, Katherine . . . since Laura's death?"

"As well as you might expect. It's never easy losing a family member, even though my birth mother was someone I hardly knew." She remembered her manners. "How have *you* been?"

"Oh, busy as usual. I meet myself coming and going these days." Natalie handed her the glass of water, then motioned toward a vacant table in the center of the room.

Katherine sat down and took a sip, knowing how it felt to be that busy . . . to fall into bed at night, completely exhausted from the day's activities. She'd grown up that way, getting up nearly as tired as she'd gone to bed. But those days were far behind her now.

"I was hoping I might be able to help out with your younger patients," she offered.

Natalie seemed pleased. "Client volunteers are always welcome. We do offer a concentrated two-week training program, and an interview is required along with an application."

"I'll be glad to do whatever is required."

Natalie poured herself a cup of coffee. "We're shorthanded at the present time, so I can set you up with the screening right away."

"Thank you. It means an awful lot to me." Katherine felt out of control suddenly, an unexpected lump forming in her throat.

"Are you all right?" Natalie's gaze narrowed, and she reached over to cover Katherine's hand with her own.

"I'm looking forward to getting out around people again," Katherine admitted. "The mansion, as big as it is, is quite confining at times. I don't know how to explain it, really."

Natalie seemed to understand. "Yes . . . I imagine it would be, by contrast."

"I'm also thinking of starting a quilting class. I want to set up frames in the manor library. Know of anyone who might be interested?"

Natalie's eyes grew big. "Are you serious? You're going to teach traditional Amish quilting patterns?"

"Beginning with the popular Ninepatch and working our way up to one of my favorites—the Country Songbird," she replied, growing more excited about the idea as she watched Natalie's face.

"Count me in. When do we start?"

"Right away. As soon as I can round up a frame or somebody to build me one."

Natalie blew on her coffee. "I know of several Amish settlements in and around Canandaigua. Someone from our fund-raising committee might know who does that sort of thing."

"Really?"

"Oh, absolutely. One of the reasons is that we have specially handmade quilts—some are Amish-made, I believe—displayed on the wall in each patient's room."

She'd never thought of doing such a thing with a quilt, though she could see why English folk might choose to. "What a nice way to decorate."

"Oh, it certainly is. Quilts are warm and cheery; often tell a story. We even have a few with the creators' names sewn right on the individual squares . . . really lovely."

They talked more about Katherine's idea to offer a class for beginning quilters at Mayfield Manor. Natalie's response was so surprisingly positive, Katherine felt spurred to act quickly. Along with her volunteer work at the hospice, the quilting class would help crowd out nagging thoughts of

Dan. Such a wonderful-good plan it was.

On the return trip, Theodore slowed the limousine to a stop in front of the post office, waiting for a red light. Spying people rushing in and out to mail their letters and packages, Katherine's thoughts wandered back to the letter she and Rosie had concocted for Mary, and wondered whether or not it had been delivered to the Hickory Hollow address.

She could only hope that her friend might receive it with all the love that was intended, and that it might not pose a problem for one so dear.

CHAPTER NINE

❖ ❖ ❖

Mary's bedroom—with only a bed, a small table next to it, an upright cane chair, and a narrow dresser with a medium-sized mirror attached—was nearly bare. She wasn't bothered by the room's simple furnishings. Rather, she liked the openness, preferred the expanse of the hardwood floor to fancy rugs and coverings.

She wrapped herself in a quilt and sat on the edge of her small bed, *kischblich*—silly—with delight. Tomorrow, *here*, in this house, she would come face-to-face with John Beiler again. Oh, she could hardly stand the thought of wasting the night by sleeping through it, not with the moon coming in through the window like a spotlight on her soul!

The quilt dragged behind her as she went to the window and stared out at the barnyard and on past the tobacco shed and beyond, where the land lay open in wide, sweeping patches. Snow lay heavy on the ground and in the distance, against the evening sky, two bright stars grinned down at her.

It was cold in the room, yet she shivered with joy, remembering the obnoxious way her muscles had tensed up on the ride back from the bank with Bishop John last Saturday afternoon, already one week ago. Seemed like just yesterday, and she held her breath in anticipation of the People coming for preaching tomorrow. More than that, she hoped to hear for certain that the bishop was actually going over to Schaefferstown, to attend the funeral of an old preacher friend. She'd overheard such talk at the General Store two days ago when young Levi Beiler, while chatting with Preacher Yoder, had said that his father was off to a funeral come Monday.

Her ears perked up right good as she crouched down behind a row of sacked sugar, eavesdropping on Levi and the preacher.

"I s'pose your pop'll be needin' someone to watch over you younguns while he's gone," said Preacher Yoder.

Levi nodded absentmindedly, reaching over to lift the glass lid off the peppermint sticks. "Daed's got someone in mind for us, all right."

Mary's heart leaped up at the boy's words. Who was the bishop thinking of asking? Did John have her in mind to stay with his brood?

She turned from the window and scurried across the floor, removing the quilt she'd wrapped herself in and placing it on top of the pile of quilts that draped over the single bed. Then, because the floor was ice-cold, she slipped under the sheets to say her prayers. The Good Lord would surely understand. This night, this moonbeam-filled night, she would pray under the warmth of her mamma's and Mammi Ruth's quilts, thanking the Lord God heavenly Father for His watchcare over her life. And . . . over John's.

Around midnight, Mary was still lying awake, wide-eyed in the scant light of a fading moon. She had devised various ways lately to occupy her mind when she suffered from insomnia. One way was to think of the days when she and Katie were little girls. Her favorite memory, among many, was the summer night they'd sneaked away from a picnic at the Lapps' place. Making sure no one noticed, she and Katie had run down the mule road that led to the cornfield, past the clearing, and toward the deep, wide pond with its cloistered island.

Under a fingernail of a moon, they'd rowed out on the slow water in the old boat, whispering and giggling to each other. When they reached the middle, Katie decided they wouldn't row all the way to the island but should stop and just drift along, lying back, staring up at hundreds of light points in the silvery sky.

Neither of them spoke for a time, then Katie sneezed, and the sound echoed across the water like ripples. Mary got the giggles all over again. And they sat up and faced each other, best friends, listening to the peaceful night sounds of talk and laughter carrying across the water, coming from the Lapps' farmhouse nearly a half mile away.

"Wish someday we could marry each other's brothers so we'd be sisters," Katie said softly.

"It don't matter really. We're already closer than that, jah?"

"Sisters in our hearts," Katie whispered, her eyes shining back at Mary.

"Right ya be," she agreed.

Mary closed her eyes, thinking of her dear sister-friend, and when she did, tears squeezed through her eyelids onto the old feather pillow.

Right ya be. . . .

Quickly, she thought of another way to fall asleep. She would say her Amish rote prayers over and over—several times in German, three times in English. If that didn't make her tired enough, she'd think of everything that had happened to her from the day she could actually remember things, which, she supposed, was around age four or so till the present time.

Try as she might, it seemed the years got all jumbled up in the routine of Amish life . . . over and again the same things. Getting up, making breakfast, choring inside and out, putting up quarts of food, helping other women can *their* harvested produce, sewing, mending, cleaning, baking, cooking, going to church every other Sunday, visiting, and going to bed. Not till Katie ditched Bishop John and got herself shunned had Mary ever noticed any departure from the rituals of her life. Not that there needed to be anything much more interesting than daily living, not really. But it *was* a noticeable thing—Katie leaving the bishop behind on their wedding day like she did. If nothing else, the sad yet surprising tale gave the women something to wag their tongues about. But it gave Mary much more than that. In her grief for Katie, she'd found hope.

So right then and there, in the darkness of her silent room, she decided she must *not* tell the bishop or anyone else about the letter from Rosie Taylor, who lived somewhere up in New York.

❖ ❖ ❖

Sometimes Samuel Lapp would read out loud to Rebecca on a Sunday evening when the house was quiet and they'd all had their share of seconds at dessert. She especially liked hearing him read from the many columns in *Die Botschaft*, a weekly newspaper for Old Order Amish and Mennonite communities.

"Listen here to this," her husband said with a chortle. "This 'un comes from Kutztown . . . seems there was an awful big commotion over at Luke Hoover's pigsty the other night. Sounded like one of his pigs was in serious trouble, a-howlin' and complainin' over in the hog house. And then if Clarence Leid's fussy old rooster didn't start a-crowin' and offerin' his sympathy to the noisy pig. 'Course the duet didn't last too much longer as the rooster seemed to out-howl the sow. And that was that."

Rebecca sat quietly rocking while her husband had to put down the paper and remove his glasses. He was laughing so hard his eyes were moist, but she tried not to gawk. Part of her had listened, taking in his words as he read the true anecdote. And she'd heard enough to offer a slight smile at the amusing story, nodding occasionally when he glanced over at her as he read.

Yet her heart seemed like a big chunk of ice, hard and cold. And the more she wished it would melt and leave her soft the way she used to be, the harder it felt.

When he'd composed himself, Samuel glanced over in her direction. "Now, what do ya think of that?"

"Well . . ." She pushed a little smile onto her face. "If you're tryin' to get me to laugh, ach, there's just not much that strikes me funny these days." She could've gone on to say what the reason was, but she figured he ought to know by now.

Samuel nodded, picked up the paper, and read to himself all the rest of the evening. She didn't blame him for it, not one little bit. The man had had his own share of sorrow over their daughter's rebellion and ultimate shunning. When she'd upped and left town, Rebecca knew he had suffered terribly, but here lately she just assumed he was handling his loss pretty well, in a manner of speaking. There were the upsetting occasions when he'd raise his voice to her or their sons, getting angry over hardly anything at all, far as she could tell. The look on Eli's and Benjamin's faces would tell her that they, too, knew something was still bothering Samuel awful much. Probably as much as it bothered all of them.

She leaned her head back on the rocking chair and sighed. And far off in the distance she heard a hoot owl calling for its mate from the trees beyond the creek.

❖   ❖   ❖

Her new grandbaby, Daniel Fisher—named for his uncle Daniel, who everyone thought was dead but had turned up alive—was howling like that sow her husband had read about the night before when Rebecca Lapp entered the kitchen door of her oldest son's house bright and early Monday morning.

Annie, her daughter-in-law, greeted her, waving her into the kitchen. "Baby's got the colic, I daresay." Reaching into the cradle, Annie lifted the bundle up into her arms.

Rebecca took off her wraps as the little one continued to wail. "Has a tummyache, all right." She went over and rubbed his tiny back in circular motions. "This'll sometimes help relieve the gas. Try that." And she stepped back, letting Annie take over the gentle patting.

Meanwhile, she went into the front room, where two large quilting frames were set up and ready for the womenfolk who would be arriving later, after breakfast. "Mary Stoltzfus won't be comin' over today," she said, going back to the kitchen.

"Jah, I heard. Seems she's been asked to stay all day with John Beiler's children." Annie's face blossomed into a big smile. "Suppose the bishop's taken a liking to her?"

Rebecca sat down at the long table, a frown appearing as she sighed audibly. "Your guess is as good as mine, but you know the sayin' same as I do: 'One who wastes time wastes life itself.' Wouldn't expect John to want to remain a widower much longer."

Annie shook her head, still rubbing the baby's back. "He's not gettin' any younger."

"No, none of us are that."

Daniel stopped crying and made sweet little sucking sounds. "Guess now he might be gettin' hungry," said Annie, preparing to nurse the baby.

"I'll do your dishes for ya." And Rebecca went to the sink and drew the rinse water.

"Denki, Mam." Annie sighed. "It's mighty hard keeping everything clean around here with a little one . . . and another one already on the way."

"You ain't tellin' me anything I don't know already." Rebecca clearly remembered what it was like having three children right in a row—all of them clamoring for attention while the housework and chores piled up. But not for one minute had she regretted birthing three fine sons and, later, embracing the infant Katie as her own. No, given the chance, she'd do it all again. Only one thing would be different if she could change things. She would have destroyed the satin infant gown that had stirred up such commotion with Katie, leading her away from the People—up to that English woman in New York. As much as she'd loved the perty rose-colored dress, she knew, for sure and for certain, the fancy little thing was the reason why her secret—her and Samuel's—ended up having to be told. Now the baby gown was gone, tricked out of her own hands by Ella Mae Zook. No wonder folks called her the Wise Woman. She wasn't just wise, she was shrewd. And more than ever, Rebecca suspected her of being in cahoots with Katie. Why else had she entertained the shunned Daniel Fisher in her Dawdi Haus several weeks ago? Why else had she told him where to go and look for Katie?

Once the womenfolk started coming for the quilting frolic, the tormenting questions subsided, and she set to sewing her straight, tiny stitches on a brand-new quilt to be given to one of Annie's cousins as a birthday gift. For the first time in a long, long time, she came ever so close to volunteering a story. "I'll try to tell one today," she said hesitantly. "It may not happen. I just don't know yet. . . ."

Annie and the others burst into applause, grinning and cheering her on like nobody's business. She felt her cheeks flush with embarrassment, but when she opened her mouth to recite the opening lines of an old favorite, she knew she wasn't quite ready. Someday she would spin her tales again, 'cause this was a gut and right thing. Something she'd yearned for—honest-to-goodness missed—but just couldn't bring herself to do. Not just yet.

❖   ❖   ❖

Mary met the bishop's four older children at the back door as they came in from school. Jacob, the youngest, held her hand as they stood there, propping the storm door open. "How was school today?" she asked as they filed in, one by one.

Nancy and Hickory John launched into a long description of what they'd studied. But the minute Susie stepped into the utility room, she started bawling her eyes out.

"What'sa matter?" Mary asked, brushing stray hairs from the girl's forehead.

Susie hitched up her skirt tail and pointed to her skinned knee. "Oooow! I hurt . . . myself . . . awful bad!" she wailed.

Mary knelt on the floor, eye level with the six-year-old. "Let's see how *awful* bad it is."

"I . . . I falled down and skinned my knee." Susie leaned down and showed her the wound, crying all the while.

A quick look and Mary saw that a scab had begun to form already.

"It hurts!" Susie fussed some more.

Levi rolled his eyes and pursed his lips, as though he knew something about the injury but wasn't saying. He pulled his boots off and lined them up next to Hickory John's.

It was Nancy who offered the telling explanation about her sister's accident. "She fell outside during recess this morning. And she never told the teacher about it . . . so *now* she's cryin'."

Mary gathered the tiny girl in her arms. "Aw, you held

in the pain all this time? Well, come on in and have some hot chocolate. That'll help better'n *anything*."

Nodding, her lower lip protruding, Susie took Mary's hand and went without further complaint to the table, scooted onto the bench, and waited with glistening eyes for her cocoa.

Several hours later, with Nancy offering to help, Mary set a fine table and served up a delicious batch of chicken and dumplings.

"You should come on over more often," Nancy said, grinning at her across the table. "Daed likes gut cookin'."

"Sure does!" little Jacob said. "And me too!"

Susie, her knee scrape forgotten, nodded her head up and down. "We need a mamma . . . real bad."

Mary grinned, growing more attached to the Beiler children with each minute that passed.

Hickory John spoke up. "When's Daed due back?"

"Sometime tonight," she told him.

Nancy smiled and ducked her head. "Best save some dumplin's for him," she said softly into her plate.

"Gut idea," Levi agreed, though he never once looked up at Mary.

Sitting there with the children scattered around the table, their hands busy with dinner, their faces bright with hope, she knew for sure and for certain that this home was where she belonged—what her heart was longing for.

Sighing, she decided yet anew that she would not answer the warm and honest letter from the stranger named Rosie, who'd written her in Katie's stead. There was only one way she would ever consider doing such a thing. Bishop John would have to remove the ban on talking to Katie of his own accord, without any mention of it from Mary.

CHAPTER TEN

❖   ❖   ❖

The search for Laura's journal continued all week long. Even after Katherine tired of rummaging through the two large attics, Selig and Garrett continued, with Fulton's and Rosie's help.

"I suppose it'll turn up if the Good Lord wants me to find it," she said at last.

Rosie encouraged her not to worry. "I'm sure it's around here somewhere."

All at once Katherine was struck with concern. "Could it be . . . do you think Dylan knew about Laura's diary and took it with him when he moved his things out?"

Rosie turned quickly to look at her husband. "What do you think of that, Fulton? Is it possible?"

The butler stood tall and, shaking his head, assured Katherine and Rosie that could not be the case. "Certainly not. What use would he have for it?"

"None, unless he thought it might lead him to secret accounts or such things," Rosie added with a groan. "But, of course, that would have been long before Laura had any accounts of her own."

"You're right." Fulton sat in a tufted Victorian chair near the butler's pantry just outside the kitchen. He scratched his head, glancing up at the staircase nearby. "I don't believe Dylan Bennett had any idea the young Laura's diary even existed."

Rosie placed her hand on his shoulder. "She must have packed it away safely with other treasures from her youth."

"Should I call Mr. Cranston?" Katherine spoke up. "Would *he* know anything about it?"

"I doubt it. The diary is over twenty-two years old. I'd have to say there's little chance an attorney would be privy to it."

While Fulton was talking, Katherine had the feeling, once again, that Lydia Miller would wholeheartedly suggest going to prayer over the lost journal. "God cares about every detail of your life, Katie," she'd told her on several occasions.

Still, Katherine continued to look in every closet, search every nook and cranny of the old mansion, not bothering God with such a mundane thing as the lost diary of a teenage mother-to-be, even though that mother had been her very own.

❖　❖　❖

Four cars were parked in the circular drive in front of Mayfield Manor ten days later: Natalie Judah's and the vehicles belonging to three other women who'd responded happily to the quilting class ad in the Canandaigua newspaper. Katherine was overjoyed with such interest in her free class. In fact, she stood where Fulton usually positioned himself, personally greeting each lady at the front door.

She had all of them gather in the drawing room to get better acquainted before asking Garrett to bring in some hot tea and pastries.

"So good to see all of you here," Katherine said, standing near the fireplace and leaning against the mantelpiece. She introduced herself first, then Leoma, Natalie Judah, Missy

Braun, Elizabeth May, and Rosie's sister, Ada. "All future quilters," she said of them.

They smiled, nodding. The ladies exchanged pleasantries, and Katherine discovered that Ada and Elizabeth had taken a quilting class together years ago but hadn't run into each other since. "We probably need a refresher course," Ada spoke up, casting a smile at Elizabeth. "But since Katherine used to be Amish, well, maybe we'll actually remember better this time."

Used to be Amish.

The phrase took Katherine quite by surprise. Probably because she'd never heard herself referred to in that way before. At any rate, she stood there, preparing to teach the fundamentals of quilting, when a fleeting memory surfaced and she recalled a month of school days. At just sixteen, she had served as substitute for the regular Amish teacher. Once again she was an instructor, only tonight the topic for discussion did not involve the three R's.

The evening proved to be a lively one, and even though some of these women had come to her as strangers, Katherine felt, midway through this first quilting session, that she really liked these fancy English ladies and hoped there might come lasting friendships out of their time together.

❧ ❧ ❧

The remaining weekdays were spent attending the training sessions at the hospice. Natalie Judah was always jovial and kind, grateful for Katherine's interest in the hospice. Glad that her birth mother had had the opportunity to know the nurse before Laura's passing, Katherine derived great strength from Natalie. After only a few days, she was also becoming a dear friend.

When Katherine had finished up her two weeks of training and sailed through her exit interview, she was delighted.

Her schedule was set for Mondays and Wednesdays, two hours each day.

"I'd like you to read to Willy," said Natalie on Katherine's first official day as a volunteer.

She followed a nurse's aide to the common area, eager to interact with one of the patients. Willy turned out to be the blond boy she'd seen on the day she'd inquired about volunteering. He was a beautiful eight-year-old, diagnosed with a malignant brain tumor. Willy's eyes, blue as they were, filled her with compassion, for she could see the agony of cancer imprinted there.

She sat with him in the sun-filled gathering area, getting acquainted. "What's your middle name?" he asked her after they'd exchanged first and last names.

"I was never given a middle name," she told him.

His eyes widened. "Really . . . no middle name?"

"Is a middle name very important?"

"Well . . . maybe." He broke into a smile. "I've got *two* middle names."

"You do? Well, I think that's very nice. What are they . . . if you don't mind telling me?"

He seemed more than happy to tell her. "My name is William James Lee Norton. I have my dad's name, my grandpa's name, and my uncle's name."

She couldn't help smiling. She had her birth mother's *choice* of a name, but that was the extent of it. "I like all of your names, Willy," she commented, wondering why she was so drawn to the youngster.

Later, after they'd discussed favorite colors and foods, and the best kinds of smells, books, and animals, he asked out of the blue, "Are you married?"

She had to chuckle. "Not yet, but I hope to be someday."

"Then will you have lots of children?" His face was full of questions as they sat side by side on the wicker settee.

"If the Good Lord sees fit, I suppose I will."

"It's one of your wishes, right?" He reached for a small ball with his foot, his legs limp as wilted celery.

"A wish?" she said. "Well, I guess I never thought of having children as being a wish."

Willy asked if she'd help him sit on the floor so they could roll the ball back and forth. Carefully, she lifted him down and got him propped up on the floor with several pillows. Then she sat on the floor opposite the bright but fragile boy and pushed the ball gently, glad she'd worn woolen trousers instead of a skirt.

"My father says that God gives His people the desires of their hearts," young Willy continued, "if they're linked up with Him."

Linked up with God?

Katherine had never heard such talk. Especially coming from one so young . . . one so desperately ill.

On Wednesday, Willy talked even more openly, and Katherine remembered hearing or reading—or maybe it was Dan who'd told her this years ago; she couldn't recall which—that "a little child shall lead them." Honestly, she didn't feel as though she needed to be led anywhere, so she didn't quite know from where such a recollection had sprung. Or why.

As far as she was concerned, she was right where she wanted to be, enjoying every minute of her high-society English life, partly due to Justin Wirth and his many contacts and friends.

Katherine turned her attention back to Willy, and when he'd tired of their checkers game, she slowly wheeled him over to have a close look at the aquarium. Several large blue and green fish caught their interest, and one very fat brown snail, too, which they quickly agreed to name Fred.

When it came time to say good-bye, Katherine was reluctant to leave the boy. With all of her heart, she wished she could do something significant to make Willy's cancer go away—and never return.

On the ride home, she forced her thoughts away from Willy, daydreaming of Justin, yet careful to conceal her smile from Theodore's view.

Just last Friday she had dined with him at Belhurst Castle, a turreted, red Medina stone structure located in Geneva, less than a thirty minutes' drive from Mayfield Manor. It was the romantic setting he had promised her before the crippling snowstorm.

The cordial waiter had chosen a table for two, situated near a window in the banquet hall overlooking the shores of Seneca Lake. The breathtaking vista and sweeping expanse of snow-covered lawns gave Katherine the notion that she *was* a princess, dining in a real castle.

Justin, dressed impeccably in a double-breasted navy blazer and tan slacks, was very attentive—more so than ever—leaning toward her at one point as they sat across from each other at the candlelit table. "They say an Italian opera singer once lived here. Have you heard the story?"

She shook her head, but her gaze was riveted on the handsome face, the azure eyes, as he told the haunting tale.

"A Spanish don and his ladylove lived here long, long ago." His voice was softer now. "The couple ran away from home . . . an ill-fated romance, some say."

"And they built this castle?" She felt as if she might be the runaway ladylove, especially tonight, so far removed from the cloistered life of the Amish. "They came here to hide?"

"Yes, amidst secret tunnels and buried treasure, they hid here . . . from their own people."

She looked about her at the flagstone floor, the stone walls, the high windows, wondering about Justin's simple story. "Is it really true?"

He smiled, offering her a mischievous wink, and her

pulse quickened. "No one knows for sure," he said.

When the waiter came back to take their order, Justin was the perfect gentleman, ordering the salmon dinner she chose from the menu. She felt helpless to slow her heart to its normal pace, sitting there, her eyes fixed on his face, his hands—the well-bred, attractive man whose words flowed like warm honey, whose gestures were artistic, as enchanting as this mysterious place.

He had reached for her hand and held it all the way back to Mayfield Manor as they rode in the moonlight. Later, upon their arrival, he got out and opened the door of the limousine, asking the driver to stay put as he walked her to the door. "The castle was the perfect setting for our first dinner out together," he remarked as they made their way to the double doors of her mansion.

"Yes." She could hardly speak past a whisper.

Turning to face her, he took both her hands in his. "I hope one day we'll return."

"To the castle?"

"As runaway lovers," he said, smiling down at her in the light of the rustic lamppost.

Surprised, she didn't know what he meant exactly, but she liked the sound of his voice in the stillness. So quiet, she felt as if the earth held its breath.

Then he kissed the back of each of her hands. "I'll call tomorrow," he said, smiling down at her.

"Good night," she said, turning toward the door lest he reach for her, sweeping her into his arms unexpectedly. Oh, as much as she might've welcomed it, she was hesitant. Something held her back, though she was not sure what.

"Until tomorrow," he said. "Good night, dear Katherine."

She smiled to herself, hearing his footsteps on the pavement. Turning for a parting glance, Princess Katherine leaned against the heavy door that led inside to her very own castle, her heart filled with longing for the next glimpse of her artist prince.

Not until she turned off the lamp beside her bed did she even once think of Dan. And because of that, she assumed she was moving away from the initial shock—pushing her pain far away from her, pushing away the realization that out there in the world somewhere her dear first love was alive and well.

In her silent rote prayers, as she had always learned to pray at bedtime, she thought of young Willy, wondering if his wish might come true . . . if *he* was to have his heart's desire. She tried to pray for the poor, sick boy but felt every bit at odds with it, the same as she'd felt about praying in that way back at Lydia Miller's when she'd first tried.

Once asleep, she dreamed of Justin. He was planning a picnic in the snow . . . for her and Willy. Mixed-up and hazy, the wintry, pastoral dream was filled with spicy ferns growing ankle-deep out of a dense snow crust, ending with Daniel Fisher arriving just as they were putting the food away, packing up, ready to go home.

Gasping for breath, she woke with a start and sat up in her bed. "He's still . . . in my dreams," she whispered, hand at her throat.

Fully awake, she climbed out of bed, slipped into her bathrobe and house shoes, and made her way through the bedroom to the sitting room. There she stopped and stared at the dying embers in the fireplace, then headed out into the hallway, her steps guided by low-burning wall lamps.

A late-night snack might help her forget the peculiar dream. Oh, she longed for one long night without thoughts of Daniel intruding on her sleep. And one pleasant day without the memory of his eyes probing hers, his words burning into her soul.

"I don't mean to take up much of your time," he had said in her parlor. The scene had replayed itself a thousand times

in her mind. He wasn't only taking up her time, he was disrupting her life.

"I've been waiting a long time to see you again. . . ."

She sat at the table where her domestic help always ate their meals, except for the one snowbound night in the library. Clapping her hands over her ears, she longed to stop his voice. More than anything.

Little Willy had said something about God giving His children the longings of their hearts. Well, now was a good time for the Good Lord to start, she decided. Because if God didn't stop the memories, heal her immense pain, how was she ever to focus her romantic attentions on the dashing, very *honest* Justin Wirth?

She folded her hands in front of her. "Please, dear God, will you make the past die? Make *my* past go away," she said softly into the darkness of the kitchen.

Then, weeping, she nearly forgot where she was. In the dim light, the enormous kitchen almost looked like her mamma's, and for a brief, intangible moment, she was sitting on the wooden bench next to the trestle table, wishing Rebecca might come and find her out of bed in the middle of the night and make her some warm, soothing cocoa.

CHAPTER ELEVEN

◆　◆　◆

Mary had promised herself that she would try to not think about the bishop so much. 'Course, it was next to impossible to keep that promise really. Every waking minute he was on her mind. She could only hope that he was pleased with the way she'd looked after his children.

She arose at four-thirty, eager to help with breakfast, and even volunteered to assist her father with milking chores.

"No . . . no, you stay in where it's warm," he said, hurrying out the back door into the predawn blackness.

"Are ya sure?" she called after him, experiencing such a surge of energy she could hardly contain herself.

Abe turned around, staring at her from the bottom of the snowy steps, a frown pinching his brow. "Goodness' sakes, Mary, ya haven't helped with milkin' for several years now."

"Well . . . just thought I'd offer." She knew her words must sound awful peculiar; still she waited, wondering if he'd change his mind.

Her father shrugged, turned, and shook his head as if to say he wasn't about to try to figure out his youngest offspring, which didn't discourage her one little bit. She rushed back into the kitchen to help stir up some milk and flour and eggs, making ready for homemade waffles.

Even as she stirred the mixture, John Beiler was a big part of her day, of her thoughts, and she felt like a young girl again, getting ready for the Christmas Eve program at school . . . or something just as exciting. She hailed him from past days, recalling the fun, the laughter . . . jah, the love that was beginning to flower between them.

And there was to be yet another get-together. The evening she had prepared to leave the bishop's house, after John had arrived home from Schaefferstown, he'd invited her on a sleigh ride. "For just the two of us," he whispered as she stood in the privacy of the utility room, pulling on her mittens.

"Where will we meet then?" she'd managed to ask.

His eyes sparkled as he smiled down at her. "Can ya take your Dat's horse and carriage over to the bridge at Weaver's Creek?"

"Jah . . . I think so."

"We'll leave the buggy there. The horse will be all right tied up to the fence post." He paused for a moment, his eyes searching hers so much that she felt she might blush right there in front of him. "Meet me after nightfall . . . about six-thirty."

She smiled, imagining the sleigh ride, bundled up in her warmest coat and winter bonnet, maybe even snuggling a bit under the furry lap robe.

"What're *you* smilin' about?" her mamma said, staring over at her from across the kitchen.

Mary straightened, turning away, so her mother and grandmother wouldn't see the heat rising into her face. "Oh, was I smiling just now?"

Mammi Ruth cackled, going about the chore of setting the table. "She must be thinkin' on her new Beau."

Not to reply would mean acknowledgment. So Mary spoke softly, keeping her face to the wall as she stirred the flour and baking soda into the bowl with swift, hard strokes. "What new Beau?"

Now both women were hooting with uncontrollable laughter. Mary had to smile herself. She couldn't help it; the corners of her mouth turned up at will. But she was able to hide the jubilant grin from the women most dear to her. She did it merely by facing away, fixing her eyes on the waffle batter.

❖ ❖ ❖

She accepted John's extended hand, allowing him to pull her up into the box-shaped sleigh filled with sweet-smelling straw and more lap robes than she could count.

"Nice to see ya, Mary."

"And you too."

He helped spread the fur-lined blankets over her legs before taking the reins in both hands. "Ready?" he said.

"Jah."

The tinkle of bells echoed in the night as the moon peeked through trees, casting silvery shadows on the ground. Mary heard the swishing, crisp sound of the runners cut through hardened snow, and the icy earth glistened under ten thousand stars.

She laughed right along with John as the horse seemed to fly over acres and acres of snow-laden fields, pulling them through space, away from their work and toil, away from those whose eyes might pry, those suspecting that love just might reside in the chill of the wind on this night.

John leaned his head back at one point, sniffing the cold air. "Smell that?"

She did the same, breathing in deeply. "Ach, it's skunk."

They had to laugh again, pinching their noses shut. After the smell had dissipated, they rode on in silence. Mary, content enough just to be sitting next to John this way, squeezed her mittened hands under the heavy blanket on her lap.

It seemed as if eternity might pass before John spoke again. Oh, how she longed for it, to hear his voice so very close to her ears. *So close. . . .*

When John let go of the reins with one hand and reached behind her, putting his arm around her, she felt as if she might cry, so in love with this man she was.

"A right-gut night for a sleigh ride." He turned to face her. "Ain't so?"

Her eyes met his. "Jah, right fine," she whispered.

Then John moved closer, pressing his forehead gently against hers. The motion tilted her winter bonnet back a bit, but she didn't mind, didn't even bother to put up her hand to steady it.

"I'm a bit old to think of goin' for steady, ya know," he said, his breath warm against her face.

She knew. "If ya say so."

He sat up straight just then. "Well, what would ya think of marryin' your bishop in the dead of winter?" His voice was strong and confident, taking her by surprise.

Her heart beat wildly. "Marryin'?"

"I want you for my own . . . for my wife, Mary Stoltzfus." His eyes were wells of affection.

"Oh . . . I . . ." Her throat felt like cotton. "I—"

Gazing intently on her face, he reached up and traced her hairline with his fingertips. She held her breath, and his bare hand cupped her trembling chin. "It must come as a surprise to ya, Mary. I'm sorry if I—"

"I'm . . . I'm as happy as can be," she said softly, so as not to break the spell, her eyes searching his.

Then slowly his lips found hers in a tender kiss. He backed away, looking deep into her eyes yet again. "Oh, Mary, I want to make ya happy. Honest I do. . . ."

Before she could answer, his lips met hers again—a lingering kiss to seal their unspoken commitment.

Mary wasn't sure how long they snuggled that way. For all she knew, the horse might've lost his way for the lack of direction on the part of the driver, yet Mary cared not how many sweet kisses her beloved showered upon her that night, his strong arms enfolding her in his loving embrace. Nor could she think clearly of anything but of her longing to be near him, for ever and always.

❖   ❖   ❖

It was well past eight o'clock when they turned back toward Weaver's Creek, to her parked carriage and the poor abandoned horse. "Sugar might be too cold to be trottin'," she said, glancing up at the moon.

"We were gone longer than I thought," John said, getting out of the sleigh and throwing one of the lighter blankets over Sugar's back. "That oughta help. Just let him go at his own pace. And . . . if ya don't mind, I'll follow you out to your lane."

"Denki. That's kind of you." She wished John would come and give her a parting kiss before they went their separate ways. But she knew it was best that they not show affection right there on the road. Too many courting couples out on a night like this. Too many eyes . . .

He helped her into the cold buggy, then went to the fence and untied her father's horse. "Why don't ya use one of my blankets? Already warmed up."

"Gut idea." She had to smile as he jumped up into her carriage unexpectedly, wrapping her up in the furry thing, treating her as tenderly as a child.

"This'll keep ya warm till you're home." He turned, looked both ways up and down the road, then sat beside her. "I'll be missin' ya, Mary. I will." He took her in his arms and gave her a long good-bye kiss. Her head was swimming, though she did not pull away first. "Good night, Mary, dear."

"God be with you," she said, completely out of breath.

Grinning, he backed out of the buggy and stood there in the snow, waving. "Meet me here again?"

"When?"

"Tomorrow, maybe?"

She nodded, wishing the night might never end or, better yet, would depart on swift wings of day until Sunday evening could come.

❖　❖　❖

Katherine had been completely surprised by the letter in the late afternoon mail. Because of her scheduled plans to have the quilting class meet again that evening, she purposely waited until the ladies left for home, before ever sitting down with the envelope postmarked Newark, New Jersey.

Sighing, she leaned against the plump antique chair just a few feet from her bed. She might've guessed Daniel would pursue her, especially after the way she'd dismissed him. Though, thinking back on it now, she wished he had done so years ago, long before she'd discovered that her Amish upbringing had been a fakery. That she was truly English.

Unsure of herself, she held the envelope in her hand, studying the handwriting. She'd know it anywhere. The old feelings stirred within her, and she hardly knew what to do.

Slipping a finger under the loose part of the flap, she opened the envelope, her breath coming more quickly now. *Dare I do this?* she wondered.

She hesitated, eyes scanning the return address. So this was his residence, the place where he'd hid from her all these years? In Newark, New Jersey—not far from Lancaster County. She almost laid it down or threw it away, still uneasy about holding the envelope in her hands.

Was she giving Dan a second chance, another opportunity to hurt her, by reading his letter? She laid the envelope on her lap, staring at the formally draped window across the room.

Was it the right thing to do? A soft chuckle escaped her lips. *The right thing.* The very words that had always defined Mary's position in life. Her friend would probably say to go ahead and open the letter, find out what Daniel wanted to put in writing. Mary, it seemed, was still advising her in spirit, though they were miles apart. Friends for life, in spite of the shunning. Connected in spite of all that had transpired.

Her dearest friend would say to read it. So she did. With shaking hands, she unfolded the letter.

Thursday, March 7

Dear Katie,

Nearly two months have passed since I saw you in Canandaigua. At the time, I worried that I might upset you unduly, and as it turned out, that was the case. You were not only upset, you were clearly pained at my visit, and for this, I am truly sorry.

No amount of asking on my part can make it possible for you to forgive me, though I could only pray that it would be so. You see, I have never stopped loving you, and hard as I try to think of you as Katherine Mayfield, it is difficult for me to remember you as anyone other than the dear Amish girl I first fell in love with that day many years ago—when we were but children. Perhaps I never told you about the first time I saw you standing there by the old buck stove in the schoolhouse. Your hair was not yet in the traditional bun, but pulled back with braids wrapped around your little head. You must have been no more than seven, but I can't be sure. If I'd had any sense I would have recorded the day, the year, the moment. I never told you of the feeling I had that day, but it has never let go of me since

131

that time. To think that all those years from my nineteenth birthday until now have been wasted, literally a great waste of our love. And now, here we are, once again separated.

I take all the blame for this, Katie, as I tried to tell you when we met briefly, and you may not accept it now as you did not then. How can I tell you? What I did was wrong. I should have returned to my father that very day, made things right with him, turned from my rebellion, and then, after much prayer and counsel, left the Amish church. Instead, things turned out much differently for me—for everyone. Someday I hope you'll allow me to tell you the whole story, everything that happened.

In the meantime, I have found a love I've never known . . . this I find in the Lord Jesus. And if nothing ever comes of my love for you on this earth, it will not be for naught. You see, Katie, I pray that you may find this same joy and peace that I have. It is not bound up in the rules and requirements of a church. My happiness is in knowing my sins are washed away, my name written in the Lamb's Book of Life. You can have this peace, this assurance of salvation that we were taught to believe was wrong, even prideful. The truth is, God's Word clearly states the way to redemption—through faith in Jesus, the Savior. If you ever yearn to know more, read the book of John in the New Testament. You'll find there what your heart searches for.

I don't mean to sound like a preacher, but I cannot keep this peace to myself. Truly, it passes all understanding. It is this Good News that compels me to witness of Jesus' love for you.

Yours always,
Daniel Fisher

P.S. Do you ever play the guitar I gave you?

Had she known the contents of the letter, she might never have opened it. Slipping the letter back inside the envelope, she tried to push his written words out of her mind. The man was clearly insane . . . declaring his love to her in a letter like this.

And telling her what to believe about God, of all things!

She wondered where such boldness had come from, for she had not remembered him being quite this way as a youth, well . . . maybe he *had* been more brash than most, now that she thought of it.

There was no need to belabor this. She went to her bureau drawer and placed the letter inside, beneath the satin baby gown still wrapped in tissue paper.

❖   ❖   ❖

Justin called as he had promised, inviting her to tomorrow evening's symphony concert, followed by a reception in honor of a retiring violinist. She agreed to go, thinking that another evening spent with her dashing boyfriend might lay all her troubles to rest.

Had she been a praying woman, she might've mentioned this in a prayer to the Almighty. But she was far too suspicious of such praying—to plead for mercy or help from the Creator of the heavens and the earth. Besides, how could she really know if God was as intimately involved in her life and in her plans as both Lydia Miller and Daniel Fisher seemed to think? She considered this concept, so foreign to her way of thinking and to her Amish background, and recalled Laura's glowing deathbed description of her love for God's Son, even going so far as to ask Katherine if she, too, knew Jesus.

At the time, Katherine had been moved to tears, but now she was able to think more rationally about the matter and wondered if her heart had been so touched then because she was attending the death of her birth mother. Surely, that's all there was to it.

CHAPTER TWELVE

❖   ❖   ❖

Every other Sunday was always spent visiting in Hickory Hollow, and Mary could hardly wait to take an afternoon drive to see Rebecca Lapp. It seemed—if she could believe the hearsay—that Katie's mamma was slowly inching out of her depression over the shunning and whatnot all.

Mattie Beiler had been heard telling Preacher Zook's wife at the General Store that Rebecca nearly launched off on one of her stories back last Monday at Annie Lapp's quilting frolic. In fact, she'd come *that* close to actually starting one of her old familiar yarns.

Praise be! Mary thought it right-gut news, but she just had to see for herself. So she hitched up Sugar and hopped in the carriage.

"*Hott rum!*" she called to the horse, flapping the reins lightly. He turned to the right and hurried down Hickory Lane.

Rebecca did seem mighty glad to see her. Mary could tell by the way the woman greeted her with an enthusiastic, "Wie geht's, Mary? Gut to see ya."

She went inside, letting Rebecca assist with hanging up her coat, scarf, and outer bonnet. "Denki," she said, following the older woman into the warm kitchen, where cherry

135

pie and vanilla ice cream were already spread out on the table, almost as if she had been expected.

"Sit down and have something to eat," Rebecca invited.

Mary glanced around, surprised to see that Samuel wasn't sitting in his usual spot—the hickory rocker near the woodstove. "Isn't your husband at home?"

"He's out checking on Tobias, our pony. The poor thing's got a stiff leg or some such ailment. Samuel and the boys are having a look-see."

Mary remembered the pony. Satin Boy was the name Katie had given Tobias, right out of the blue, around the time she started obsessing on fancy things—out and out disobeying the Ordnung. At least that was the way Mary remembered it.

"It's awful nice of you to come," Rebecca was saying. "Since our daughter left, I don't see too terrible much of you, ya know."

Mary nodded. "I'll hafta remedy that, I 'spect. It's a shame we don't talk more." She was working up to telling the woman about Katie's letter—that her shunned daughter had inquired of her. But Mary felt she ought to wait till she knew, for sure and for certain, that it was the right time to bring up the subject. And that Rebecca would keep it quiet.

"Care for a piece of pie?" asked Rebecca, positioning the knife over the crust.

"Jah, looks delicious."

Rebecca dished up a hearty serving of the homemade dessert, piling a big scoop of ice cream on top, after getting the nod from Mary.

The two women enjoyed the sweet pastry together, smacking their lips in the quiet of the kitchen, a room filled with the smells of yesterday's baking. Mary wondered how terribly much Rebecca must miss her daughter's help around the house, especially in the kitchen, preparing food, baking bread and things.

"I . . . uh, don't really know how to go about sayin' this, Rebecca, but . . ." She paused a moment, noticing instant concern creep into the woman's hazel eyes. "No, no," she assured her, "it's nothing bad I have to tell you, not at all. I received an unexpected letter from a stranger in New York . . . someone who knows your daughter, is all. Anyways, the woman—her name was Rosie Taylor—wanted me to tell you that Katie, er, you know—Katherine—was worried about you, is thinkin' of ya. Guess she heard from Lydia Miller that you weren't feelin' all that gut for a spell there."

Rebecca put both hands in her lap and blinked several times in a row, creating an awkward silence. At last she spoke. "You say my daughter sent a letter written by someone else . . . to you?"

"Jah, but she was awful careful about it—didn't want to cause trouble here in the Hollow. So I guess I'm thinkin' we should keep this under our hats, ya know . . . not mention it to anyone."

Rebecca smiled slightly. "Probably a gut idea."

They finished eating their pie, stealing glances back and forth. Finally, Mary got up the nerve to say something else. Something just as important as letting Rebecca know that Katie was thinking of her, missing her. Something she'd *thought* of discussing with the bishop but had only mentioned to her own mamma. No one else.

"I was wonderin'," she began again. "I thought maybe there might be a way to correspond with my dear friend up there in New York if . . . well, if I might speak to Bishop John about the possibility of being allowed to talk to her, or just maybe even write to her . . . lift the talking part of the shunning. That way the People might be able to have some influence on the poor shunned girl."

Rebecca's face brightened. "How do ya plan to go about such a thing?"

"Well, I don't rightly know, but I'm hopin' something—

some powerful-gut idea might come to me when . . ." She almost let it slip that she was going to be seeing the bishop privately or some such revealing comment. "*Whenever* it is that I might have a chance to speak to the bishop about it." It was a feeble attempt to cover her tracks. Watching the expression in Rebecca's eyes, she was pretty sure that Katie's mamma didn't suspect much of anything from the slip of Mary's tongue.

Sighing softly, Rebecca gathered up the plastic dessert plates and rinsed them off. "You and the bishop seein' each other some?" she said from the sink.

Mary's heart leaped up at the question. So Rebecca Lapp was smarter than she thought. "Oh, ya know . . . after Preachin' services and all." That sort of answer might not satisfy, but it was the best she could do without lying.

Turning now, Rebecca looked her square in the face, the dishwater dripping down off her wrists. "Then . . . are ya sayin' that you think ya might be able to get my shunned daughter to see the light and return and confess on bended knee?"

"I can only pray so."

"But if she did do all that—come back to the bishop and the People and repented her sins—she wouldn't have the opportunity to enjoy the blessing of marryin' Bishop John, after all. That is, if he'd even have her back."

Mary felt like a fool. Why *had* she bothered to bring the topic up? She wished she'd never said a word about it.

Rebecca continued. "You must be thinkin' that by speaking the words of the Ordnung to my girl, it could bring her back, only to have her suffer the pain of singleness all the rest of her days. Or maybe you're hopin' she and Daniel will find each other out there in the world and return together." She crossed the kitchen to come to the table, a fierce look on her plump face. "Well, if that's what you're a-thinkin', Mary Stoltzfus, let me tell you right now, that's no way to treat a best friend . . . takin' her prospects for a husband right out from under her nose."

"I . . . uh, I don't think you understand, Rebecca," she said, trying her best to talk sense to the woman.

"No, *no*. You listen to me! You know what you're doin', Mary, and I don't like it one bit. It's not becoming to Amish ways, neither." Rebecca's face was flushed pink, her eyes moist with angry tears, welling up and threatening to spill. "If you ask me, I think you must've been waitin' all along for the bishop. You waited till my girl left town to make your move."

Mary was horrified, shocked. She could scarcely breathe now; her heart pounded hard beneath the bodice of her dress and apron. "That's not true. Honest it ain't." She might've tried to explain further, but she heard the sound of the men coming in the back door, the clump of their boots on the utility room floor, the banter between them.

"You best be goin' now," Rebecca said sternly, turning her back to tend to the dishes in the sink.

Mary rose and left quickly. She never said a word of thanks for the pie, not a word of greeting to Samuel or his sons. And she didn't speak softly to Sugar as she hitched him up to Dat's carriage. It was all she could do to get herself inside the buggy and covered up for the cold ride home.

Then, seeing the heavy lap robe John had loaned her the night before, she gritted her teeth and found the reins, shaking more from the stinging words than from the chilling breeze.

❖   ❖   ❖

Katherine marveled at the concert hall—the lovely seating, the large stage framed with enormous velvet curtains. She hadn't recalled ever being inside such a fascinating place but didn't let on to Justin, who was dressed in a tuxedo for the evening event.

Glad that Rosie had helped her choose the perfect dress for the occasion, Katherine settled back in the cushioned seat, reveling in the dissonant, yet pleasant sound of the string section tuning to the first violinist's instrument. *Wonderful-gut*, she thought, ready for a night of music.

Justin glanced at her, offering a gentleman's smile. Once more she understood her attraction to this man, her charming date. He was more than attentive, always thinking of her, it seemed. Always willing to offer her an interesting time. Yet she wondered how he might feel if he knew that she felt awkward in his high-society circles, that she was still trying to acclimate herself to the newness of her life.

Rosie's words had come to her on several occasions since the maid had uttered them frivolously, then had apologized speedily. *Justin Wirth has noticed your aristocratic roots. . . .*

Sitting here next to him, she wondered just what role her inherited wealth had played in influencing Justin. Would he have been attracted to her had she been just an ordinary Plain girl?

Then she recalled how their eyes had met on Christmas Day, how he had known, almost by instinct, that she was Laura's daughter. He was a good man, through and through, she told herself.

Before the lights were lowered and the orchestra director took the podium and raised his baton, she read the program and notes carefully, thrilled that there was a piece by J. S. Bach. His music soothed her wholly, and she contemplated her state in life—*this* present time of her life—content to be wearing the satiny dress, delicate shoes, and glittering jewelry at her throat and on her wrist.

Sighing, she folded her hands over the program, wondering what lovely things the night might reveal. She didn't have to wait long. As the lights went down, Justin reached for her hand and caressed it during the first piece. Try as she might, the music got lost in her head somewhere; she could scarcely hear it for the beating of her heart.

❖　❖　❖

John was waiting at the appointed spot in the road when Mary reined in Sugar, pulling the horse and carriage over to the shoulder. Instead of anticipating the secret rendezvous, she was dreading it. After thinking through Rebecca's harsh comments, she felt at odds with herself and with her and John's budding relationship. Truth be told, she'd just as soon have stayed home tonight, sitting under the gas lamp in the kitchen, cozy by the fire, reading.

But she was here as she'd said she would be, and by the looks of John's cheerful countenance, he was delighted that she was.

"I thought the day would never end," he said, helping her down out of the carriage. "I've missed ya so."

She nodded, keeping her chin up, so to speak, putting on a happy face for the bishop, who was kind enough to help get her settled in the straw-laden sleigh and wrapped up with the same furry lap robes as the night before.

The moon was the slightest bit rounder tonight, and John made note of it to her. "Such a shame the children aren't out enjoyin' the evening with us."

"How're they doin'?" she asked, glad for this topic instead of romance.

"Ah, gut . . . right fine, they are. Eager for their old Daed to find 'em a mamma, I 'spect."

She grimaced at his words. Was that all she was to him—someone to take care of his young?

Unable to think clearly, she felt herself stiffen, relieved that John hadn't felt at ease enough with her to slip his arm around her just yet.

The silence between them was deafening, and she wished now she'd never gone to see Rebecca Lapp. What *was* she thinking? The woman was completely daft; at least it seemed so. For as much as the womenfolk had said she was improving, Mary knew better. She knew now firsthand that Katie's mamma had not totally recovered from the loss of her daughter. No, she was clearly suffering from deep grief—and worse. *Senseless* and *absurd* were the words that came to mind regarding Rebecca's harsh comments to her.

Shadows from the moon played tag with the horse-drawn sleigh as it sped over fields and down the glen, deep into the Hollow, past the rickety covered bridge at Weaver's Creek, where several open buggies—courting buggies the Englischers like to call them—were parked off the side of the road to accommodate smooching. Past ten or more farmhouses, all Old Order Amish, and she knew they were because not a single electrical wire ran from the road to the house.

"You're awful quiet," John remarked. "Somethin' bothering ya?"

She had no idea what to tell him. "Best to be silent if there's nothin' to say."

John pulled on the reins, halting the horse. He turned to her, wearing a concerned frown. "Mary . . . darling, what is it?"

Hearing her name coupled with the endearing term caused her to feel renewed compassion for him. She kept her eyes on her lap as she began. "If my shunned girlfriend returned . . . what would happen to . . . you and me?"

He sighed. "Are ya wonderin' if I'm still in love with her?"

"Well, I'd hardly think so, not after last night." She was thinking of his kisses, his declarations of love. "It's just that, well . . . folks talk, ya know. And maybe they're wonderin' if she *did* return and repent anytime soon, whether or not you'd rather have *her* for your wife."

"Nonsense," he exclaimed. "The woman's as disobedient as any I've known, and I have a strong feelin' she'll always be struggling with it, even if she does return and make things right."

It wasn't exactly what Mary wanted to hear. She'd longed to hear that John loved *her* . . . not Katie. But he hadn't said that, not in so many words. It made her wonder if his choice in a wife had more to do with devotion to God and the church than it did with love.

"What if there was something we could do? What if *I*, her best friend, could do that something to bring her back to the fold?"

She felt him reach under the blankets and find her mittened hands, taking one of them in his own and bringing it out into the air. He held it against his heart. "Are ya askin' for special treatment for Samuel Lapp's daughter?"

Now was her chance; it might be her only one. Yet she didn't want to tie her acceptance of his marriage proposal to her request for leniency on Katie's behalf. 'Twas a ticklish situation, and she had to be mighty careful what she said. "I'm thinking of a way to admonish her . . . instruct her, ya know."

"It was a harsh thing I did, not allowing the People to speak to her." He fell silent and let her hand go.

Quickly, she put it back under the lap robe, thankful that there was no real breeze to speak of tonight. "What if some of us could write her, speak to her in love about her rebellion?"

He wrapped his arms around her. "If this is what you wish, Mary, I will allow it."

She relaxed in his arms. "I want it more than almost anything."

"Then let it be so," he said. "I will lift the speech ban . . . because your heart is pure. And mine was filled with anger, wrongly so." His confession surprised her.

"Oh, thank you . . . John. Thank you ever so much!"

They embraced, and she felt as if her worries were far behind her as he leaned down to kiss her cheek, then her lips. "I do love ya, Mary," he whispered.

"And I love *you*."

With one arm around her, the other holding the reins, John drove through the night, her head on his strong shoulder. Ach, she was more than happy and could hardly wait to write and tell Katie the good news.

As for Rebecca, well . . . Katie's Mam would just have to wait and hear about this wonderful-gut turn of events at the membership meeting after Preachin' come Sunday. Jah, that was the best way.

Chapter Thirteen

❖   ❖   ❖

The hospice was especially quiet on Monday morning. Katherine had gone early, taking her guitar along, hoping to play soft music to entertain the patients as they ate their breakfast in the family-style eating area.

First, as was the procedure each time she came, she was given the update on all the inpatients. Two patients had passed away since her last visit, sadly enough. Willy, however, had remained the same.

When she asked permission to play, Natalie was thrilled with the idea. "Feel free to bring your guitar anytime you come, Katherine. Music is good therapy for the patients."

One of the nurse's aides took her back to the dining room and introduced her to the patients. "This is Katherine Mayfield, and she would like to play some breakfast music for you."

Some of the patients clapped, but most of them just smiled up at her. For a moment, she wondered if maybe *this* was the reason she had come to Canandaigua. Maybe this, in God's providence, had been the real purpose for her search so far from home.

Willy's eyes lit up when he saw her, and she played

several old tunes from Hickory Hollow days, then got brave and actually sang along.

The boy's face beamed with approval and afterward he asked about the songs. "How'd you learn to play like that?"

"Oh, I had a little help, I guess you could say."

"From your daddy, maybe?"

She chuckled. "No, my father didn't help me play music."

"Then who?"

"A good friend of mine."

A broad smile broke out on his face. "Your boyfriend, right?"

He had her, but she wouldn't admit it.

"What's his name?" Willy probed.

This conversation was going too far, too fast. But, looking into his curious eyes, she decided it wouldn't hurt to share a bit with the boy. "Dan. That was his nickname."

"What happened to your Dan? Did he help other people learn to play, too, besides you?"

She hadn't ever thought of that, really—had never wondered about it, come to think of it. "I don't know, but maybe he did. Dan was like that . . . always enjoyed being around lots of people, eating and talking, and sometimes just being quiet with a good friend."

"I think you must've loved him," Willy said softly.

She was startled by the comment. But she wouldn't deceive this wonderful boy, this adorable child who was dying a little bit every day before her very eyes. "Yes, I loved Dan very much."

"Then why didn't you marry him?"

"He went away . . . for a long, long time."

"Too long?" He stared at her, waiting for an answer.

"Maybe so." It was surprising that she'd allowed herself to be pulled into such a conversation. But there was something innocent and sweet—trustworthy, too—about Willy.

And each time she had come to visit, to cheer him with her presence, she was aware that *he* had encouraged *her*. Yet, sadly enough, his determined spirit, his will to live, seemed to be fading. She could see the light slowly going out of his eyes.

Today, though, while she played the guitar, she'd noticed a flicker of vitality in him. She hoped her eyes weren't playing tricks merely because she longed to see him improve, growing stronger instead of weaker. Natalie had suggested in passing that music possesses a healing power. She wondered if Dan had ever heard such a thing. Thinking about it now, she was startled that her former love had come to mind at all.

She remembered Dan's postscript at the end of the unexpected letter. He was still thinking of the guitar, it seemed, inquiring of it, pondering the past firm connection between them. Was their mutual love of music still weaving their lives together, like an ancient tapestry loom?

She glanced at her watch. "It's almost time for me to leave," she told Willy.

"Aw, do you have to go?"

"My ride is probably here." She didn't want to mention that she was a lady of means, that she had a private chauffeur who took her anywhere she pleased. None of that was important to her friendship with the boy. Or to any of the other precious patients in this secluded retreat, where they came to spend their last months, weeks, and days being nurtured and loved, even by volunteers who had more than just time to give.

"Before you go, can I hold your guitar?" Willy asked, trying to scoot forward on his chair.

"Sure." She positioned it carefully on his lap, steadying the instrument in his hands. "Would you like to pluck a string?"

He nodded his head up and down. "Wait'll I tell my

brother . . . Josh will be so jealous."

Katherine put the pick in his right hand, pressed his thumb over it, and guided his hand to the middle string. The string hummed softly. "You have a nice touch, Willy James Lee," she said, grinning at him.

His face was filled with surprise and delight. "You remembered?"

"Of course I did. How could I forget such wonderful-gut names?"

"You think they're wonderful . . . really?"

She looked at him, his hair catching the light as it swirled in ringlets at the nape of his neck. And his sweet countenance. "*You're* wonderful, Willy," she replied.

He reached for her hand and clutched it. "I think *you* are . . . just plain Katherine."

They burst into laughter, although Willy had no idea why it was that she was so tickled at his comment.

Later she read to him from the Bible at his request and afterward recounted several of the many old tales from Rebecca's storytelling repertoire.

As she was preparing to leave he asked, "Do you think I could learn to play the way you do?"

"I don't see why not. I'll do my very best to teach you, all right?" Her heart was warmed by his reaction, and once again she saw the faint sparkle of energy in his eyes.

"Why are you so nice to me?" he surprised her by asking.

"Well, I'd like to think I'm nice to just about everyone."

"Everyone? Even Dan?" he asked without blinking.

She waved her hand at him. "I was *always* nice to Dan . . . yes."

On this day especially, it was difficult to say good-bye, and she wondered if this was what it might've been like having a little brother. An English brother with two middle names. . . .

❖ ❖ ❖

On the ride home, Katherine had a yearning for Theodore to drive her to the outskirts of town. "To see the landscape," she said, hoping to stumble upon Mr. Esler's farmhouse. She'd hired the Amishman to construct the quilt frame, and the day he delivered the pieces and put it together, he'd mentioned that his wife sold homemade preserves.

"Do you think we might be able to find the Eslers' place?" she asked Theodore.

"I'll certainly do my best." He pulled over, stopped the car, and took a map out of the glove box. "Where is it these folks live?"

She told him as best she could, from having heard Mr. Esler describe the rural location. Theodore pinpointed the spot on his map and folded it so the specific section was visible. Then, sitting tall and proper in his black overcoat and hat, he signaled for the left turn and pulled away from the shoulder and onto the highway.

They rode past several miles of sweeping fields, covered with snow, and she thought of the many times Samuel or her oldest brother, Elam, had taken her and Rebecca on sleigh rides down across the glen and up over the high meadows of Hickory Hollow. And there were several times, too, when she and Mary had taken the pony, Tobias—before she'd changed his name to Satin Boy—out on a snowy day, going from farm to farm, loading up the pung sleigh with schoolchildren.

She squeaked a chuckle in the back of her throat, realizing that they had never once missed school for bad weather while growing up in Lancaster County. Public schools often had to close due to drifted roads, but never Amish schools. Outsiders might scoff at the Old Ways, wondering why Plain folk didn't seem to care about "catching up" with modern technology, but when it came right down to it, the horse-drawn sleighs came out way ahead of the snowplows and the street crews during the worst of winters.

Katherine had to smile at her memories. Sentimental, perhaps, though she cared not to admit it to anyone who knew her here in New York. Not when she had every possible convenience at her disposal. Fancy and modern.

When they arrived at the Amish farmhouse, she instructed Theodore to pull in to the barnyard. The layout of house, barn, and sheds seemed all too familiar, and for a moment she wondered if these folk might be related to some of her own Plain relatives.

"I won't be long." She reached for the door handle before Theodore could jump out of the driver's seat and come around to assist her.

"Katherine, please, let me help," Theodore argued.

"No . . . no, I'm perfectly fine." But she thanked him, nevertheless.

A sign that read "Tourists Are Welcome" invited her to ring the bell at the back door, connected to a screened-in porch just off the kitchen area, similar to the long utility room she was accustomed to in Hickory Hollow.

The plump woman who came to the door and greeted her reminded her of the old Wise Woman, only about forty years or so younger and maybe the same number of pounds heavier. She was rosy-cheeked and smiling, wearing a long blue dress and a black pinafore-style apron over it. The veiled head covering was only a slight bit different—a few less pleats sewn in—but otherwise, the woman might've been part of Katherine's former church district in the Hollow.

"I'd like to buy some jellies," she said politely, trying not to gawk, for she was keenly aware of how it felt to be stared at, up one side and down the other.

"*Kumm mit,*" the woman said, sporting a cheery smile and inviting Katherine inside.

The kitchen was large with a checkered pattern on the linoleum floor, a black woodstove in the corner, and a trestle table surrounded by long wooden benches. The room was very much like the one she'd grown up in—baking, cooking, and canning with Rebecca and, oftentimes, with many other women from the community. A scenic calendar hanging from a door that surely led to a cold cellar caught her eye. She felt a rush of overwhelming feelings. Mixed emotions, true. Yet a surprisingly strong tug that she could not deny.

"Do you make strawberry rhubarb jam?" One of her favorites. "And apple butter, too?"

"Jah, I have plenty of those on hand. How many jars do you want?"

She had to stop and think. "Oh, I'd say three of each. That'll be enough for now."

The portly woman scurried over to a corner cupboard there in the kitchen and opened it to reveal fifty or more jars of preserves. She counted them out, placing them in a sturdy brown produce bag, similar to the ones Rebecca gave to summer tourists who purchased her delicious fruit preserves and jellies.

"Thank you ever so much," Katherine said, taking a fifty-dollar bill out of her wallet.

"Oh, goodness me. Don't ya wanna write me a check instead?"

"No . . . is cash all right?" she asked, fearful of offending with her show of wealth.

The woman grinned. "Ach, you'd be awful surprised how many folk ask to pay with check. Never seem to have much cash, them locals."

She remembered, all right. "Well, have a nice day." Then, before she left—"Go ahead and keep the change."

"Oh my, no . . . wouldn't think of it."

"Well, just remember all those customers' checks that never cleared the bank," Katherine said, observing the sudden odd expression on the woman's face.

"How would *you* know about such as that?"

Katherine touched the woman's elbow. "Please . . . just save it for a rainy day." And with that, she left.

The drive home wasn't half as exciting, although she told Theodore all about the Amishwoman and her reaction to getting the extra money for her jellies.

"Sounds as if some folk take advantage of the gentle people," he said, referring to the Amish.

"Sadly, they do."

"It's troubling, to say the least. Why aren't people more considerate of each other?"

Her feelings exactly. But she was no longer thinking of the many cheap tourists roaming about. Her thoughts were on the most considerate person she had ever known. Mary Stoltzfus.

She longed to hear from Mary, though if she'd had better sense, she might've guessed that her friend wouldn't risk her good standing in the community to write a reply to a letter written by a stranger. Maybe Katherine herself should've written directly. But, no, if that had been the right thing to do, she would have done it in the first place.

Still, she was more than anxious to have some word from Mary . . . or anyone else back home, for that matter.

CHAPTER FOURTEEN

❖   ❖   ❖

Katherine's quilting class met again on Wednesday evening. She was excited to see the women picking up speed with the placement of pieces and working with the tic-tac-toe shading pattern in general.

"It's like following a recipe," Natalie Judah remarked, looking pert in her kelly green pants outfit. "So I guess anyone can learn to quilt, right?"

Rosie and Leoma exchanged glances, shrugging. "Speak for yourself," Rosie said, laughing.

The other women studied the copies of Katherine's sketches of what the finished Ninepatch should look like.

Later she showed them the beautiful Country Songbird pattern. "I love to make this one," she said, pointing out the striking redbird appliqués interspersed with flowing vines and graceful green leaves throughout.

"It looks very difficult," Ada remarked. "Can we really learn to make it, too?"

"If we work together as well as we have been, I don't see why not," Katherine replied.

"A challenge, to be sure," said Leoma.

The women were nodding in agreement.

"How much would a quilt like that sell for?" Elizabeth

asked, sitting across the frame from Katherine.

"Oh, probably over a thousand dollars for a queen size, at a store catering to tourists. If you knew where to go—to a private Amish residence, for instance—you'd only pay about five hundred dollars."

They talked about what to do with the Ninepatch quilt the seven of them were already in the process of making. "*If* we ever finish it," Natalie said with a grin.

"Maybe we could sell it to raise money for the hospice," Katherine suggested.

Missy, Elizabeth, and Natalie immediately decided that was a good idea. Leoma, Rosie, and Ada didn't seem to mind either way. "We're just thrilled to have the opportunity to learn firsthand from someone who knows what she's doing," Ada said, acknowledging Katherine.

"Yes, thanks for being Amish," Missy teased, offering a smile.

Katherine didn't quite know how to respond. Truth be told, if Missy, or any of the other women gathered here, had the slightest idea what she'd experienced for having been an unyielding Plain woman, maybe they wouldn't be so quick to jump to conclusions. But, of course, they couldn't possibly know. They had no way of understanding the rigid, nearly unattainable, expectations placed on one growing up in a cloistered society. So she said nothing.

"What made you leave your people?" asked Elizabeth.

Katherine noticed Natalie's concerned look but took the question in stride. "I wanted to find my birth mother, Laura Mayfield-Bennett. My search brought me here to Canandaigua and this mansion."

Several of the ladies looked surprised. "So you were adopted by the Amish?" asked Elizabeth.

"Yes, as an infant, but I wasn't told until just last year." She was beginning to feel uncomfortable about exposing her past.

"Oh . . . I know just how you must feel," Ada offered. "One of my cousins recently found out she was adopted. She's in her late forties."

"Why would parents keep something like that from their child?" Missy asked, frowning as she looked across the frame at Ada.

Ada shook her head. "In the case of my cousin, she never felt connected to her family. I guess, from what she says, she always sensed that she didn't really belong."

Didn't belong . . .

Katherine wondered if her quilting class was turning into the type of therapy sessions she'd recently read about in the newspaper. Was this how English folk aired their pent-up emotions?

Natalie, being the professional she was, must've picked up on Katherine's mood. Because before you could say *Geilssch wanz*—horsetail—she had steered the conversation away from adoption to the nasty weather and news of another storm front heading their way.

In more ways than one, Katherine was mighty glad the nurse had joined the group.

❖   ❖   ❖

When Daniel arrived home after putting in another long day at work, it was coming on toward twilight, and the city lights were beginning to twinkle up and down his street.

Sorting through the mail, he scrutinized each return address and the handwriting as well, hoping for a reply from Katie. But, as had been the case each day, nothing had come from Canandaigua. If he'd been honest with himself, he might've realized that Katherine Mayfield was not about to write a letter back to him. He was simply not going to hear a word from the woman he'd once called his sweetheart girl.

His boss, Owen Hess, and his wife must have observed

his pensive mood the last few times they were together. Owen had gone so far as to invite him to their home for dinner, talking of including Ruth Stine, *if* Dan would agree to a semi-blind date.

Ruth was a year younger than Dan. A devoted Christian, she believed in waiting for God's choice in a mate. She had literally given up on the idea of dating, and Dan couldn't blame her for that. The social scene in some of the churches tended to lean more toward worldly, selfish motives. The Mennonite way taught that a woman, no matter her age, was to abide under the protection of her father's roof—physically live in the house of her parents—until such time as God brought along a life mate of His choosing.

Ruth was trusting the Lord for His will in the matter, and Dan was aware of it. Not only was she devout in her faith, she was a beautiful woman of humility and grace.

"Thanks for thinking of me," he'd told Owen.

"Pray about coming, why don't you?" his boss replied.

Dan had prayed, though not in regard to developing a friendship with Ruth. He'd fasted and prayed for Katie. And because his affections were still very strong for her, he felt it unwise to accept Owen's kind invitation.

As far as he knew, Katie had never come to faith in Jesus as Savior and Lord. He'd inquired of the Wise Woman about Katie's beliefs, but Ella Mae seemed hesitant to say for sure, one way or the other. The assurance of salvation issue was a touchy one. He knew this to be true, because he'd been brought up to believe that such doctrine was a disruption to the community. "It is a manifestation of conceit, not humility," his father had said when first they'd discussed it years back.

Dan had tried repeatedly to show his father the passages of Scripture stating the truth of the gospel, that Christ had come to bring salvation . . . eternal life. But Dan's words had fallen on deaf ears.

Tired and hungry, he wandered out to the kitchen and warmed up some leftovers. He would not permit his mind to dwell on the fact that Katie apparently had not felt inclined to reply to his letter. He'd waited five long years to approach her. She was entitled to take her time about responding.

❖　❖　❖

Snow was falling gently as the People made their way to the Preaching service over at David and Mattie Beiler's house on Sunday. Mary sat in the back of the enclosed carriage with Mammi Ruth, while Dat and Mam sat in front.

The thought crossed her mind that she could easily spill the beans and let them in on what they were going to hear from the bishop about Katie Lapp, when the adults met for a membership meeting after Preachin'. But she held her tongue and did the right thing—kept all of it to herself.

She was overjoyed that John had been mindful of her request, and she figured he loved her an awful lot because of it.

The membership meeting didn't last very long, especially once the People realized how adamant John was. Mary, too, could see it all so clearly—the look on his face, the sound of his voice, the hushed awe surrounding the moment.

It was his apology that came as a surprise.

"I stand before you today to ask your forgiveness for the hasty and indignant way I dealt with Katie Lapp's shunning. It was an unjust thing I did, and I pray that none of you will follow my example in this," he said, standing before the membership.

Mary felt her burden lift as she sat on the hard bench next to her mother. She listened attentively as Bishop John explained that the shunning itself was to be kept in force.

"As stated in the Scripture, we will not keep company with such a sinner, no, not eat with such a one." Still, he was lifting the worst part.

Rebecca's face radiated pure joy, and Mary couldn't help but notice how the dear woman sat just a bit taller than before. Glory be! They could communicate with Katie!

Mary wondered if Katie's mamma would ever forgive her for agreeing to marry the bishop. Whatever time it took, whatever words were required, she'd see to it that there were no hard feelings festering between them.

If Katie ever *did* come back and repent, Mary knew she would wholeheartedly welcome her friend—without reservation, encouraging Rebecca to think wonderful-gut thoughts about the possibility of Katie getting married, no matter what age she might be at the time. 'Course, there was always Daniel, that is if he'd been able to locate her. But Mary wasn't about to hold her breath for *two* shunned young people finding the courage to confess. Usually, the way it worked, only one might be willing—at least, that's how it had been in a good many cases over the years.

As Mary sat there, she noticed that Samuel Lapp's eyes were moist, and his cheeks twitched with emotion. She was careful not to stare, even though a large group of men sat on the opposite side of the house, and it was next to impossible *not* to observe his facial expressions.

The first thing Mary wanted to do after the common meal and the visiting and after they all left for home was to write Katie a letter. She felt like a young girl again, just thinking about being allowed to correspond freely with her bosom buddy. Sure, she'd offer words of spiritual assistance, but she'd be sharing other things, too. Plenty of things.

❖   ❖   ❖

Sunday, March 15

My dearest friend,

I have the most wonderful news for you. The bishop has lifted the Ban a little. The People are allowed to communicate with you! I'm mighty happy about it, because I've wondered how to let you know that I got your letter (the one Mrs. Rosie Taylor was so kind to write me). Thank you, Katie. It meant ever so much to me for you to be so cautious that way.

Rebecca and I had a nice chat last Sunday afternoon— one week ago today it was—and her eyes lit up when she heard that you'd asked about her. Of course, you wouldn't have any way of knowing what your poor mamma's been through since you left. Even Bishop John went to see her to try to help her, so depressed she was. But now, honestly, I think I see a change coming. I wouldn't be a bit surprised if Rebecca wrote to you sometime soon.

We all believe that in time you'll see the error of your ways and rejoin your Amish family here in Hickory Hollow. Until then, I remain your faithful friend,

Mary Stoltzfus

She took time to read what she'd written, second-guessing herself about not having told a speck of news regarding her romance with Bishop John. The more she pondered the letter, the more she supposed *that* news was not the best thing to be writing just yet. She could only hope that Rebecca wouldn't go and let the cat out of the bag.

As for informing Katie that Dan was alive, well, she'd thought long and hard about trying to explain the mighty strange story in a letter—as confusing as it would sound to Katie—but she chose not to. Chances were, Dan had already located his beloved by now.

❖   ❖   ❖

Mattie Beiler had made some hot tea, the mint kind her mother always loved. "Here now, this oughta get ya warmed up," she said, setting the cup and saucer in front of Ella Mae.

"Jah, somethin' oughta." The old woman leaned over the table to sip her tea, but her hands were shaking. "Goodness' sakes, what'sa matter with me?"

Mattie took the teacup from her and set it down on the table. "Here, let me help ya, Mam." Then taking a good hard look at her, Mattie asked, "Have ya been feelin' poorly all day, Mam?"

"Ever since after Preachin'," I guess."

"That long? During the meal, too?"

"Jah."

She wasn't surprised that not a single complaint had come from Ella Mae. The woman was a stoic when it came to physical ailments, of which there were very few for her advanced age.

Ella Mae began to shake her head back and forth, her eyes blinking fast. "Aw, probably nothin' to worry about much." More sipping, then she tried to add some honey to the hot liquid, but when it came to stirring the tea, the spoon jiggled about in her gnarled hand.

Mattie sat down at the table, noting that her Mam didn't seem quite as alert as usual. "Would ya like to lie down a bit?"

Ella Mae looked at her, eyes smooth and shiny—almost glassy. "M-maybe s-so," she mumbled, her words coming thick.

"Mamma?" She leaned over next to the white-haired woman, touching her hand. It felt damp to the touch and Ella Mae's breathing seemed irregular, as if she had to pant for breath.

"O-oh" came an uncontrolled sound, deep and frightening. And Ella Mae slumped over, her body falling forward on the tabletop.

Mattie ran to the back door. "Something's wrong with Mamma! Come quick!" she called to David, who was busy outside, folding up long benches from the Preaching service and putting them back in the bench wagon with several other men.

Her husband hurried inside, going over to lift Ella Mae out of her chair. "Don'tcha worry none, Mam," she heard him saying as he carried the Wise Woman out of the kitchen to the Dawdi Haus adjoining theirs.

Mattie followed close behind, fretting that her mamma was going to die of a stroke. Right here in the house where, not but a few hours before, they'd had a right-gut Preachin'. Where their bishop had come clean with the most startling personal confession she'd ever heard; all that business of lifting part of the Ban from Katie Lapp and whatnot all.

Ella Mae continued making that horrifying low-pitched groan. It came right out of the depth of her being. A painful, treacherous sound.

Mattie had seen enough of this sort of thing to know what was happening. Too many elderly aunts and uncles had ended up this way. And now *her* mamma.

The thought crossed her mind to ride for a telephone—to one of her Mennonite neighbors. Such times as this, a phone would come in mighty handy. But her mother had repeatedly expressed her desire that when the time came, she did not want to be sent to some English hospital, wired up to contraptions to keep her heart beating against its will. "I'd rather die in my own bed," she'd always said.

Because of that, Mattie dismissed the notion of using anybody's telephone at all.

"Be gentle," she advised her husband and pulled back the bed quilts and other handmade coverings.

Leaning down, David lowered Ella Mae into her bed. Mattie couldn't help thinking, with a chilling shudder, that it was much like the lowering of a coffin. When she'd covered her mother carefully, tucking her in almost as if she were a child, Mattie slid a chair over next to the bed and sat there, holding her breath as the left side of Ella Mae's facial muscles began to weaken and sag.

Mattie appreciated her husband's comforting hand on her shoulder as he stood behind her, watching . . . waiting.

CHAPTER FIFTEEN

❖   ❖   ❖

The weather was cold and gray for a full week, and Katherine was glad to have another social event to look forward to at the end of it. She had read and reread the letter from Mary more times than she could count, for it brought a great sense of relief.

Shortly after Mary's letter had arrived, she marveled to receive one from Rebecca as well, though her mamma's letter seemed less spirited, more of a means to admonish and instruct than to convey compassion. And there had been news of Ella Mae, who'd had a bad stroke. Katherine wondered how the dear woman was doing. Surely the womenfolk would assist her in her recovery. They were known to be able to bring a body near back from the grave.

There'd been no mention of Dan's visit to Hickory Hollow, though, which made her wonder. Still, she cherished the letter with all her heart.

Katherine sensed a mysterious stirring in the air, though she couldn't quite put her finger on it. She had not known of a bishop—not anywhere in Lancaster County—backing away from his initial declaration of shunning. Never—*niemols!*

She couldn't help but wonder what was happening in

the Hollow. Was Bishop John floundering as a leader? If so, wouldn't Mary have said something?

To clear her head, Katherine bundled up and headed outside to walk the grounds, though some patches were too deep with snow to explore.

She went around to the south side of the mansion, where Rosie had told her there was a little lily pond surrounding a small fountain. "You'll enjoy sitting out there with a good book come summer."

She smiled at the thought of warmer weather, thinking that the expansive lawns might be just the place to bring Willy for a picnic. That is, if she could get permission from the hospice. On second thought, Mayfield Manor would be a perfect picnic spot for any number of terminally ill young children. She could hardly wait to discuss the idea with Natalie.

❖　❖　❖

Justin was indeed charming as he sat at the end of the elegant table that evening. It was the occasion of his cousin's birthday, and the evening was complete with a roving string trio, and later, dancing. Never having attempted to dance ballroom style, Katherine declined Justin's cousin's invitation as politely as she knew how, which may or may not have been a slap in the face to the guest of honor. She couldn't tell for sure by the way Justin continued to make conversation with several others at the table, never so much as raising an eyebrow.

Observing his interaction with others, she was learning a great deal about her handsome Beau. She hadn't known it before, but just this night she discovered that he was fluent in two other languages besides English. Not to let that tidbit of information get the best of her, she boosted her morale with the fact that *she* was fluent in two. Thankfully, Justin wasn't the type of person to reveal the secret Plain past of his date. He carried on, smiling often and throwing her an occasional wink.

Clearly, she felt like a fish floundering on a beach somewhere, what with the blue-smoke, high-society atmosphere. Especially tonight. Even the chandelier over her head far surpassed the exquisite one in the dining room at Mayfield Manor. She was dressed appropriately for the occasion, so the feeling she suppressed had nothing at all to do with the way she'd arranged her hair in a lovely updo, secured with one of Laura's diamond-studded combs, or the gown she'd chosen with matching heels and bag. No, it had more to do with the awkward way she felt while in such grand and fancy surroundings, her own mansion not included.

She wondered if she was trying too hard to fit in with Justin's friends and his extended family. So far, he had not mentioned taking her to meet his parents, though she almost expected it, in lieu of his recent comments about their "future together."

She honestly felt as if he might be getting close to a proposal of marriage, and the thought of it made her tingle with expectancy. Perhaps, in time, he would present her with a beautiful ring, too, just as everything else she'd ever really dreamed of had seemed to wend its way to the doorstep of her life.

❖   ❖   ❖

The drive over to Ella Mae's took less than five minutes, and Lydia Miller was thankful for a warm car on such a cold day. Peter, her good-natured husband, had consented to drop her off for a visit with the ailing Wise Woman on his way to town. "Do you think she'll even know you?" he asked as they turned into the lane leading to David and Mattie Beiler's big farmhouse.

"If it's as bad a stroke as some are saying, maybe not. But that won't scare me away," she answered truthfully. "I can still pray for her whether she knows me or not."

Peter nodded, then got out and went around to help her out. "You won't be able to phone me when you're ready to leave, but maybe you can visit with Mattie for a while, and then I'll be by to pick you up." He glanced at his watch. "Say, in about an hour from now?"

"Suits me fine," she said as he leaned down to peck her cheek.

"I'll be in prayer for you, dear. And for your friend."

She waved. "See you soon."

At the door, Lydia was greeted and made to feel at home by Mattie and several other Amishwomen who were close relatives of the David Beiler family, but none that Lydia herself had ever met.

Mattie, talking softly, led her through the front room to the door that connected the main house with the smaller addition. "I s'pose you should know that she can't speak at all," Mattie cautioned as they went into the main floor bedroom. "But Mam loves havin' visitors, so don't let that hinder ya one bit."

Glad she could be of some help, whether spreading cheer or just sitting by Ella Mae's bedside, Lydia prayed silently that she might be a blessing to the woman.

"I'll give ya some time alone with her," Mattie said, closing the door behind her as she left.

The room was serene and dim, and Lydia felt she ought to tiptoe, which she did, but then stopped and stood at the foot of the bed, looking down on her friend's thin frame there under several layers of cozy quilts. "Hullo, Ella Mae," she said softly. "I heard you could use some company, and, well . . . I'm right here."

The Wise Woman's cheeks were sunken and drooped, her eyes glum, yet she blinked as if to say, "Glad ya came."

Lydia pushed the chair closer to the bed so that it was right up next to the mattress, where she could comfortably reach out and hold the paralyzed hand, stroke the limp arm. "I've been thinking and praying for you every day since I heard," she said.

Leaning forward, she put her face up close to the wrinkled one. "The Lord's presence is here, Ella Mae, right here in this room."

Minutes passed. Lydia remained silent, squeezing the fragile hand in hers. Ella Mae's loving hands had helped many a person with domestic chores over the years: sowing seeds in charity gardens, harvesting, canning and preserving, quilting, mending—even churning butter on occasion. They'd touched many a little one's head, gently blessing her children, grandchildren, and great-grandchildren with her generosity and love. And her hands had helped weather the storms of life, soothing the brow of her dying husband and years before that, of Essie, her twin sister.

Now it was Ella Mae's time to be touched with tenderness. Lydia was content to reach past the stiff immobility, past the deadened limbs, and communicate God's love.

As she held the misshapen hands, the bluish veins bulging up past the surface of crinkled skin, she prayed aloud, "Dear Lord Jesus, thank you for Ella Mae's life, that she has lived it for you—helping others, offering her life as a sacrifice to those who have come, searching for truth. I pray a special blessing over this your child. If it be your will, bring her out of this condition. Allow her to regain the use of her hands and limbs, her voice and her mind. I pray this in Jesus' name. Amen."

As she stood to leave, she was aware of Mattie's presence. "Oh, I didn't hear you come in," she whispered.

"Your prayer was awful perty," Mattie replied. "Thank you, Lydia. You're a . . . kind woman."

She nodded, feeling a bit uneasy. No one had ever complimented her on a prayer. "I . . . I hope Ella Mae—*both* of you know that the Lord understands what you're going through."

Mattie's eyes were bright with tears, yet she didn't make an attempt to hide them, and when she blinked, they spilled over and coursed down her face. "We don't often hear that kinda thing about the Good Lord. It would be awful nice to know that what you say is true about almighty God bein' interested in each and every person's life. I'd give just about anything to know for sure and for certain. . . ." Her voice trailed off.

Lydia went to Mattie and reached for her hands, holding them in both of hers. "Oh, but you *can* know. You can!"

Nodding her head, Mattie's lip quivered, unable to speak.

Lydia glanced over her shoulder at the sleeping Ella Mae. "Your mamma knows. She's filled up to the brim with the love of the Lord, Mattie. That's why people are drawn to her. God's given her a great gift of wisdom."

"Jah," Mattie said, brushing the tears away. "I remember the day things changed for the better for Mamma. It happened weeks before my father died of a heart attack. She'd met up with some churchgoing folk in town somewheres. Never really said who they were or what had kept her so long, but I saw by the shine on her face that somethin' was different. Not long after, that same kind of joy showed up on Dat's face . . . and 'twasn't but a few weeks later, and he up and died."

Lydia paid close attention to this story, though she'd suspected as much for years.

Mattie sighed, adjusting her apron. "Thinking back on it, I suppose Mamma felt she had no choice but to live out the rest of her life in the Amish church."

"Well, I can understand that."

"She probably should've turned English on us and followed her heart to the Mennonites," said Mattie with a dainty smile. "I 'spect the thing that kept her was the Meinding. Our bishop's mighty hard on the People, ya know. Doesn't bat an eye 'bout puttin' the Ban on someone who shows signs of arrogance—which is what John Beiler would've said about Mamma if ever he'd known."

Lydia couldn't help but think that the Wise Woman had made a difficult choice, yet prudent—following the Lord by serving the People right in her own community.

When the time came for Lydia to say good-bye, it was like leaving behind a thirsty woman in a desert. Mattie's heart had been softened by Ella Mae's stroke.

"Come by for pie and coffee," Lydia offered. "Come anytime at all."

"Denki . . . I just might do that."

Lydia prayed that she would.

CHAPTER SIXTEEN

❖   ❖   ❖

Katherine was more than eager to attend church with Rosie and Fulton Taylor. The Lord's Day morning had started out quite early, with her trying to read another one of the old classics she'd found in the manor library. Yet she turned the pages without reading it. Such a peculiar feeling she had, like she was marking time, waiting for something to happen, perhaps something unforeseen. Though she was not impatient about whatever that something might be, she felt a lurking sense of excitement residing in the back of her head, though she had no way to comprehend it. Not one iota.

Were the letters from Mary and Rebecca the reason for her aloofness, her disinterest in the book she held in her hands? Odd as it seemed, she felt she was stepping toward a new phase of her life, not knowing where it might leave Katherine Mayfield's hopes and dreams.

She shrugged off her brooding feelings and went to find Rosie to say that she would like to go to church today.

Not two hours later, she entered the doors of the beautiful sanctuary, recalling that the last time she'd come here, she was saying a final good-bye to a mother she'd barely known.

Having never visited any church except the Mennonite

meetinghouse in Hickory Hollow, she was in awe of the windows—cut up in little parts of colorful glass and put back together like a quilt—the massive pipe organ, and the sloping aisle that created a carpeted path through the many cherrywood pews. Surely she had noticed such beauty on the day of the funeral, yet she vaguely remembered.

"Himmel," she whispered to herself, following Rosie and Fulton to their pew. She sat next to Rosie, with Fulton closest to the aisle, and sang along with a few of the hymns, though she didn't know many of them. As she tried to follow the notes on the staff, she thought again of Dan, who had first taught her to read music.

The music presentation by the choir, followed by an organ solo, set her spirits soaring. She could hardly wait to try out the melodies on her guitar.

But it was the sermon that touched her most. The pastor's delivery and style was so foreign to her, so entirely different from what she'd grown up with in the Amish church. Yet she was captivated by the message on the love of God . . . a *personal* heavenly Father who adored and cared for His children. This message about a God who was involved in her life—she'd kept hearing it, from Dan and then little Willy and now the minister. Could it really be true?

She thought of Lydia Miller, too, knowing that her cousin would approve of such a sermon. The more Katherine listened, the more the minister explained, the less heretical the idea seemed to her. What *was* strange was hearing Scripture passages she'd never known existed.

Quickly, she scribbled down the references on the bulletin she'd received from one of the ushers. She had to read them for herself, wanted to hold Laura's Bible in her hands, to search out some of these verses she'd never heard read by any of the preachers in Hickory Hollow.

Well, now she would. Hearing the minister expound on the verses was shaping something life-giving inside her, a craving in her heart for truth—something she'd experienced as a child on several occasions but had had no idea what to do about it.

She was ever so glad she'd come and could hardly wait to tell Justin. Maybe *he* could bring her next week. Yes, that's exactly what she'd do. She'd invite him and they would come together.

❖   ❖   ❖

The minute she arrived back at the mansion, she rushed off to the south wing. There, in the stillness of her suite, she wrote two short letters—one to Mary, the other to Rebecca. She described what she'd encountered at church, not hesitating in the least. The bishop would probably slap the no-communicating part of the shunning back on her when he found out, but she *had* to share it.

Dinner was served in the dining room at her request, and she spent much of the time discussing the church service with Garrett, Theodore, Leoma, and all the others. She noticed Rosie and Fulton nodding in agreement, but they seemed a bit surprised when she came up with the idea to bake up "a batch of goodies to take to the children at the hospice."

Garrett was all for it. "What's your pleasure, Katherine?"

She paused to recall her favorite sweet treat as a child. "Mississippi Mud."

"I beg your pardon?"

Several of the maids were chuckling.

"It's the perfect thing for children—rich and gooey, just right. They'll love it!"

Garrett appeared to be flustered. "I don't believe I know of a recipe for . . . uh, this mud treat you mention."

"Mississippi Mud," she said again. "I'll write out the

recipe for you. I have it memorized."

"Very well," he said, concentrating on the prime rib steak on his plate.

"In fact, I'll help make it," Katherine offered. She didn't go on to say that this gesture of kindness was only the beginning of her plan to share her wealth with the people of Canandaigua.

❖ ❖ ❖

Rosie waited until her husband's hands were free of clean table linens before sneaking over to give him a hug. "I'm so excited, Fulton!"

"Over me?" He grinned, bussing her cheek.

She poked him playfully, wriggling away. "You know what I'm talking about, now don't you?"

"Yes, I believe I do. And isn't it remarkable what a single church service can do for a person?"

"I daresay it's been a long time coming for our young mistress." She followed him out of the dining room and down the long main hall. It was her assumption that if a person mulled and puzzled over something as important as everlasting life long enough, and was open to God's leading, he or she would ultimately find it. Katherine, in Rosie's opinion, had been searching for truth all her young life. "I suspect the prayers of certain key people, not only Laura's, have played a part in what may be happening."

He gave her an approving wink. "Once again, I believe you are right, my dear." And he hurried into the kitchen.

❖ ❖ ❖

Promptly after the noon meal, Katherine headed to the library—down the main hall, past the grand staircase, and to the left. She located a section where numerous Bibles were shelved. She had no idea which one had been Laura's personal Bible, or even if she had had a favorite. So Katherine chose a large leather-bound King James Version and carried it off to her room.

Finding her notes scrawled on the church bulletin, she began to look up the minister's sermon text. *Behold, what manner of love the Father hath bestowed upon us, that we should be called the sons of God. . . .*

She read the verse a second time, letting the words sink into her heart. Tears clouded her vision as she contemplated what this very Scripture might've meant to her as a child. Oh, to have heard this verse at the knee of Dat or Mam— such words that had endured thousands of years since the Bible was written. *The test of time*, Preacher Yoder might've said, if only he'd known.

To think that the minister who said this phrase had been anointed by the almighty God himself! Reading the passage again and again, she began to know, without a shadow of a doubt, that if she had read the complete Bible while growing up—perhaps even owned a Bible—her whole life might've turned out much differently.

Quickly, she went to the dresser drawer where she kept the handmade baby dress and found Dan's letter, scanning it again for the sentence that had pricked her heart when the letter had first arrived. *I have found a love I've never known . . . this I find in the Lord Jesus.*

She wondered if this discovery had something to do with the restless anticipation she'd experienced earlier today. She thought of Laura's sunny disposition. In spite of the woman's debilitating disease and constant pain, her mother's day-to-day dealings with the servants and the domestic help were exemplary of godly love. And she had prayed for Katherine's salvation, of all things! Rosie had talked of it on several occasions. Laura, though she was dying, had spent her morning hours talking to the Lord . . . here, in this room.

She read again each of the Scriptures, this time out loud, and as she did, God's Word sprang to life in her, and she began to weep.

Chapter Seventeen

❖   ❖   ❖

Before the mixing of the muddy Mississippi confection ever began on Monday morning, Katherine placed a phone call to Natalie Judah. She told her of the plan to surprise the children, and without the slightest hesitation, Natalie sanctioned the idea.

"I'll make the delivery sometime this afternoon," Katherine promised.

"What a thoughtful gesture," said Natalie. "I'll alert the other nurses so they're aware of your coming."

"I almost forgot to ask—will this cause a dietary problem for any of the children?"

"Better bring along the recipe."

Katherine agreed, grinning to herself. She'd mentioned the name of the treat, and Natalie, misunderstanding, had asked her to repeat it. But Katherine made it clear that the dessert recipe was an old Amish delicacy. "It's been in my adoptive family for hundreds of years," she explained.

This comment seemed to spark the nurse's interest even further.

"I'll make copies for anyone who wants one," she volunteered.

Overjoyed, Natalie thanked her. "Say . . . maybe we

could have an Amish emphasis this year at our annual bazaar. It's coming up on May first."

"Maybe sell our class quilts?"

Natalie laughed about that. "We'll have to hustle in order to finish the Country Songbird pattern."

"If we work fast, we can do it." After hanging up the telephone, Katherine scurried off to help Garrett and Selig make the mouth-watering recipe.

It was while they were making the syrup, while the brown sugar and butter were boiling, that the rich and sweet aroma transported her back to Rebecca's kitchen when Katie was just six years old. . . .

A stiff wind blew flakes of snow mixed with sleet, making tapping sounds on the windowpanes and the storm doors. The sun, hiding behind the heavy layers of snow clouds, refused to shine. Still, Mary and her mother and grandmother had come to help make four double batches of the tasty dish she loved better 'n most anything.

Katie and Mamma washed their hands at the sink, then tossed the hand towel back and forth merrily before starting to melt and brown the butter.

"Won't Dat and the boys be excited?" Mamma said.

Katie giggled. "Jah, and they'll prob'ly finish off the whole dish before we can ever get seconds," she said, standing on a chair to reach the top of the counter.

She held a long rolling pin in her little hands and was making ready to help squash the graham crackers when it came time. Later, she would help her little friend Mary spread the crumbs all over the top of the gooey dessert. But the best part of all was the lip-smackin' session just around the corner—eating the delicious dish.

Mary scooted a chair over next to her. "I'm almost as tall as you," she said.

"Almost, but not quite."

They leaned close together, taking turns trying to measure each other, but they giggled so much they couldn't stand up straight long enough.

"Ach, hold still now, and I'll see where your forehead comes on me," said Katie.

Mary sucked in a deep breath and held perfectly still until Katie got the job done. "Half a head shorter," Katie announced, to which Mary blew all her air out. "And ya have bad breath, too!" she hollered, then burst into laughter again.

"Miss Katherine?" Selig said, waving a tea towel in front of her face.

"Oh . . . er, what?" A bit startled, she apologized for daydreaming. "I guess this recipe pulls me right back to my childhood."

"We had a feeling you might've gone back and decided not to return," Garrett teased her.

Selig and Katherine joined in the laughter. What a wonderful-good time they were having. She could hardly wait for the "mud" to cool.

◈　　◈　　◈

The children who could respond with spoken praise for her surprise treat did so.

Willy was especially expressive, his fingertips covered with graham cracker crumbs. He put up both thumbs and wiggled them in the air. "Can you teach my mommy how to make this stuff?" he asked.

"I'll see that she gets this recipe—good enough?" Katherine folded the piece of paper in half and placed it on a clean spot on the table.

They talked about his weekend, what he did on Sunday.

"Mommy and Daddy took turns reading my Bible to me," he told her, his eyes wide.

"I'm glad they did." She paused, remembering the church service and the Scriptures she'd looked up afterward, and how moved she was by the message of God's love.

"My brother came to visit me, too." Willy's expression was serious. "Josh looked real sad, though."

She knew he was speaking of his older brother. "I'm sure he was very happy to see you."

"Josh thinks I'm going to die, but I'm not. I'm going to get well and go home again and . . ." He stopped in mid-sentence.

Katherine's heart ached for the little boy. So young to be dealing with issues of life and death.

"I want to get well," he whispered, as if confiding a secret.

"We all want you to."

When it came time for him to rest, she wheeled the boy down the hall to his room. Colorful balloons floated gently in the corner near the window, and a lovely handmade quilt covered a portion of one wall. There was a recliner and a hide-a-bed for family members who wished to spend the night. Bright and cheery, Willy's room was filled with large, graceful ferns and freestanding plants.

She helped him into bed, pulling the covers up for him. "Sweet dreams, now."

"Aw, we didn't have time to play guitar today," he said suddenly, as if it were terribly important to him.

"I'll come again on Wednesday," she said. "You can learn to play another chord then."

He nodded reluctantly and reached his arms up for a hug. "Good-bye, Katherine. I'll miss you."

She leaned down and caressed his head. "I'll miss you too, Willy."

"Come back tomorrow, okay?"

"I'll see what I can do," she said, knowing that it would mean changing the schedule and having to get permission from the charge nurse. A bit complicated, but she would talk to Natalie and see what could be done.

On the drive home, she wished it were midsummer so she could take her young friend outside. They would sit in the shade of a maple tree, enjoying the fragrance of garden phlox and honeysuckle vines, feel the warm breeze, and watch the sun cast short shadows on the birdbath in the courtyard behind the hospice. As it was, she feared Willy might not live long enough to see July come at all.

Later Theodore drove her to the mall, where she found a gift shop. She wanted to purchase several cards for the sick boy, but as she was standing in front of the "Get Well" section, she noticed two Amish teens enter the store. Their dresses were similar to those worn in Lancaster County, and the connection instantly drew her to them.

"Wie bischt?" she said, forgetting she wasn't dressed Plain, let alone Amish, and that these girls might be frightened by a greeting from a stranger who spoke their language.

They *were* shy, lowering their heads, eyes cast down.

Katherine stepped back a bit before she made a complete fool of herself. "Uh, sorry. Have a nice day." She turned to go, the cards for Willy still in her hand.

"Didja forget to pay?" the older Amish girl called.

Katherine felt her neck and cheeks grow warm. "Oh my, yes. I certainly did. Thank you ever so much."

The girls glanced at each other, grinning. Then one spoke up, "Weren't you out at our place buying jam the other week?"

Katherine couldn't believe it. These girls looked an awful lot like Mrs. Esler. "Yes, I bought the jellies. Are you related to her?"

"We're her youngest daughters," said one shyly.

"Jah, we spotted you from the front room that day," said

the other. "We had an old quilt that was worn through, so we were puttin' some new batting in, which was why ya didn't see us. Usually we help Mamma with the jam and jelly business."

"Well, that makes sense, then."

The younger girl was eyeing her. "Do ya have any need for a good homemade quilt or two, miss?"

She smiled. "To tell you the truth, I'm working on one right now myself—along with six other women." She didn't say she was teaching a quilting class, though. "Have you ever made the Country Songbird pattern?"

Their faces brightened as if they'd just met up with an old friend. "Jah . . . we know it well. In fact, Mamma said just the other day we oughta start one of those with the birds all in blue."

She stood there, enjoying the company of these Plain girls immensely. Suddenly, she thought of the hospice bazaar. Here might be a way to finish the quilt in time for such an event.

She stuck her neck out even further and explained the craft show fund-raiser and what it would mean to the terminally ill children who were inpatients at the hospice. "If we could finish the quilt, I think it might bring quite a lot at the bazaar on May first."

The girls were still smiling. A good sign, she thought.

"How would you like to help finish the Country Songbird? I'd be happy to pay you to work with us."

They were shaking their heads, sharing sober expressions now. "We wouldn't think of takin' pay for it. But we'll hafta talk to Mam first," said the younger girl.

Katherine opened her purse and looked for a piece of paper. Quickly, she jotted down her address and phone number. "Won't you keep this handy, just in case?"

"Denki. We have a telephone . . . for the jelly business. So we can call and leave you know."

Katherine was so thrilled to have met these kindred spirits, she came close to walking out of the store again without paying for the cards. Fortunately, she caught herself. "I'll look forward to hearing from you, then."

Later, she realized that she'd fallen back into the old speech pattern—adding "then" to the end of her sentence. It was plenty obvious to her that Rosie had been right when she'd said it would take some time getting used to the way English folk speak.

Still, she hadn't remembered feeling so completely comfortable with anyone. Unless it had been the day she'd stopped in at the Eslers' home to buy rhubarb jam.

Justin would find this amusing, she was quite sure. And she would tell him—the very next time he phoned.

❖ ❖ ❖

Sitting at her writing desk, Katherine's mind was awhirl. She signed the cute card and wrote Willy's name on the envelope, wishing there was something she could do to add days and weeks to his life. Even years. But the tumor in his brain was inoperable, Natalie had said. "Our mission here is to make our patients as comfortable . . . as *contented* as possible."

If money were the obstacle to his health, Katherine could've helped cure Willy easily enough. She would have given up her inheritance in order to give the darling boy his health. With all her heart, she wished it were possible.

❖ ❖ ❖

Willy was smiling for her the next day. He held her colorful elephant card in both his hands, too close to his eyes, it seemed to Katherine.

She glanced at Nurse Judah, wondering about it.

"It's all right," Natalie whispered, nodding her head. "He can see the words best that way."

A pain stabbed in the pit of her stomach. How long before the sunshine boy would go blind from the tumor? Or worse?

She stooped to open her guitar case, but Willy began to moan and the card fell to the floor. Before she could retrieve it or offer to play a soft, sweet lullaby, Willy rang the call bell. The nurse in charge arrived in seconds, and Katherine left the room.

Hours later, upon her return home, she went immediately to the drawing room and started a fire on her own. She began to play her guitar, remembering snatches of the hymn melodies she'd heard at Rosie's church. After several unsuccessful attempts at finishing, she turned to her old songs, strumming hard as she sang.

Rosie inched her way into the room at one point, during an interval of silence between songs. "Are you feeling all right, Katherine?" she asked, a deep frown on her face.

"Well . . . no."

Rosie crept closer. "Is it the hospice child? Is Willy worse?"

Her throat closed up, the lump stinging hard against the glands in her neck. All she could do was shake her head back and forth.

"Oh, dear lady. I'm so sorry." Rosie came and put her arm around Katherine's shoulders. "May I pray with you?"

She agreed, sobbing silently into her hands. Rosie's prayer was short but it calmed her, gave her hope. "Thank you," she said much later. "Suppose I've been needing that."

"The cry or the prayer?" Rosie offered a box of tissues.

Looking up, Katherine nodded. "Jah, I 'spect I needed both."

Rosie smiled down at her. "There is still a good portion of Amish in you, I daresay."

"Puh . . . I said it that way just for fun."

"Are you positively sure?"

She brushed the tears away and moved closer to the fireplace. "I met two Amish sisters yesterday . . . at the card shop in the mall. They might come and help us finish the quilt in time for the hospice bazaar."

Rosie offered her another tissue to blow her nose. "That would be lovely, having more Amish folk around here."

"You think I'm going home someday, don't you, Rosie? Back to Hickory Hollow?" The question came clear out of the blue; she wasn't sure where.

"Well, I wouldn't be too surprised perhaps."

Katherine shook her head. "This is home to me now. I love my mother's mansion . . . and everyone in it."

"If you returned, where would that leave your Justin Wirth?" It was as if Rosie hadn't heard Katherine's comment about the beautiful estate.

"This mansion . . . *and* Mr. Wirth are absolutely wonderful," she insisted, and the thought of Justin all dressed up, sending his enticing smiles her way, made her heart flutter.

Rosie's eyes twinkled mischievously. "Has he popped the question yet?"

"Popped . . . what?"

"Has Justin asked you to spend the rest of your life with him? You know, say 'I do' in front of a preacher and a churchful of witnesses—be his Mrs. Wirth?"

She gazed at the ceiling, trying the name on in her head. "Mrs. Katherine Wirth. Hm-m, sounds pretty, don't you think?"

Rosie's eyes narrowed. "And are you ready to change your name again?"

Katherine turned and stared at the fire, purposely ignoring the pointed question. "Justin's a good man. I have a feeling he'll take me somewhere very special to dine when the question pops out."

They laughed together, Katherine reaching out to grasp Rosie's sturdy hands. She clung to her housemaid as one might hold fast to an older sister, and felt all the better for it.

CHAPTER EIGHTEEN

❖ ❖ ❖

Rebecca was indeed surprised and happy to receive yet another letter from Katie. But she was alarmed at her daughter's comments about the worldly English church she'd attended. All that music—*Ei, yi, yi*—and the apostasy that minister had preached from his pulpit. It broke her heart anew to think that her girl was outside the fold—farther away than she'd feared.

She sat right down and started writing, never once thinking that she might oughta wait a few days before penning her thoughts.

Wednesday, March 25

Dear Katie,

I'm awful worried about you. Wish you'd be more cautious about the kind of meetings you go to with your English friends.

How's the weather there? We've had our share of cold and snow here.

Nothing much new, except that I've been going over to help Mattie exercise Ella Mae's limbs, trying to get the muscles to come to life again so she can at least feed herself. But it's a right slow process, as you probably remember from when Mammi Essie had hers back years ago.

187

*Mary said she didn't say anything in her letter to you
about Daniel Fisher. Maybe it's because he's shunned, too,
only the situation's much different with him. His Pop's terrible troubled over it. That's all I better say. Mattie said
that Ella Mae told her that Dan stopped in to see her before
he left again for New Jersey, that he was heading up north
to look for you. Have you seen him yet?*

*Such a story Daniel has to tell. I suppose you've heard
it all by now anyways. It is sad, really, when you think of
it. The poor fellow . . .*

*Well, news is all, so I best sign off. Never forget how
much all of us love you. The People want you to do what's
right under God and the church. (Bishop John stands
waiting and ready to hear your confession, dear girl.)*

Your Mam

She sealed the envelope and got it right out in the mail
before she could change her mind about some of what she'd
written.

Because she was in a hurry, she chose Daisy, who could
trot no matter the weather because she was young and
downright spirited. The snow stung her face and the wind
whipped at her skirt as she hitched up the horse to the family carriage. She was determined to get over to Ella Mae's
and help Mattie with afternoon chores as well as exercising
the Wise Woman's arms and legs some.

The ride took longer than usual due to the blizzard-like
conditions. She could scarcely see the outline of Daisy's
head, one horse-length ahead. Heavy, thick flakes blanketed
the road, drifting up in uneven piles, but she persisted, shivering beneath the furry lap robes.

Only one other buggy was parked outside when Rebecca
arrived at the Beiler home. One of Mattie's married daughters maybe.

Sure enough, when she got herself inside and out of the
biting cold, Anna was boiling water for peppermint tea.

"Wouldja care for some?" she asked, big brown eyes smiling.

"Jah, I'll have some, with plenty sugar."

Mattie looked up from the table where she was sitting with young Sally, choosing a pattern for a quilt. "You look like ya could use a gut hot drink about now."

She nodded. "It's awful bad out, making like it's gonna dump heavy on us."

Young Sally glanced up, smiling. "Ach, a blizzard? Yuscht what we need to have us a school vacation."

Rebecca eyed her. "Your Pop has a right fine sleigh, don't he?"

The girl nodded, looking mighty sheepish.

"Well, then, I don't 'spect there'll be any chance of school closin'—no matter how gut and hard the snow comes," Rebecca said, taking a sip of the tea.

Sally scrunched up her face and got back to her quilting work. "Jah . . . maybe."

Grinning at her, Mattie hugged her granddaughter to herself, holding her there for a moment. "This one needs extra learnin', if ya ask me."

"Maybe Sally just oughta have herself a taste of summer school come July," said Anna sternly. "Then maybe my daughter won't dawdle so during the school year."

The awkward subject was soon dropped and the conversation turned to Ella Mae. "How's she feelin' today?" Rebecca wanted to know.

"Oh, she's itchin' to talk—tries her best to make little grunting sounds, tryin' hard as anything to communicate," Mattie said. "Poor thing's havin' a time of it."

Rebecca was sorry to hear it. "Would she like some tea?"

"Well, you know as gut as I do how she feels about a hot cup of mint tea." Mattie pulled herself up off the table bench with a sigh and went to pour her mamma some.

Rebecca spoke up. "I'd be glad to take it over to her," she

said. "And while I'm at it, I'll have her doing her daily calisthenics."

Young Sally giggled, and Anna said 'twasn't funny being two months shy of eighty and having just suffered a stroke.

"Sorry, Mamma," Sally said, wearing a repentant face.

"You best be" was all Anna replied.

Something about feisty Sally made Rebecca think of Katie at that age. But she brushed the thought aside and took a tray of tea, honey, and some fresh cream across the house to the Wise Woman.

❖   ❖   ❖

Katherine did tell Justin about the Amish girls at the gift shop when he phoned her after lunch. "I wish you could've seen me there talking with them. It was the oddest thing, really."

It was hard for her to know what he was thinking or how he might look on the other end of the line, but she was happy to hear the cheerfulness in his voice. "It's intriguing, this recent connection with the Amish . . . after your church shunned you, Katherine. I'm a bit surprised that you are still drawn to Plain folk."

She understood his reservations. "I suppose it does seem strange, but I really don't have any animosity toward my People. I don't dislike them . . . not at all." She was thinking especially of Mary.

"But you can never go back, can you?" The words were confident, pointed.

She was silent. In such a short time, Justin had come to know her heart better, it seemed, than almost anyone. "That's true, I can't go back. I'm someone altogether different now."

"Well, if that's settled"—he chuckled—"why don't we plan a trip together?"

190

"A trip? Where?"

"Have you ever heard of Niagara Falls? It's a true wonder of nature."

"And only a short drive from here—am I right?"

He laughed again, and the warmth of it was merry in her ear. "Only about an hour away. We could leave in the morning, spend the afternoon, and dine somewhere lovely at sunset."

She wondered if this might be the location for a marriage proposal, though she supposed it might be just another opportunity to spend some time alone together. "Sounds wonderful," she heard herself saying.

He explained that he was nearing the completion of a new oil painting and that he'd need another few days—"at the most a week, though I doubt it."

"Whenever you're ready," she said, smiling to herself.

"In the meantime, let's have lunch somewhere exotic. Tomorrow?"

"Tomorrow's fine, thank you."

"I'll come by and pick you up around eleven-thirty?"

"All right."

"Good, I'll see you then." He paused. "I miss you, Katherine."

Her heart danced in her chest. "I'm looking forward to seeing you, too."

They said good-bye, and she hung up the phone, more than eager to see him again.

❖　❖　❖

Katherine kept her word, but when she went to visit Willy, he was scarcely aware of her being there. "Is he slipping away?" she whispered to Natalie, who was administering his afternoon shot.

"I'm afraid it's just a matter of days now," Natalie replied, gently easing the needle out of his vein.

"And he was so happy about . . ." She paused, trying to compose herself. "He was talking about going home and . . . and . . ." She simply could not go on.

Willy's mother and brother came in the room just then, and Katherine felt she should leave. Before she could do so, the petite woman with shoulder-length blond hair spoke up. "I want you to know how much our Willy has talked of you, Katherine." She smiled, glancing down at the guitar case. "He was telling his father and me just last night that he's decided he doesn't want to play a harp when he goes to heaven."

"Oh?"

"Willy wants to play *guitar*."

"For all the angels," said Josh, straight-faced.

That brought a smile to Katherine's face, and she wanted to tell them what an amazing boy Willy was. "He's a delight—a ray of sunshine in many ways," she said, keeping her comment short and to the point for fear of breaking down emotionally. Quickly, she exited, giving the little family some privacy.

Standing in the hallway just outside Willy's room, she breathed in deeply, wondering why she felt even more at a loss for words than she had when Laura lay dying. Willy was so terribly young—hadn't even had a chance to live—and now his life was ending.

She busied herself reading to several other patients, passing out cups of water in the common room, and sitting silently in the darkened room of another cancer patient. Hoping for another moment or two with Willy before she left for the day, Katherine was happy when his mother and brother came looking for her.

"We're going to the cafeteria for a snack," Willy's mother said. "Would you mind playing your guitar softly in the room until we return?"

"It's no use," Josh spoke up, his countenance glum. "Willy won't hear it anyway. He's dangling somewhere between earth and heaven."

Katherine cringed, remembering Nurse Judah's remark—that the boy might have only a few days at the longest.

When Mrs. Norton and Josh left, Katherine slipped back into Willy's room. He was lying very still in his bed, his little arm wrapped lovingly around all three of his teddy bears. Going over to stand at the side of his bed, she noticed the elephant card in his right hand.

In the quietude, she played a new song for him—a lilting, happy tune she composed as she went along. Strumming softly, she pictured a meadow with daisies and a hot sun high overhead. She and Willy were romping through the high grass, their faces flushed with the heat of summer.

"Are you married, Katherine?"

She could hear his innocent words, could see his blue, inquisitive eyes. Sweet . . . dear Willy. Dying.

She wished his cancer might go into remission, then he could be the boy who carried the ring at her and Justin's church wedding—the ring bearer, she thought it was called, though she couldn't be sure. Such a selfish thought; at least it might seem so to anyone who didn't truly know her.

"Will you have lots of children?"

She played on, changing keys as she sang the song just for him. It was a song of sheer joy, for the boy had given her much in the way of friendship, and on several occasions he'd offered her hope. Yet *she* had been the one volunteering to encourage *him*!

"God gives His people the desires of their hearts," he'd said once, startling her by adding something so profound that she could hardly comprehend it. *"If they're linked up with Him,"* he'd said.

At the time she had seen the sincerity in his eyes. Now,

thinking back to that moment, she wondered why such great faith hadn't given Willy *his* heart's desire. Could it be that the all-wise, all-knowing heavenly Father had a better plan for the child? Was *that* the reason Willy was dying?

Katherine played her guitar as beautifully as she ever had, thinking that it might very well be the last time. Her fingertips tender, she played till both Mr. and Mrs. Norton and Josh returned. Again, they thanked her for showing kindness to their son.

"I'm happy to have spent so much time with Willy," she said. "I can't begin to tell you the many things he's taught me."

His father nodded. "We're very proud of him."

When they'd said their good-byes, she excused herself and went to page Theodore, waiting outdoors where she could breathe the crisp, cold air. Her head needed a good airing out. "Dear Lord, must you take Willy now?" she prayed, reminding God of the child's youth. "He doesn't want to die. Please, could you reconsider?"

For the first time in her life, she did not feel that such a prayer was bossy or presumptuous.

CHAPTER NINETEEN

❖ ❖ ❖

Katherine took the call in the library, where she'd spent most of the morning reading.

Natalie Judah was on the line. "Hello, Katherine. I called to tell you about Willy Norton." She paused briefly. "I wanted you to know before you come in on Monday."

Katherine braced herself. "Yes?"

"The boy passed away in his sleep early this morning" came the report.

Silent, Katherine let the message seep into her consciousness. *Willy James Lee . . . gone.*

"Katherine? Are you all right?"

Immediately, her thoughts flew to Willy's parents and brother. "How's the family taking it?"

"Our spiritual-care people are with them now," Natalie assured her. "The family has a strong faith."

"Yes," she whispered. "Yes, I know."

After she had said good-bye, Katherine put in a call to Justin. She didn't feel much like having lunch with anyone today, exotic dining room or not. He answered on the first ring.

"I'm very sorry to cancel our luncheon date," she said. "But I don't believe I would be good company for you." She went on to tell him about Willy's passing.

"I'm sad to hear that, but perhaps you'll change your mind in a few hours. Why don't you page me later? You might feel like having something to eat after all."

It was generous of him to offer, she thought, extending himself that way. "Yes, well, I might, but I hope you won't be offended if I don't . . . not today."

"It's entirely your choice, Katherine. Whatever you decide, my dear."

"Thanks for understanding."

"Certainly. We'll talk later, or maybe tomorrow—as soon as you feel up to it."

When they'd hung up, she sat there in the stillness. Feeling suddenly hemmed in, the towering library shelves seemed to close in on her as she brooded. The tea table, with her books scattered on it, was near the fire, and a plate of cookies and other sweets enticed her to linger awhile.

Getting up, she wandered over to the windows, staring up at a clean sky. Only an occasional puff of a cloud, far in the distance, caught her attention. Yet she watched them drift, break into pieces, and float aimlessly across the expanse of blue.

She thought of Willy's passing in light of her Amish upbringing, and it wasn't so unnatural to think in terms of death being all wrapped up in life—merely part of the cycle we humans must celebrate. Funerals, as seen through the eye of one who'd experienced a good many of them in Hickory Hollow, were a gathering together of loved ones and friends to rejoice in the life of the deceased, no matter how short or long. No weeping and wailing over the loss of one of the People. "For every soul who goes, another will be born to take his place," Samuel Lapp used to say.

No, she would never want to wish Willy back. With the Lord's blessing—and Willy certainly seemed to have a corner on that—the boy would find his own mansion in paradise just fine.

Still, she felt overcome with grief. Another loss, one so close to the other. And she supposed—had she been given to drinking wine—that she might have been tempted to drown her sorrow. Instead, she turned to Laura's books, and for the next several hours lost herself in classic literature.

It was much later, after Justin had called to check up on her, that she felt compelled to visit her birth mother's grave. A quick call to Theodore brought the limousine promptly around to the front entrance.

There was precious little talk between herself and the chauffeur this time, even though a hint of spring in the air served to evoke frivolous chatter on the part of Theodore, the day being warm in contrast to the severe weather of past weeks.

"I certainly wouldn't think it would be much longer until spring is more than official," said Theodore, looking dapper as usual. "We're on the downside of bitter weather, if I do say so myself."

He had a pleasant pattern of speech—a kind of good-natured, yet British way of bantering—with or without the listener ever having to interact. The sound of his voice was as warm and welcome as her long-deceased Dawdi David's approach to loafing around with other Amishmen. They'd huddled together on many a springlike day, sitting out under the shade of their gnarled oak tree on a low wooden bench, chewing the fat—some of them chewing the tobacco leaf, too.

Katherine listened without comment. After a time, though, she was less aware of his soft patter and more absorbed in her own private thoughts.

The cemetery was several miles from town, situated off one of the county roads a bit. The burial place—removed from urban life, yet accessible enough for visitors, be they mourners or merely lovers of nature—was as serene as it was haunting.

Huge iron gates yawning open reminded her that it was also quite secluded and separate from the rest of Canandaigua. This, she was fairly certain, was the reason Laura's parents had purchased burial plots here years ago.

The trees seemed taller than she'd remembered. Today they created an entangled sanctuary of branches high above the gravel road that stretched, narrow and bending, around the sections of the graveyard.

She imagined the place in full summer, the orchard to the south filled with bees moiling the magic of pollination, the lovely, fragrant smells, the margin of woods to the east where tall goldenrod and ironweed would bloom tawny gold and sky blue come autumn, where starlings bickered and swallows swooped down to say hello.

Katherine, awestruck by her surroundings, had never felt so vulnerable, so breathless, in the Amish cemeteries in Lancaster County. Yet she simply could not shrug off the heaviness as she donned her snow boots and left the limousine to search for her birth mother's headstone.

Minutes later, she stood in front of Laura Mayfield-Bennett's grave and silently read the words etched on the stone. " 'But the salvation of the righteous is of the Lord: he is their strength in the time of trouble.' "

The salvation of the righteous . . .

These words, read by one of the ministers at the funeral, had been ever so dear to Laura. Reading them again, Katherine felt the vigor, the unexpected drawing power.

Dropping to her knees in the snow, she began to share her secret grief. "Oh, Mother, I never understood the things you said as you were dying. Not fully. You were such a kind and compassionate woman. Everyone who knew you says so. I only wish I might've known you longer . . . better."

She sighed. "There's a dear little boy. His name is—

was—Willy, and I came to love him in spite of his terminal disease. But now he's gone. I never, never dreamed I could care so much for a child . . . one who was not my own."

Pausing, she heard the gentle wind in the trees, the hushed reverence around her. "Willy has two middle names, Mother. Something I've never heard of, but he has them all the same. Surely Willy James Lee must be skipping down the golden streets, playing ball with the other children in paradise along about now. I was just hoping that you might be able to look out for him, dear Mother. He was such a fragile boy. Will you care for him for me?"

She couldn't quite get out *until I can come and watch over him myself.* Feelings of unworthiness kept her from voicing it, though she knew that someday she would have to reckon with her choice: either for or against the blessed faith of both young Willy and benevolent Laura. She could not continue on much longer, torn between her unyielding past and the indoctrination of her childhood and the gentle, life-giving passages of God's Word. And she was puzzled as to why it seemed that at every turn she kept stumbling into some biblical reminder of divine love.

Chapter Twenty

❖　❖　❖

The day trip to Niagara Falls fell on the following Sunday, much to Katherine's dismay, although when she mentioned attending church, Justin promised to take her the next opportunity he had.

"The Taylors—Fulton and Rosie—go there," she told him, hoping to engage him in some conversation about his religious beliefs.

"Ah, churches . . . they're a dime a dozen around here." His comment left her cold, though she continued to pursue the topic.

"Did your parents ever teach you about God when you were small?"

"Not, perhaps, as much as yours did, though I did attend an occasional summer church camp." He smiled at her from behind the wheel of his own car. They'd decided to abandon the limousine and chauffeur, giving them more privacy for the day. Actually, it was Justin's idea, and Katherine was rather glad about it.

"Church camp? What was it like?"

He mentioned a few hair-raising scenes of boys catching toads from the creek and hiding them in the girls' quarters, but nothing of spiritual substance.

"What made it church related?" she inquired.

He reached over and took her hand. "Is everything all right today, Katherine? It seems you've talked of nothing but church and God since we left town."

She nodded. "Yes . . . I'm curious, I guess you could say."

He squeezed her hand. "Your loss of young Willy, is it?"

Tears sprang up unexpectedly. "I . . . I miss him . . . terribly," she stammered.

Justin pressed the turn signal and pulled over on the shoulder, slowing down gradually, then coming to a complete stop. "Katherine, darling." He gathered her into his arms, and she wept for the little boy who'd seemed to know her heart with such ease. "His pain is past," Justin whispered into her hair.

She snuggled next to him, her face against the smooth lapel of his overcoat. "I never thought he'd die. . . ."

"Sh-h, now, don't say more. You'll be fine, Katherine. I'll take good care of you."

When she'd regained her composure, the subject of Willy seemed to fade naturally, and she hoped her emotional state hadn't altered the course of the day.

"I want to show you my art studio sometime," he said later as they entered the Niagara Falls tourist area and headed for the lookout tower. "Would you like that?"

She smiled, glad her tears were over. "Very much."

"My painting is nearly complete now, and I'd like your opinion of it."

Hearing that he wanted to include her in his professional life—even just showing her around his work studio—was an exhilarating thought. "I'd be happy to see your work."

They found a parking spot close to the lookout on the American side, and Katherine was in awe of the movement of the vast river as it plunged over the falls. Even at this distance, the mighty surge of power was riveting.

Standing next to Justin, she felt a bit nervous at the

thunderous roar. To think that stunt men had braved tight-ropes and barrels and lived to tell about it!

"What are you thinking?" he asked, slipping his arm around her shoulders.

"This place . . . it's the most unbelievable sight I've ever seen."

"There are many wondrous and scenic spots in the world. This happens to be one of my favorites, close to home." He turned to face her. "It's only the beginning of what I want to show you, my darling."

Her heart beat wildly as he caressed her face with his hands, leaning down for their first kiss. His lips were sweet and lingered gently. Smiling into her eyes, he said, "Some-day we'll bring our children to see the majesty of these falls."

Our children . . .

She had to suppress a giggle. Justin was taking much for granted. He hadn't even asked her to marry him yet!

They strolled along the walkway, Justin's arm curved protectively around her waist. Nothing more was said about their future for the rest of the excursion. No "popping of the question," as Rosie had so humorously called it.

Katherine fell into bed late that night after enjoying another candlelight supper with fine food and music, won-dering what Justin had said or done to cause her such dis-satisfaction. Thinking back through the entire day, she knew she ought to have been on "cloud nine," as Rosie or Leoma might say. But something was troubling her, and she couldn't put her finger on it.

◈　◈　◈

Rachel Esler called first thing the next morning, and for a moment, Katherine wasn't sure who was on the line. "Who did you say you were?"

"Ach, I'm sorry" came the Amish reply. "Guess I must've

forgotten to tell ya that we met over at the mall at the card shop. You gave your phone number to my sister and me."

Katherine now knew exactly who was calling. "Of course I remember you, Rachel. You had me stumped there for a minute, because you sounded like one of my relatives—back in Pennsylvania."

"Jah, I see. Well," the girl continued, "I wanted to let ya know that my sisters—all three of them—and our mother would like to help you finish off your Country Songbird quilt for the hospice bazaar."

"Really? You do?"

"For sure and for certain" came the familiar reply. "We could come for two or three hours at a time but only on weekdays."

"I understand," she said. This was too good to be true!

"So when do ya plan your next frolic?" Rachel inquired.

Frolic? Katherine hadn't heard the word in ages. What a lovely sound—so charming, she nearly forgot to answer the caller's question. "Uh . . . *when?* This Wednesday evening, we'll meet again."

"Gut, then." Rachel went on to ask if there would be enough people in all to have twelve quilters.

"Let's see . . ." Katherine thought for a minute. "There's seven of us here and five of you. Perfect!"

"We'll see ya after supper on Wednesday then."

"Thank you, Rachel. Good-bye."

She spun around, twisting the phone cord about her. "This is wonderful-gut," she announced so loudly that Rosie and Leoma leaned their heads into the French doors.

"Sorry," she said, untangling the cord while the housemaids exchanged comical glances.

"Must be something about Justin Wirth," she heard Rosie say as the women turned to leave.

Katherine had herself a good chuckle—somewhat subdued, however—over that. Wouldn't the ladies be surprised to meet their new quilting comrades?

❖ ❖ ❖

The studio tour was enlightening, and Justin was quite the humble host as he showed her around the next weekend. Most remarkable of all was his oil painting of Mayfield Manor—Katherine's estate.

"Oh, it's amazing," she cooed, looking closely to inspect the detail, then stepping back to survey the grandeur. "You really captured the feel of the place."

He smiled, standing off to himself in the corner, where books on castles and bridges stood on a display shelf, facing out.

"I mean it, Justin. You're branching out, aren't you?"

His arms were folded tightly against his chest, his expression serious and subdued. "I've always been most interested in portraying people, but more lately—and I'm not exactly sure why, unless it has something to do with the splendor of your mansion—I've become fascinated by architecture and nature."

She went to him, resting both hands on his folded arms. "So *that's* why you took me to Niagara Falls. You're going to paint it, too. Am I right?"

He unwrapped his arms and pulled her close. "What do you think? Is it a good idea?" he asked, his lips pleasantly close to her face.

The smell of his breath, his musk cologne, all of it made her wish he'd say how much he loved her . . . ask her the important question. Instead, he waited for her response, gazing down into her eyes.

"I, uh, should think the water would be hard to paint, especially because it's moving so quickly," she managed to say.

Gently, he brushed the tip of her nose with his lips, gave

her a loving hug, and led her by the hand to his easel. There, he began pointing out various brush strokes that would lend themselves well to depicting the motion of the Niagara River. "So you see, it *is* possible to capture such energy and movement with paint," he said quite adamantly.

"Yes, I think I see that." It was obvious the man was fond of his work, and rightly so, for he was as talented as he was admirable. And at that moment, Katherine was altogether sure he was the dearest man in all the world.

CHAPTER TWENTY-ONE

❖   ❖   ❖

The pipe organ enthralled Katherine with a piece she'd never heard before—*The Palms*—though she wondered if Justin's presence on this day, Palm Sunday, might not have enhanced the musical experience for her.

Churchgoers thronged the chapel, joyfully looking ahead to Easter. Katherine heeded the minister's message, hoping to discuss some of the Scriptures with Justin over dinner.

The topic that seemed to be most interesting to him, however, was another trip. "To Toronto, Canada," he mentioned as they dined. "What do you say, Katherine? Will you come with me?"

He told her of his plan to sketch one of the cathedrals there. "We could have a lovely time, just the two of us."

She felt somewhat awkward about it, unsure of the travel plans. "I . . . wouldn't want to miss out on my scheduled days at the hospice or the quilting sessions," she told him.

"No, no, I don't want you to forego any of your plans." He brushed aside her unspoken concerns. "We could leave on a Friday evening, after your quilting group and return by Sunday night."

She didn't need to remind him that they weren't married; therefore, she would not feel comfortable sharing a hotel room with him. Miraculously, she didn't have to bring up the subject. He must've seen the puzzlement on her face—she didn't really know how he knew—but he winked at her and assured her that they'd acquire separate rooms.

"Could we wait to go until after Easter?" she asked, longing to attend church on that special day.

Justin's response was not as animated as she had hoped it might be, but he agreed to postpone the trip. So it was set. He made all the necessary arrangements in regard to accommodations; Katherine merely had to alert her domestic staff.

Rosie raised her eyebrows when Katherine filled her in on the details. The maid's eyebrows stayed up when Katherine explained that she'd toured Justin's art studio as well.

"Hm-m, it's starting to sound more serious between the two of you," Rosie said with a curious smile.

"I think he must love me, or he wouldn't be spending so much time taking me to dinners and nice places."

Rosie's eyes penetrated hers. "But do *you* love him?"

"I care for Justin very much, if that's what you mean."

"Does he share your interest in church?" The question was as pointed a comment as Rosie had ever made.

Katherine didn't quite know how to answer, other than to be completely honest. "I suppose not."

Rosie said no more. Katherine, however, felt she wanted to defend Justin's lack of interest in religion. After all, America was the land of the free, wasn't it? Yet something kept her from speaking up, something desperate and hidden from view.

❖ ❖ ❖

The afternoon sky was featureless, but the road that stretched ahead for miles took Dan past two covered bridges, a single one-room schoolhouse, and numerous farmhouses. He recognized the private lanes leading into his relatives' barnyards—knew them like the back of his hand. Yet coming here, uninvited, on an off-Sunday, posed definite drawbacks for a shunned member of the Amish church.

Starting out first thing after church, he had decided it was high time he laid eyes on his namesake, four-month-old Daniel Lapp. Impulsively, he'd set out for Lancaster County, not bothering to stop for lunch. Annie would be surprised, he knew, but she wouldn't turn him away, not even if Elam were home. He could count on her warming up some left-overs for him, too, though she'd not let him eat at the same table. Without question.

Her face brightened pink when she spied him at the door, then paled considerably when he bent down to kiss her cheek. "I've waited too long to see my young nephew," he said, apologizing for not letting her know ahead of time. "Hope it's not an inconvenience."

"Puh! Come on in, Dan." She quickly closed the door behind him. "Elam might not be too happy about havin' you here much—not too long, anyways—but *I'm* glad you came!"

He understood. "I'll stay only a short time," he promised, following her into the kitchen.

She set to work immediately, pulling food out of the pantry. "You must be starved, drivin' all that way."

"I'll eat whatever you give me." He glanced around at the familiar trappings of the kitchen: the corner cupboard that housed the big German Bible and other books, the typical calendar hanging on the back of the cellar door, the trestle table in the middle of the floor, the woodstove, the hickory rocker, and the dark green blinds wound up tight and high at the windows. One Amish kitchen was like any other, comforting and familiar.

Annie called to Elam in the front room. "Daniel's here for a visit."

Thinking it was nice that she hadn't said a "quick visit," Dan felt more comfortable, though he knew they wouldn't feel too kindly about him wearing out his welcome—being under the Meinding and all.

"Would you like for me to get the folding table out of the cellar?" he offered.

Annie shook her head. "You sit yourself right down at the big table, Dan. Nobody's gonna be sittin' there with ya anyhow."

She looked so young to be married and a mother already, he thought. And if he wasn't mistaken, she wore the blush of motherhood on her cheeks and in her eyes—he'd seen it enough times to know that she was probably expecting her second baby come early autumn.

"Well, Daniel, what brings you here?" Elam asked, standing in the doorway between the kitchen and the front room. His high forehead and blond hair immediately reminded Dan of Rebecca Lapp, though the lack of a smile hid the dimples so prominent on his mother's face.

"I came to meet your son . . . my nephew."

"Let's see if the baby's awake." Elam left the kitchen and headed for the stairs.

Annie smiled sweetly. "I'm sure Daniel's up." She glanced at the day clock high over the sink. "It's been an hour or more since I put him down for a nap. Such a gut baby . . ."

Soon Elam came downstairs carrying the blanketed bundle.

"Ach, hold him up," Annie said, going over and leaning on her husband's arm. "He's right big already. Jah?"

They removed the blanket, and Elam held little Daniel up in the air, the baby's feet kicking and his arms flapping about, till Annie rescued the poor thing. She reached for him and cradled him in her arms, coming around to the opposite side of the table where Dan sat in front of a plate of chunky potato salad, homemade bread spread with honey-butter and jam, and cold slices of chicken. "Here's the little fella," she said, bringing him over to Dan.

Surprised at first, he took the squirming mass of humanity and looked into the bright blue eyes. "Hello there, young man. I'm your uncle Dan Fisher."

The baby didn't fuss as Dan expected, just stared up at him and cooed. The weight of the tiny body in his arms, the little round eyes looking back at him, and the joyful gurglings—all of it stirred something in him, and he wondered what it would be like to father and raise a fine son or two or three someday.

The shape of young Daniel's mouth and chin line reminded Dan of himself. Though he hadn't ever seen himself in pictures as a youngster, for there had never been photos taken—not even snapshots—not of any of the People all those years. Still there was something terribly familiar about the baby's facial features. He felt as if he were looking into a mirror, one that reflected the past. "All the little fella needs is a beard and we could pass for twins."

Annie agreed. "I thought the same thing when he was first born. There's a strong family likeness."

"Suppose I ought to shave my beard. That would work just as well." He was laughing now, which seemed to amuse the baby, who reached up and pulled on his beard.

"Mary's about to marry herself the bishop," Annie said, pulling up one of the rocking chairs.

Elam stood close to the table, eyeing Dan—his eyes watching the baby like a hawk. "Won't be a public weddin', this one," he spoke up. "Last I heard, they were ridin' over to SummerHill come Saturday afternoon."

"The day before Easter—ain't that nice?" Annie said.

"Speakin' of Zooks, Ella Mae had a stroke here a while

back," Elam spoke up, shifting his weight from one foot to the other. "I only say that because you two were close."

Dan caught his breath. "Will she be all right?"

"She's a fighter, Ella Mae is," Annie said. "I 'spect she'll get over her paralysis in due time. She'd wanna see ya if she knew you were in town."

Dan shook his head. "I'll have to come back and see her some other time."

"Well, then, I won't say nothin' about you bein' here."

The baby started to fuss, and Annie came quickly to take him from Dan. Holding the baby in one arm, she pulled the rocker across the floor closer to the woodstove, sat down, and began to nurse him.

Dan picked up his fork and lit in to the food his sister had been so kind to set out for him. Elam made an awkward grunt and left the room. Daniel ate in silence and Annie sat quietly; the only noise in the room came from the little one making contented sucking sounds.

"I suppose you found Katie already," Annie said softly, without looking at him.

He sighed, wiping his mouth with the paper napkin. "Turned out she didn't want to be found."

Annie's eyes were on him now. "She's a right hard one to figure."

He nodded. "She's Katherine Mayfield now . . . lives in a mansion. Even has a houseful of servants looking after her." He was thinking of the dutiful butler he'd encountered at the front door.

"I can't imagine Katie livin' that way—right fancy and all."

"You wouldn't be so shocked to see her, Annie. Under all those nice clothes, there's still a girl from Hickory Hollow. You'd recognize her. I know you would."

"What's she gonna do up there all alone?" asked Annie, rocking hard.

"The Lord's up there in New York, too. Same as He is with you and Elam and little Daniel. Prayer can change things for Katie. You'll see."

"Then what about *you*?" she asked, casting a disparaging look at him. "When's God gonna answer my prayers and bring you back home?"

He knew he shouldn't start to defend his beliefs. Not now. Not here in Elam's house. His prayers for his loved ones would be more effective than anything he could say on his first visit back since the shunning.

When it came time to say good-bye, tears welled up in Annie's eyes. "Ach, I miss ya so, Daniel. Come back to the People. We could use another gut pair of hands here in the Hollow." She reminded him that their father was getting up in years, that Dat could use more help than he was already getting.

"Sure, I'd love to come home, but I can't." His soul-deep need for family—the loved ones he'd grown up with—remained ever strong, yet he resisted explaining why he could never return to the Amish church.

She clung to him, and he hugged her hard, leaning his cheek down against her devotional kapp. "I love you, Annie."

"The People are ever so anxious to hear your confession. Please . . . don't wait too long" was her soft reply.

Elam didn't wave at him when Dan turned to go to the car. He stayed inside with the baby.

It was Annie who followed him down the back walk to his car. "Won'tcha think about it, Dan?"

"I've done all I can possibly do. The Lord's in control of my life now." He said the words, though he knew she might not comprehend.

"Will ya come again?"

He nodded, waving. "Take good care of my nephew."

That brought a smile. "Good-bye, Daniel."

Getting in the car, he turned the ignition. The engine roared to life, and his last glimpse of Annie was of her closing the back door, eyes cast down as if she might cry again. Then she was gone.

CHAPTER TWENTY-TWO

❖ ❖ ❖

With Katherine's help, Selig baked up another batch of Mississippi Mud for the quilting class. Mrs. Esler and her daughters—Rachel, Ruth, Nancy, and Anna—arrived by horse and buggy about six o'clock.

Standing at the window in the drawing room, Katherine watched as Rachel Esler helped her mother out of the buggy, followed by the other girls. One unhitched the horse and tied him to the fence post in the grassy area on the far side of the driveway.

She remembered the first time she'd ever taken a harness off a horse, the feel of the warm leather in her hands. It was a heavy chore for a young girl, so Dat had helped her. Still, something about the memory made her miss Satin Boy, her first-ever pony. She sincerely hoped her mild-mannered pet was adjusting all right without her, that Benjamin was taking good care of him.

Noticing that the group of Amishwomen was now heading toward the house, Katherine moved away from the draped window and hurried across the room to the grand entryway, to be ready when the doorbell rang.

"Please, come in and make yourself at home," she said,

greeting Mrs. Esler once again, as well as the two daughters she'd met at the gift shop.

Rachel introduced her older sisters, Nancy and Anna. "They were awful excited to come and see your mansion," she added.

"And here you are," said Katherine as the butler took their wraps. "Would you like to see the place?"

Shyly, the sisters nodded their heads. "Well, come along, then." And she signaled for Fulton to assist with the tour.

The evening turned out to be one of the most joyous ones she'd spent at the mansion—much laughter and story-telling and, of course, the delicious Mississippi Mud dessert and various flavors of coffees served up by Selig and Garrett.

Mrs. Esler and her daughters were a cheerful addition to the quilting class. In fact, in many ways, the five of them helped Katherine teach the others. All in all, it was a night of hard work and fun mixed together in one delightful package of inspiration and relaxation.

"We'll come again next Wednesday," said Mrs. Esler as they prepared to leave.

"Good Friday's a fast day for us," Rachel explained.

Katherine recalled that the Amish in Hickory Hollow also observed the day as a prayerful one. "Maybe *we* won't work on the quilt Good Friday, either," she spoke up, and Rosie, Leoma, and the other non-Amish women agreed.

When she returned to her private sitting room, Katherine found herself reflecting on Mrs. Esler and her girls. Their patient, agreeable way with English folk struck her as appealing, and she truly hoped that her housemaids and the entire domestic staff felt the same about her. Before she dressed for bed, she decided that she, too, would fast and pray come Good Friday, just like her new friends.

❖ ❖ ❖

It was the bluest, clearest day of April. Each breath Mary took in was as sweet as could be, for it was her wedding day. And the day before Easter, of all things.

She and Bishop John had agreed that they'd get married in SummerHill, not but a few miles from Hickory Hollow, across the highway, up Snake Road, out past Hunsecker Mill Bridge, and on over to Preacher Zook's church district. It made right-gut sense to Mary, too. After all, John had already been through his share of wedding services, the last of which had turned into a miserable day for all concerned. No sense going to all the trouble of a full-blown wedding. Besides, it being the wrong season for a wedding in Lancaster County, this was the best way.

The children—all five of them—rode to Preacher Zook's big farmhouse with them in the enclosed buggy. The day was warmer than any she'd experienced in ages, and because of the springtime weather, Mary thought it must surely be a good sign. She could only hope that it was, for she'd waited her whole life long for this one, special day.

She turned to look over her shoulder at the bishop's children, sitting so tall and straight, going to their Daed's wedding. *I hope I can be a wonderful-gut Mamma to them*, she thought almost sadly, ever so sorry for the lonely years they'd been without Miriam, their dear mother—John's first wife.

When it came time for her to say "jah," promising to be loyal to John Beiler, to care for him in all hardship, affliction, illness, weakness, or faintheartedness, her heart opened up with great love and compassion for this man. She would show him the kind of affection that he deserved, no matter that he'd shunned her dearest and best friend. No matter that he was thought of as a rigid, *standhaft* bishop. Sure as the dawn, she desired to love him, to serve him, to be his faithful wife till the day she died.

After the short ceremony, Nancy and Susie both kissed

her cheek. Hickory John, Levi, and young Jacob shook her hand, but Jacob sneaked in a quick hug when no one was looking. "I've got me a mamma now," he said, then scampered off to play outside with Preacher Zook's children.

Mary had to smile. "And I've got me a family of my own," she whispered, watching as Jacob's little legs carried him across the barnyard.

Turning back to her handsome husband, she wondered how on earth she could break this news to Katie, especially now. She'd heard from Annie Lapp that Dan had been in town last Sunday, and from what he'd told his sister, the poor lad was heartsick over Katie—not being received too well by her and all.

Was it the right thing to share her joyous news, let Katie know that her friend had found true happiness right here in Hickory Hollow? Because it sounded, for all the world, as if there was someone awful sad and alone up there in New York.

CHAPTER TWENTY-THREE

❖   ❖   ❖

On Easter morning, Katherine arose early and hurried to the closet. She slipped into her warmest robe and house slippers, then scurried to the kitchen at the other end of the house. Gut! No one was about.

Opening the refrigerator, she took out the square plastic box the florist had delivered to her yesterday afternoon. Eager to see the lovely corsage without being observed, she decided to take it to her suite. Back in the privacy of her own room, she opened the lid and lifted the delicate arrangement of tiny pink rosebuds and a sprig of the daintiest baby's breath she'd ever seen. The fragrance was as pure as any rose her Amish mamma had ever grown in the family rose garden. Maybe all the sweeter because it came from Justin.

The card that had arrived with the corsage had thrilled her upon first reading it. *Wishing you an Easter filled with love. Yours always, Justin.* Even more thrilling was the fact that he would be sitting beside her in church!

Written in his own hand, the words now delighted her once again, and she savored the prospect of a lovely day.

Outside, the air was warm and breezy, and the sky was

as blue as a robin's egg, with not a hint of rain. A perfect Easter Sunday. Justin drove her to church in his own car, and she was secretly glad they could talk without being overheard by a chauffeur.

Glorious music, both choral and organ, filled the church before and after the sermon. Katherine battled thoughts of Dan upon hearing the offertory—*Hallelujah, What A Savior!*—a hymn she'd sung at some of the livelier Singings at SummerHill get-togethers during her teen years. But she couldn't allow anything or anyone to spoil her day with Justin, and she tilted her head slightly to breathe in the sweet scent of the flowers pinned to her cream-colored linen blazer. Glancing down, she smoothed her tea-length floral skirt, marveling again at the feel of the lovely fabric, so unlike the coarse and heavy homespun dresses of the past.

She daydreamed periodically during the sermon, though she wouldn't have wanted to admit it to a soul, this being a house of worship. Yet she had difficulty keeping her eyes fixed on the pulpit, so preoccupied was she in scanning the sanctuary and thinking how nice it would be to have her and Justin's wedding here. A candlelight service . . . in the fall. Yes, that's what she would like. Her vows to Justin should take place at dawn, just as the earth held its breath, awaiting the sun's rays; the emerging of little birds from their nests, the mist hugging the trees at the gossamer first light of daybreak.

She glanced at Justin to her left, wondering if he, too, might be thinking similar thoughts. He caught her eye and smiled, then reached for her hand. Katherine's heart beat a bit faster, and she hoped he would kiss her again, sometime today. Easter Sunday . . . after dinner perhaps.

◈　　◈　　◈

"Ach, I've never missed an Easter Sunday Preachin' in

all my born days," Ella Mae complained, her speech still awkward.

"It's out of the question, Mamma."

"But I'm feelin' gut already."

"Sorry, Mam. You best stay home today."

She wanted to fuss some more, make a bigger bother about not getting to go to Preaching, but she knew by the determined look on Mattie's face, not to mention the frustrated sighs, that her daughter wasn't going to budge an inch.

"You've had a bad stroke, for goodness' sake," Mattie said, straightening the quilt at the bottom of the bed.

"I won't enjoy bein' alone." Her final attempt at guilt. There was no reply, though, and she figured Mattie was trying to make a point by shuffling out of the room and down the hall.

The house was mighty quiet with everybody gone over to Jake and Becky Zook's—her son and daughter-in-law's place. Ella Mae felt just awful about it, missing out on Easter the first time ever. "I oughta up and die," she said, chuckling a bit. "Would serve 'em right for leavin' me behind like this."

She didn't feel quite bad enough to die, though. With all that exercising of arms and legs her friends and relatives were insisting on doing, she was actually improving, even getting her speech back little by little. And best of all her mobility.

Scooting herself up in bed, she reached behind her and folded her pillows in half to support her back. It would do her good to read away the hours, help pass the time till David and Mattie returned. 'Course, they wouldn't be so unthinking as to stay for the common meal after the sermons. No, they'd come on home, and Mattie would fix up some cold cuts, maybe even warm up some potato soup. Jah, she'd like that just fine.

The book she chose to read was one Lydia Miller had

brought over just yesterday. Lydia had always been a faithful friend, but here lately—ever since Ella Mae's stroke—the dear girl had come nearly every day, bringing flowers from an English florist or her own homemade soups or an occasional book. Goodies, too. Jah, Lydia knew what made her smile.

The book she held in her hands was far different than anything she'd ever read. It was a small book, told from an Amishwoman's viewpoint, about how she witnessed to the folk who came to her bed-and-breakfast establishment. Ella Mae had to smile when she read the prologue, describing the real-life woman. It seemed downright uncanny that something like that was going on right here in Lancaster County. Maybe because she'd thought of doing something very much like it, back years ago.

As it turned out, she'd opened her heart and her hearth to many a weary soul, eventually relinquishing the idea of an Amish B&B. Still, she found the reading interesting—oh, so true. The woman, who'd assumed a pen name, had the right idea. A wonderful-gut idea it was to pass along the love of the Lord. 'Course, she didn't suppose the woman had to contend with such a strict bishop as John Beiler. But from what she knew of marriage, she figured the bishop was long overdue for some tender, loving care. Maybe just the thing to soften him up some. She only hoped that young Mary was up to the task of keeping a husband happy and five *munder*—oh, so lively—children well fed. Still, if anyone could do it, she s'pected plump and perty Mary Stoltzfus was the one for the job.

Ella Mae reined in her wandering thoughts and got into the book real deep, turning one page after another, laughing here and there, imagining herself doing just what the B&B owner had done.

The pages captured and held her interest until she drifted off—not quite knowing when it happened or if she'd read through to the end of the book. But when she awoke with a start, she found the book half covering her face, open to a page toward the back.

"Dear me," she mumbled, sitting up. "Wonder what time it could be."

She listened, hearing voices in the main house. David and Mattie were home. She wouldn't call out to them, she decided. She'd sit, silent as a snipe, and wait for the report of the Preachin' service she'd missed.

❖ ❖ ❖

Katherine was excited about the upcoming trip to Toronto, although she wasn't sure why. She had only the vaguest idea of what to expect from such a trip. Time to talk and share each other's goals and hopes for the future was high on her list.

"I'm thinking of painting your Songbird quilt when it's finished," Justin said as they rode along the highway, heading north. "I think it will be a unique approach to art."

She was surprised. "I never would have thought of such a thing, but it sounds interesting."

Justin turned and winked at her. "Think about it. When have you ever seen a rendering of an Amish quilt on canvas?"

It was an absolutely wonderful idea. Katherine could hardly wait for him to begin, but the quilt itself had to be completed before Justin could paint it. And there was the matter of the hospice bazaar. "How will it work—if the quilt's going to be sold in a few weeks?"

"Oh," he said, frowning. "I hadn't thought of that."

They discussed his exciting idea, thinking of various ways to approach the problem. Katherine suggested taking a photograph, but Justin didn't think he could capture the essence of the quilt from a photo. Finally, Katherine said,

"Maybe you could sketch the pattern ahead of time. You could come to my quilting class and begin a pencil drawing as we work."

He nodded, grinning. "Splendid idea!"

She didn't say so, but she was thrilled at his response. Having Justin come to the mansion two or three hours on Wednesday and Friday evenings would be delightful. She was glad she'd thought of it.

❖   ❖   ❖

The first few hours in Toronto were spent locating one particular cathedral, then taking photographs of it for Justin's file. Katherine enjoyed watching him angle the poses with his expensive camera, but most of all, the trip gave her ample time with her Beau.

While there, she began composing a letter to Mary, anxious to tell her about her new love and inquiring about life in Hickory Hollow.

By the time they returned to Canandaigua, she realized how much she had enjoyed Justin's company. So much that she had not thought of Dan Fisher. Not even once.

Chapter Twenty-Four

❖ ❖ ❖

Days and weeks sped by, and with the delicate shifting of the season to summer, Katherine began to enjoy the warmer weather, though the temperatures weren't nearly as hot as she remembered them in southeastern Pennsylvania—not for late June. Still, she had plenty of picnics out-of-doors, several with her new friends—Rachel Esler and her sisters—and two barbecues for the terminally ill patients at the hospice.

And there was a steak fry for two. She and Justin had spread out a blanket on the south lawn near the lily pond, behind the mansion, enjoying the birds and sky and laughing softly. They talked about anything that came to mind, then sat quietly, reveling in the warmth of the still air and the music of nature. To top off the day, Justin had presented her with a delicate gold locket in the shape of a heart, which she'd worn ever since.

The quilts—the Ninepatch *and* the Country Songbird— were long since completed, with the expert help of her Amish friends. Justin's painting of a colorful quilt flapping on a clothesline, as well as his version of Niagara Falls in full moonlight, left exhibitors standing wide-eyed and Katherine herself in awe of his talent.

She couldn't imagine a life more blissful. Yet she found herself thinking of Mary's letters almost daily, even discussed her concern with Justin one evening as they ate apple pie and ice cream on the screened-in, second-floor balcony high above the estate grounds.

"Mary seemed almost reluctant to mention her marriage to John," she said, recalling the letter that had come the week after Easter. "I hope she isn't worried that marrying the bishop will change our friendship."

Justin's eyes were intent on her. "Mary means a lot to you, doesn't she, darling?"

"We're as close as sisters."

"The way I see it, if the shunning didn't keep the two of you apart, neither will a new husband."

"I hope not." She described for him the bishop's severe course of action once it was clear that she was not going to confess—about not having destroyed the guitar.

"Sometimes people change," he said, his soothing voice attempting to console her.

"You don't know John Beiler."

"No, but I know what love can do, especially for an unfeeling sort of man." He continued on, telling her about one of his uncles on his mother's side. "The man was the harshest fellow you'd ever want to meet. Even young children shied away from him. Dogs cowered, cats hissed. . . ."

She thought about that. "What made him change?"

Justin smiled. "It may be hard to believe, but I think for him it had to do with finding the right woman, though I wouldn't say the perfect mate is always going to alter someone's bad behavior. In the case of my uncle, though, it did."

She pondered Justin's true-life story. Hard as she tried to imagine it, Mary's patient, loving ways would never be apt to transform the bishop of Hickory Hollow, not entirely. Yet the more she thought about Mary married to John, the more she suspected that her friend was the force behind the lifting of the talking aspect of the shunning. Surely *that* was the truth.

For the first time in many weeks, she thought of Dan. How severely had John Beiler shunned *him*?

❖　❖　❖

Mary didn't have time to go out and get the mail—not a minute to spare—until nearly four o'clock. By the time she wiped her hands on a towel and ran outside barefooted, it was almost time for afternoon milking. 'Course Hickory John, Nancy, and Levi were probably already out in the barn bringing in the cows. No need to be frettin' over that chore. Bishop John's children pretty much knew what to do and when to do it. Just keeping up with the mountains of laundry, the constant cleaning and cooking, and whatnot all, left Mary near breathless most days. Still, she wouldn't have gone back to being a single lady for all the world. Her life revolved around her husband and his children, and if anyone had asked, she would've declared she was the happiest woman alive!

Now with summer in full swing, she was worn to a frazzle, so hot and humid it was. Fanning herself with a hankie, she sat down to catch her breath and read a letter from her rich and fancy girlfriend.

Tuesday, June 30

Dearest Mary,

Will you be happy for me if I tell you that I think I know who I'm going to marry? His name is Justin Wirth, and he's an artist—paints beautiful oil paintings. I don't remember when I've ever been so happy, Mary. Honestly, it's strange this feeling I have about Justin. We talk for hours about most anything, even personal things these days. I'm so glad that I can share this with you freely and do hope that you won't worry about my future with an Englischer.

I don't know how you'll be able to come for my wedding, though I'd feel completely lost if you weren't here to share my joy. Do you think John would consent to let you ride the bus?

When I look at the sky, I never see a single cloud—even when they're scattered everywhere! Oh, Mary, did you feel this way when first you fell in love with John? Did you?

More than anything, I wish I might've witnessed your vows, seeing the precious little Beiler children gathered all about you there in Preacher Zook's front room. How sweet that they could share the special day with both you and the bishop. Although I have written this before, I will repeat that I have no hard feelings about you ending up with John. I trust he treats you with the kind of love that you deserve, my dear friend.

> *Forever and always,*
> *Katherine*

The porch swing creaked a long time after Mary finished reading. Pushing her bare toes against the wooden floor, she sat quietly, taking in the cornfield across the road while Katie's letter lay in her lap. She remembered the summer days of her childhood, growing up with Katie Lapp—the girl with all the adventuresome ideas. Like the time they played hidey-seek in the cornfield, the stalks being so thick and all, neither of them could find the other. By dinnertime, she was gut and lost . . . and crying her eyes out.

She had to smile a little, thinking back to what Samuel Lapp had said about Katie playing in the cornfield with her girlfriend. "Best be careful, girls." He'd looked mighty serious, almost worried. " 'Tis a gut way to get yourselves harvested."

Of course, they'd burst out laughing at what he'd said,

and *he* had, too. But Mary never let Katie talk her into playing in the corn again.

She sighed, ignoring the flies and several mewing barn
cats looking for a handout. Katie was gonna marry a right
fancy artist, she said in her letter. Sure sounded like she was
just gonna forget all about her Plain upbringing, keep on
turning her back on redemption, and be right contented
with her new English life.

Mary sighed so hard she pushed all her wind out, then
all of a sudden realized that Jacob was hollering for her out
back. Quickly, she returned the letter to its linen envelope
and hurried down the porch steps, around the side of the
house, past her pansy garden, and to the barnyard to see
what on earth was ailing her stepson. Later on, when she
had time to sit a spell, she would read the letter again—and
decide what, if *anything*, she could do about it.

CHAPTER TWENTY-FIVE

◈   ◈   ◈

Along toward the end of July, the lima beans were coming on mighty strong—and the ripest red Early Girl tomatoes a body ever did see. A group of women sat under the elm tree at Mattie's place, *blicking*—shelling limas—and slapping at mosquitoes.

"What's anybody hear about our wayward girl?" asked Ella Mae, sitting in a chaise lounge, doing her share of work.

Mary looked over at her and shook her head gloomily. "Last she wrote—oh, several weeks back—she was planning on gettin' married."

"Married?" said Ella Mae.

"Jah."

Rebecca started hacking, another one of her coughing fits, so Rachel Stoltzfus went inside to get her a glass of water. Meanwhile, Lydia went over and sat beside Rebecca, patting her lightly on the back. "Don't you worry now, the Lord's got His hand on your girl's life," the Mennonite woman was saying, trying to soothe the distraught mother.

"But . . . but she never wrote a thing about it . . . to me," Rebecca sputtered.

All eyes were on Mary, since she seemed to be the one

with the most recent news. "She says she's in love with an artist."

"Well, what's his name, for pity's sake?" Ella Mae spoke up, wishing she didn't feel so upset and hoping it didn't show.

"Justin Wirth," Mary replied. "A nice enough *Englischer*, I 'spect."

"Puh!" Ella Mae didn't like the sound of it. Why, the girl had up and gone *ferhoodled*, for sure and for certain. 'Course 'twasn't the first time. She thought of Katie and the day she'd run off from her wedding to Bishop John. Such a case she was—all fiery tempered. Impulsive, too.

While the women talked about other things—topics unrelated to shunnings and disobedient offspring—Ella Mae fumed. Ach, she hated hearing that Katie was so awful confused—and she'd *have* to be to contemplate marriage to anyone but the boy she was meant for. The one and only fella who could make her heart sing.

She was feeling real tired now—not her fingers, from hulling limas, as much as her eyes, drowsy from the heat and humidity. She fought off snoozing like a stubborn child long past bedtime, forcing her mind to ponder the somber and complicated story of Dan and Katie, miles apart.

Her head felt right dizzy now, yet she tried to shake it off, wondering if it was a warning sign—that she might be close to having another stroke. *What if I died today?* she thought. *Would I hear the Lord say, "Well done, thou faithful servant"?*

She felt sick all over. Still, she kept hulling limas, not wanting to call attention to herself. She thought of the People—ach, she'd failed her loved ones and friends all these years. *All these years . . .*

Her whole life had been given over to kindly works, compassionate deeds. She'd leaned her ear to a gut many folk in the Hollow—more than she could ever begin to count. That was all well and gut, yet she knew she'd betrayed them, hadn't given them what their hearts yearned for: the Good News of Jesus Christ.

An orange and yellow butterfly flew over the heads of the women, lighting on Mary's shoulder briefly, though the bishop's young bride never noticed. But the Wise Woman did, and nature's caress—and the confidence in her heart—got her thinking about miracles and such, and what she could do to change things. If it just wasn't too late.

Lydia stayed awhile after the Amishwomen left. While the other guests retrieved their horses from the barn and hitched them back up to the buggies, Lydia helped Mattie take Ella Mae indoors and get her settled in a rocking chair in the front room—even though Ella Mae said she preferred to sit outside on the front porch. Mattie thought it was time her mother stayed inside for the evening and told Ella Mae so, and the older woman didn't seem to mind too much.

Lydia sat down, talking softly about the day with her Amish friend. "We got a good many limas done."

"Jah, we did."

"And lots of catching up, too." She meant that they'd gossiped plenty.

Ella Mae nodded, but her thoughts seemed to be off somewhere else.

"You all right?" she asked.

"Ach, Lyddie, I never wanted to hide my light under a bushel basket. Never, ever," Ella Mae blurted, her eyes filling with tears.

Lydia stopped rocking and placed her hand on Ella Mae's. "The light of Jesus has been shining out of your eyes for a good many years now. I knew you loved the Lord. Everyone who ever confided in you or sipped your tea knew it, too."

Ella Mae closed her eyes. "I shoulda told them about the

Lord outright," she whispered. "Shoulda passed it on."

"It's never too late for that."

"I'm a-countin' on it, Lyddie. Before I die, that's what I'm gonna do. Starting with Mattie . . ."

They were quiet then, both women rocking in the matching hickory chairs, while Mattie rattled some pots and pans across the house in her big kitchen.

Outside, a dog barked at the buggies making the turn onto Hickory Lane, and the late afternoon sun cast a fragile glow on Ella Mae's head.

❖   ❖   ❖

Thinking that she'd gone and spilled the beans in front of all the womenfolk out of turn, without ever thinking things through, Mary gently slapped the reins against John's best Belgian horse.

She examined the sky as the light began to fade ever so slightly, though there were several more summery hours till dusk. Crickets were just waiting their turn to chirp, owls eager for nightfall. She sensed the silent expectancy in the woods as the horse trotted along leisurely. Mary was in no hurry to return home. Not just yet. The children would be clamoring for attention, though she would give it graciously . . . jah, happily. But these moments—with just herself sitting in the buggy and the steady *clip-clopping* of the horse's hooves—provided time for some peaceful reflection after a long day of work and chatter.

She hoped the news about Katie's pending marriage to the Englischer up north wouldn't set Rebecca back to where she couldn't enjoy the summer. Poor dear. The last thing in the world she wanted was to upset Katie's mamma. Only the Good Lord himself had any idea of the depths of sorrow the woman had endured for having kept the adoption secret all these years—not to mention the reality of the Meinding.

Ach, she could kick herself for blurting the wedding news out like that. What *was* she thinking?

❖   ❖   ❖

Rebecca's brain felt divided in half as she drove her buggy toward the red sandstone house. The part of her that wanted to head on up to New York and talk Katie out of marrying into the fancy world kept tormenting her. The other part wanted to honor the Ordnung, wanted to heed it without question, wanted to be prayerful for Katie, hoping the Good Lord would answer her prayers and bring her daughter back home without a battle.

And how odd. She'd come that close to volunteering to tell one of her favorite stories, yet when all the dismal talk started up about Katie in love with some artist fella—English and all—she'd clammed right up again. It was ever so strange the way she *wanted* to be the storyteller, honest she did, yet something kept her from it. Something mighty painful.

And, too, she wondered about the haunting look in Ella Mae's eyes there toward the last of the lima shelling. Himmel, she worried herself almost sick over the disturbing gaze. Something was up. As sure as she knew her aunt, something was brewing.

CHAPTER TWENTY-SIX

❖　❖　❖

The minute Katherine read the letter from Hickory Hollow, she rang for Theodore, who drove her downtown to make arrangements with the hospice. "I really hesitate to ask you this, but may I change my schedule for this week?" she asked the charge nurse.

Natalie came in the office, looking glum at first, then brightening when she spotted Katherine. "You're just the person I need to talk to."

"Oh?"

"I was wondering if you could entertain the patients with your guitar tomorrow, on your regularly scheduled day."

She noticed the dark circles under Natalie's eyes. "Is everything all right? You look exhausted."

The nurse shook her head sadly. "I've had to turn three more patients away—just this week. There's simply not enough bed space."

"Where will they go?"

"That's just it. There's no other option. Many families don't want their loved ones to die in a hospital . . . or even at home, where the cares of life can weigh in so heavily. They desire the tranquil setting that we offer." She sighed.

"If we just had a larger facility."

"Maybe something will open up," Katherine said, offering encouragement, though she had no idea where such a place might be. Not in Canandaigua. Perhaps in Rochester. But that city was inconvenient for families and loved ones who lived here. She understood perfectly why Natalie's eyes were sorrowful.

"I wish I could help you tomorrow with the music, but I really must beg off. I've been called home," she explained. "An old friend has suffered a stroke and wants to see me again before she dies."

"Of course, I understand. Take as much time away as you need."

"I'll be glad to make up more than my share of hours when I return."

"That's kind of you," Natalie said, wishing her well.

Katherine left the hospice to purchase her bus ticket, though she wished she had the nerve to travel by plane to Pennsylvania. Something about flying brought back the Ordnung and its expectation, and for the life of her, she couldn't break the rules just now, not with her great-aunt possibly wasting away on her deathbed.

❖ ❖ ❖

"I'll be traveling to Pennsylvania tomorrow," she told Rosie upon returning to the estate.

Rosie stopped what she was doing, holding a handful of unpolished silver in midair. Fulton, who sat at the kitchen table sipping coffee with Theodore, turned and gawked as well.

"My great-aunt may not have long to live. It may be days or weeks . . . hard to say," she explained. "But I don't want to risk not seeing her ever again."

"I'm terribly sorry about your aunt," said Rosie, coming

over, the silverware still poised in her fist.

"Ella Mae's lived a full life, so there's no need to feel too bad."

"Well, is there something we can do?" asked Rosie, her eyes bright with concern.

Katherine couldn't think of anything, except that she would need a ride down to the bus station first thing in the morning, a matter she mentioned to Theodore.

"My pleasure." He got up and went to the bulletin board where the week's schedule was posted.

"Thank you so much," she said, including both Rosie and Fulton in her expression, and left to start packing.

❖   ❖   ❖

At the first glimpse of Lancaster County, Katherine experienced a surprising lump in her throat. Yet she couldn't help peering out the bus window, wishing the driver would speed up and deposit her on the familiar street so she could hail a taxi and be on her way to Ella Mae. And Hickory Hollow.

The bus approached the station, and she noticed the narrow streets of downtown Lancaster, the brick row houses with their tiny stoops and cobblestone sidewalks. There was something painfully pretty about the area, the familiarity of it. A rush of memories came back. Buzzing, hot summertime: the swish of skirt against bare ankles, the feel of scorching soil between her toes, the long, fun-filled days of raspberry picking with twenty or more cousins . . . the sweet aroma of new-mown hay.

She pressed her face closer to the window, longing to see Hickory Lane again, scarcely able to wait to get there.

Once she was on her way via taxi, out of the downtown area toward Route 340, she began to relax. Past Smoketown and Bird-in-Hand, past the pretzel factory smack-dab in the middle of a tourist center at Intercourse, and on to Cattail Road and the turnoff to Hickory Hollow.

"Know anybody out here in Amish country?" asked the cab driver.

She smiled at his inquiry. "Oh, a good many."

He glanced at her in his rearview mirror. "From everything I hear about Plain folk, they like to keep to themselves—don't take too well to 'Englischers.'"

"Most of the time, that's true." She didn't especially want to reveal her circumstances. Mentioning that she had been raised Amish and then shunned would open up a whole can of worms. She wasn't in the mood.

Another couple of miles—more familiar landmarks—and she was leaning forward, fidgeting in the backseat. "Would you mind slowing down a bit?" she said, as they came within a quarter mile of David and Mattie Beiler's place.

"Want me to turn in there?"

"Stop at the next lane, please. I'll walk the rest of the way." When the taxi stopped, she paid him and stepped out.

Looking around, she took in the perky pink and white petunias lined up in meticulous rows, the red roses climbing up the lattice, the newly painted white front porch, and the rustic yard bench under the age-old elm on the east side of the Dawdi Haus. Even the air smelled remarkably fresh and homey, though she wouldn't tarry on such thoughts.

"Hullo!" Someone was calling to her. "Is that *you*, Katie?"

She recognized the voice and turned to see Lydia Miller. Her mother's cousin came running across the lawn, arms outstretched. "I didn't expect to see *you* today. How in the world are you?"

"I'm fine, thanks," Katie replied, hugging her. "How's Ella Mae?"

Arm in arm, they headed up to the house. "Oh, she has good and bad days, though I think she'll perk up a bit when she sees the likes of you." Lydia stopped in her tracks. "How did you hear?"

"Ella Mae wrote . . . asked me to come."

"Ah yes, I suppose she did," Lydia said with a knowing look.

A swarm of bees flew over their heads, and Katherine held her breath and stood still automatically, the way Rebecca had taught her to do as a child. The sound of laughter—little ones at play somewhere out in the barn, most likely—caught her interest, and she wondered which of Ella Mae's great-grandchildren might be here.

At the door, Mattie's eyes popped wide when she spotted Katherine. "My goodness gracious, where'd *you* come from?"

"Ella Mae invited me for a visit."

"Ah, sounds like Mamma," Mattie said, shaking her head.

Katherine wondered about that. "Is it all right if I come in . . . just for a short while?"

Glancing over her shoulder and looking a bit sheepish, Mattie actually dawdled about whether or not to allow her entry.

Lydia was breathing hard, as though she was terribly embarrassed over it. "Aw, Mattie, it can't hurt none for Katie to visit," she said softly. "Last I heard, the shunning was lifted a bit."

Mattie waved her hand as if shooing a fly, her face languid. "What if Bishop John gets word?"

"Ella Mae will be expecting me," Katherine insisted. "I won't stay long. I promise."

Reluctantly, Mattie opened the front screen door. "I

don't want this gettin' out—don't need any trouble just now."

"I understand," she said.

Lydia stayed in the kitchen with two other Plain women, and Mattie offered to take Katherine through the front room to the Dawdi Haus.

Ella Mae was sitting in her rocking chair next to the front room window when Katherine entered. Looking up, the woman's face broke into a crooked smile. "Oh, Katie . . . Katie," she said, holding out her shriveled hand, her voice huskier than ever.

Katherine didn't bother to correct Ella Mae. Even though she very much wanted to be called Katherine, things were different here. "Glad to see you up and dressed," she said. "I came as soon as I received your letter."

Ella Mae nodded, offering a weak smile. "I hoped you'd come. Denki, I appreciate it . . . more than I can say."

Pulling up one of the cane chairs in the room, Katherine sat beside her aunt. "It's been the longest time since we've had a chat. When was your stroke?"

Ella Mae began to count on her deformed fingers, then gave up as if she couldn't recall. "Not too long ago. Couldn't talk or move my hands . . . hardly anything worked on me there for a gut while."

"Did you see a doctor?"

"No, no. Don't need no doctors when I've got friends."

She expected that. "You haven't changed a bit. Still have your spunk, that good sense of humor."

Ella Mae worked her head up and down. "You haven't changed neither . . . not really. Under all them fancy clothes, I think we've still got our Katie girl."

"Well, I don't know. I suppose there's a good part of me that's similar." She went on to say how nice it was to be back in Hickory Hollow. "Especially now. I felt like taking my shoes off as soon as I got out of the taxi."

"You came thataway? By taxi?"

"Did you expect me to ride up in a golden carriage?" She chuckled, feeling free and easy. "I left my fancy limousine back in New York. Best not to stir up the bishop, right?"

They had a good laugh over that. Then Ella Mae's voice softened, her eyes filling with tears. "There's something I wanna tell ya, Katie. I shoulda come out with it long before now." Her face was flushed.

Katherine reached for her hand. "Are you all right?"

The Wise Woman nodded but remained silent. Tears began to flow down her wrinkled face. "I never told you about Jesus," she whispered. "All these years I kept it to myself. Oh, I showed God's love to folk, sure, but I didn't say nothin' about the way He changed my life, forgave my sins . . . gave me joy." She paused, her eyes on Katherine. "Now I'm tellin' everybody I know. 'Course, the People think I'm *Dummkopp*—clear off my rocker."

"I never knew this about you," Katherine managed. "But I'm not surprised. There was always something special about you."

"Will ya forgive me for waitin' so long, Katie?"

An unsettled, prickly feeling came over her, something akin to the way she'd felt on that first visit to Laura's church. She felt her throat constrict, making her unable to speak. So she nodded, tears clouding her sight.

Ella Mae continued. "I just couldn't let myself die before tellin' you what I know in my heart, that I'm goin' to heaven someday. And it has nothin' whatever to do with pride or any such thing. I'm saved, Katie . . . I belong to Jesus."

The salvation of the righteous is of the Lord. . . .

The words on Laura's headstone echoed in her memory.

"It seems here lately," Katherine confessed, "everywhere I turn, I keep hearing the same thing—that the Lord Jesus loves me, that He died for *me*. . . ."

Ella Mae was still, eyes fixed on her.

"I knew there would come a day like this . . . sure as the heavens." Katherine searched her skirt pocket for a tissue. "I've felt it for months now." She paused to dry her eyes. "Oh, Ella Mae, I think you're right. God *is* calling me."

The Wise Woman closed her eyes, and tears squeezed out of the corners. Leaning her head back against the rocker, she remained that way without speaking—absolutely motionless—until Katherine thought she'd passed on to glory.

"Ella Mae?"

Weary eyes fluttered. "Praise be" came the raspy reply. "I prayed I'd live to see this day."

Katherine got down on her knees beside the rocking chair. Looking up at the Wise Woman, she pleaded with her; the ache in her heart had become unbearable. "Will you . . . help lead me to your Jesus?"

❂   ❂   ❂

After her tearful prayer, Katherine felt light as the clouds flitting across the afternoon sky. She stood in the window, marking the moment. She memorized the way the sun's rays cast a holy light on Hickory Lane, on the many-sided martin birdhouse in the front yard, on the wide, toothed leaves of the elm tree.

A warm breeze blew against her face and hair, and she knew she was a child of God. "My birth mother should be singing with the angels along about now."

Ella Mae cocked her head, thoughtfully. "I think I hear music."

Katherine leaned down and kissed her aunt, so weak and

small there in her chair. "I'll never forget this day . . . or what you did for me."

"What *Jesus* did for you," Ella Mae said, a smile bursting across her ashen face.

"Yes," said Katherine. "What *Jesus* did for me."

❖   ❖   ❖

She hadn't considered the idea of accommodations, though acquiring a room for a night or two would not be a problem. It was out of the question to think of staying in any of the Amish homes in the district. None of the People would risk putting up a shunned woman, especially a "saved" one.

"Will ya be visitin' Mary while you're here? And Rebecca?" Ella Mae asked as Katherine was about to leave. "They'll be heartsick if ya don't."

"I hope to see as many folk as I can." She patted the back of her aunt's hand. "I'll come again tomorrow."

"I'll be here . . . Lord willin'."

On the way out of the Dawdi Haus, Katherine waved to several of the children—young Sally Beiler and her cousins, Ben, Noah, and Jake. How they'd grown, the boys especially.

Seeing the youngsters made her think of the bishop's family, and her thoughts flew to Mary. Dare she wander down the road to the bishop's place? She could hardly contain her joy; she had to tell her best friend about this wonderful-good day. The best day of her whole life!

She followed her heart, her feet skimming the lane.

Before she knocked, Katherine peered in through the back screen door. She could see Mary scurrying here and there in the kitchen. Checking to see if John was around, she opened the door just enough for her to slip through. Then she tiptoed to the wide doorway leading from the outside utility room to the kitchen, and craning her neck around the corner, she waited till Mary might come over to the cookstove.

Just when her friend was at the right angle to spot her, Katherine cupped her hands around her mouth. "Pst!"

Mary stared, her mouth gaping.

"Kumm mit," Katherine whispered, motioning with her pointer finger.

"Katie? Is that *you*?" Mary rushed to her and embraced her in the privacy of the utility room. "Ach, girl, let me look at ya." They held on to each other's arms, twirling around.

Laughing, they hugged again. "I can't stay but a minute, Mary, but I had to let you know I'm back."

"You've come home?"

"Just to visit. Ella Mae invited me."

"Jah, she's suffered so."

She couldn't stand there discussing her aunt's stroke, not with John bound to show up soon. "Meet me at our island tomorrow morning after milking. Can you get away?"

Mary thought for a second. "John's got some horses to shoe first thing after breakfast, and the children have their outdoor chores. So, jah, I guess I can."

"Good . . . I'll see you there." She knew Mary needed no description of their childhood retreat.

"I'll be over soon as I can."

Katherine kissed her friend's plump cheek, then turned to go.

"Katie? Are ya married?"

"Not yet, why?"

Mary's eyes twinkled. "Well, ya just look so awful happy . . . that's all."

"There's a right good reason for that. I'll explain it tomorrow."

"Gut, then," Mary whispered, seeing her to the back door. "Hurry now, and God be with ya, dear friend."

"Oh, He is, Mary. He *really* is!"

CHAPTER TWENTY-SEVEN

❖　❖　❖

It was a morning of bright haze. Sunlight poured into the upstairs bedroom at Lydia's. Katherine had had only to show up on the Millers' doorstep the evening before and she was taken in with open arms. "No rent due here," insisted Peter, grinning when he first spotted her.

So she was back in her former room, high in the eaves, close to the sky . . . no, heaven. She'd had difficulty settling down to sleep after talking away the supper hour with Peter and Lydia, long after dishes were done. There was much she wanted to say, so much she wanted to hear from them as well. Questions to ask, prayers to be prayed, hymns to be sung. They were ever so delighted to hear of her life-changing experience.

Now as she sat quietly in bed, contemplating her day with Mary, she read the Bible on the nightstand and afterward bowed her head. "Dear Lord Jesus, help me to share your love with my friend today. May she have an open heart. Amen."

She decided to go barefoot—it had been such a long time. And instead of wearing her hair down, she wound it up in a bun to keep her neck cool, wrapping a sheer scarf around it. The rayon dress she selected from her suitcase was short-sleeved, a sage ground floral print with broom-stick skirt. Last of all, the golden heart locket from Justin.

❖ ❖ ❖

A big white duck waddled after her, following her all the way down the mule path, out past the thicket to the pond. She cast her gaze on the pink sky—surely a foretaste of heaven—and thanked the Lord for His fingerprints on all of nature.

The duck quacked behind her, and she turned to look down at him. He'd stopped a few feet away, his beak held up, just enough to appear inquisitive, not proud. His beady eyes were fixed on something in the distance.

"Are *you* thankful, too?" She had to laugh. Here she was, on the backstretch of her Amish father's land, conversing with a duck, of all things. Who would've thought when she left New York yesterday that her eyes would be opened to God's goodness, His love, everywhere she looked?

"Better run along now," she admonished him, hurrying to the rowboat.

Not to be discouraged, the old quacker plodded to catch up. Feeling sorry for him, she snatched him up and put him in the boat with her to wait for Mary. But he must not have wanted to be confined. Jumping out, he opened his wide wings and flapped to beat the band, landing in the water.

It wasn't long before Mary came running barefoot down the dusty path. "Been waitin' long?"

She shook her head. "Get in. We've got an island to explore and plenty of catching up to do."

They sat across from each other in the rowboat, just as they always had as children, laughing and talking, their voices echoing off the water as swallows trilled overhead.

Partway across the pond, Mary brought up Dan Fisher. "Word has it, he's given up on you."

"I suppose he has, and for all good reason." She explained about the visit in New York and his unexpected letter weeks later. "I never wrote back. Didn't see the need."

"Your lives have changed too much? Is that it?"

"Everything's changed, Mary. Everything."

"So you know all about what happened to him, then— why he decided to let us think he was dead after the boating accident?"

"Well, no. I never gave him a chance to. That day when he showed up out of nowhere . . . I was so upset, I really couldn't think straight." She hung her head, suddenly ashamed. "I asked him to leave, actually."

Mary's eyes were understanding and kind, as always. "I 'spect that's all you could do."

"Mamma wrote once that Dan's story was a sad one, but I never bothered to ask what she meant."

So Mary began to tell her everything, how Dan had wanted to spare his loved ones—all the People, really—from having to shun him. "And especially you. It would've torn his heart out, having to endure you turnin' your back on him. He'd rather have been dead."

She sighed. "Which he was to *us*, all those years."

"He thought he was protecting us, I s'pose."

Katherine pondered these things in silence and wondered how Justin might feel if he knew she was discussing her first love, all these miles away.

"You look like you just had your first kiss," Mary said, staring right at her.

"I guess I do." She stopped rowing. Now was a befitting time to speak up about the glorious thing that had happened at Ella Mae's yesterday. "I don't know if you'll understand what I have to tell you," she began. "Lately, I've been hearing, almost on every hand, that the Lord Jesus is close to us in everything we do."

Mary listened, still rowing toward the island.

Forging ahead, Katherine told about the New York minister's sermon and the very words she'd read for herself in Laura's Bible. She revealed, too, what things Dan had written in his long letter. "I understand now why he wanted to study the Bible . . . why he was always sneaking off to prayer meetings with the Mennonites."

Mary gave ear, though she wasn't as receptive as Katherine had hoped. Her reluctance came out of fear, no doubt.

"John wouldn't hear of this, would he?" Katherine asked finally.

Mary's deep frown gave her away. "You *know* what I believe, Katie. I'm trusting God for my salvation, and I do hope with all my heart that heaven will be my reward when I die."

She shook her head. "But we don't have to earn our way. Jesus died so that we could *know* our sins are forgiven—here and now."

Mary clammed up instantly. It seemed that enough seeds had been sown for one day.

Still, Katherine was bubbling over. "You must think I'm silly, talking about the Lord this way and not saying a word about confessing . . . returning to the Amish church."

"It's hard, not knowin' what to think." Mary's eyes were earnest.

The young women rowed all the way to the island. "I pray that you'll find this happiness, too," Katherine said, stepping out of the little boat onto dry land.

Mary nodded. "I'm as happy as I ever dreamed I'd be. John's a gut husband, and I love him."

Katherine said no more, lest she spoil things between

them. And when the air had cleared a bit, they began to relive the old days. They laughed together, carefree and childlike, as they ran among the willows, splashed each other in the pond, and tossed seeds to the ducks.

Out of breath, they sat on the grassy bank, overlooking the sparkling pond. They wiggled their bare toes, enjoying the hot sun.

Mary squinted up at the sky. "I 'spect it's about time I headed back home."

"Aren't much used to *duckmeisich*—sneaking off—are you?"

Mary smiled, then her face grew serious. "It's time to put away childish things. I'm a wife and a mother. I've had my fun." She picked up two pebbles and tossed them into the pond. "Won't ya come home for gut?"

Katherine's heart ached. "I'm sorry . . . really I am. I just don't see how."

Silently, they got in the boat and rowed away from the shore to the other side.

❖   ❖   ❖

Hours later, Katherine heard a knock on Lydia's front screen door and went to investigate.

There stood Rebecca. "I heard you were back," she said, her hair disheveled some, apron smudged. "I rushed right over."

Katherine opened the door and wrapped her arms around the stout woman, hugging her hard. "Oh, Mamma, I'm glad you came!"

They stood gazing into each other's eyes for a time. "I figured comin' to see ya at Lydia's was the best thing."

She knew Rebecca was referring to the Meinding, which in spite of her furtive visit with Mary was still in force. Nothing much had changed. She was an outcast of the People, compelled to meet her best friend, and now her adoptive mother, in secret.

"I wanted to see you in the worst way, Mamma—my brothers, too—but didn't want to get Dat's ire up."

Rebecca nodded, hazel eyes bright. "I figured so."

It was Katherine's idea to go upstairs to the room where she was staying. The house was peaceful and still, and the large bedroom afforded the hideaway they longed for.

Sitting opposite each other near the wide front window, both barefoot, they talked, eager to spend time together.

Katherine told her mother about her new friends, the Esler girls. "They're Amish. Funny, isn't it?"

Rebecca agreed that it was.

"I've been doing volunteer work at a hospice in Canandaigua. It's truly rewarding," she said, sharing the story of Willy and his family.

"You sound right settled at your new place." Rebecca's eyes narrowed a bit, though a slight smile presented itself.

"It's everything I've ever dreamed of—and more," she admitted.

"Home's where the heart is, ain't so?"

She had to say *yes* to that. Mamma was smart that way. "Well, sometime soon I'd like to pick up my chest of linens and things, maybe even the corner cupboard Dat made for me, if that's all right."

"Jah, that'd be just fine." Rebecca paused, her face peaked all of a sudden. "You'll be gettin' married soon, then?"

"Come fall, I'm thinking." It was enough to mention the wedding season, but she would bypass saying anything about Justin just now. "I would've written about it but didn't want to hurt you more than I already have. It's a sticky subject, I suspect."

"But ya wrote Mary 'bout it."

"Another one of my mistakes, probably."

Rebecca shook her head. "No . . . no, a body needs someone to talk to. I understand."

Ever kind and loving Rebecca. Katherine could hardly contain her feelings for the woman who'd raised her from infancy. "I miss you something awful," she confessed. "It's not so easy living far from your childhood home."

"I 'spect so," Mam replied.

The subject of her newfound joy came naturally, though Rebecca seemed mighty skeptical, hearing her daughter call herself anything but Amish. "Saved isn't for us to know," Mam argued.

Refusing to upset her mamma on this topic, she let Rebecca speak her mind, not interrupting. She could only hope and pray that in time, Mam would see the light of Jesus in her shunned daughter's eyes and want it, too.

❖ ❖ ❖

After lunch, Katherine felt restless—anxious to wander around Hickory Hollow. Lydia offered to drive her different places, but she wanted to be on her own. Reminisce alone.

She wished she'd brought along her guitar, for there was a spot she sorely missed. A very special place she hadn't laid eyes on for the longest time. This afternoon, with sun sizzling down on her bare head, she walked west on Hickory Lane, past Samuel Lapp's sandstone house, Bishop John's farmhouse, and the one-room schoolhouse, to Weaver's Creek.

Still barefoot, she scurried across the wobbly covered bridge, hearing the boards rumble gently under her feet. She cared not for splinters or nails, though her feet seemed mighty tender these days. On the opposite end of the bridge, she headed down the steep embankment to the creek below.

A cool breeze brushed her face as she stood there in the shade of giant trees, in awe of the site. Many an afternoon had been spent here during her teen years, though one clearly stood out above all others.

Lifting up her broomstick skirt just a bit, she waded into the cold creek, ignoring the age-old stepping stones and thrilling to the bold, splashing current. She did not hurry but took her time getting over to the huge boulder situated almost exactly in the middle of the rushing water.

"Ach, it looks smaller," she said aloud, eyeing the slab of rock. Without another thought, she climbed to the top and sat down.

Sunshine twinkled around her, making diamonds dance on the water, casting flickering shadows on the side of the bridge above. The boulder felt warm and hard beneath her hands as she sat there, breathing in the sweet air. She closed her eyes, thanking the Lord for all He had done in her life.

Three swallows flew into the spruce tree above her, and she leaned back to watch them spring from one branch to another as they chirped their secret language back and forth. She even tried to mimic their sounds, but her voice frightened them away.

"Sorry," she said, hugging her knees, wishing the sun would stand still and the earth would stop spinning long enough for her to share her delirious contentment with all the world.

Softly, she began to hum the love song she and Dan had created on this very location. The birds warbled along and the creek picked up the rhythm. In her secluded world, unseen by anyone but her Lord, Katherine began to sing the old song out loud. Feeling carefree, she sang it again, this time changing the words. She was creating a love song for the Lord Jesus, her special gift for Him.

It was as she finished the final phrase, just as she'd stood up to balance herself on tiptoes on the peak of the rock— just then—she heard whistling.

Quickly she crouched down, hoping she hadn't been noticed. Through the sun-dappled grove she saw a tall, clean-shaven man walking along the road, nearing the bridge. He could not be seen clearly, though she noticed snippets of blond hair through the trees. Had she been closer, she might've been able to make out who it was. Yet squinting and moving her head, trying to capture the full image, she concluded that the man was English, for there was no straw hat, no white shirt and suspenders. Curiously, she watched as he turned off the road and descended the steep bank of earth.

It might have been the vibrato in his whistle, the gait of his steps. Something. The way he carried himself erect perhaps. But in that moment Katherine knew him.

Her hand flew to her mouth. *Dan!*

Certain that she'd only thought his name, she was startled that he answered. "Who's there?"

She stiffened, wanting to hide. Had he been following her? But how could *that* be? No one knew she was visiting here except Rosie and Fulton and her domestic staff. Surely Dan hadn't gone back to Canandaigua, discovered she was here, and pursued her. Surely not!

As he came into the clearing at the water's edge, the light shone on his face. Their eyes met.

"Katie?"

They stared at each other awkwardly.

"What are you doing . . . here in the Hollow?" he asked.

"I should ask *you* that question." She felt suddenly defensive, not willing to give up her tranquil setting.

He held out his empty hands in surrender. "I'm out for a walk—nothing more."

She wasn't convinced. "So you *weren't* following me?"

Smiling now, he ran his fingers through his hair. "I was in the area . . . heard Ella Mae was ill."

Katherine didn't budge from her perch.

"Honestly, I had no idea you'd be here," Dan said, still standing on the edge of the creek bed. "How've you been, Katherine?"

She nodded, not certain of what to say, though it was lovely hearing him call her by her true name. Yet telling him how she *really* was—at least, at the present moment—would be a terrible mistake. She could say that she was feeling rather flustered at seeing him again, that she'd forgotten how handsome he was. Ach, she'd never admit such things.

Standing up, she said, "I'm fine, thanks, but I really have to be leaving now."

"Please . . . stay a few minutes, won't you?"

She thought it over. "Well, maybe. But not for long."

Dan stepped on the smaller rocks that dotted a path to the boulder. Before climbing, he stood at its base, frowning. Then, surveying it in much the same way as she had, he commented that the "ol' rock has shrunk some."

She had to laugh, sliding over to make room for him. "That's just what *I* thought."

Dan seemed pleased, nodding at her as he sat down with a sigh. "And I guess I'm getting older."

"Aren't we all?"

They chatted about Ella Mae for a while, then Dan grew quiet. He stared at their surroundings. "I miss it here. The Lord willing, I plan to set up my own drafting business here in Lancaster. Sometime in the fall, maybe, if things work out."

She was conscious of his nearness, listening as he discussed his hopes and dreams. "Will you be working with Mennonite contractors?" she asked later.

He turned to face her, leaning his arm on his knee. "Since I'm a shunned man, I don't expect to have any business dealings with Amish, at least not in Bishop John's district. But Mennonites, yes."

She smiled, fingering her heart-shaped locket. "So you're not coming back to confess?"

"My confession is before God, and I can honestly say that He's forgiven me."

"I know about divine forgiveness, too," she said softly.

His eyes blinked rapidly. "Are you . . . have you. . . ?"

"Yes, I've become a follower of Jesus. Ella Mae led me to pray a sinner's prayer just yesterday."

"That's wonderful, Katie!" He shook his head, obviously grateful. "I knew there was something different about you. But I thought it was just the sunlight."

They laughed about it, and Dan announced that they were now brother and sister in Christ. She heard the cheerful ring in his voice, glad she'd stayed after all.

One thing led to another, and she found herself telling him that she knew the truth of his lost years. "Mary told me why you stayed away. Honestly, I think I understand now."

His face was sober. "I prayed you'd forgive me someday, though I didn't expect it would be this soon."

"The Lord works miracles. Sometimes when we least expect them."

"That He does." He was grinning at her now.

Feeling a bit unnerved at his ardent smile, she stood up to stretch her cramped limbs. "Let's go for a walk."

He leaped to his feet. "C'mon, we'll go to the high meadow behind the school." It had been one of the favorite spots of their childhood.

She followed as he ran across the creek, marveling at the

coolness of the grass along the brook. Then up through the wide, grassy terrace for a good acre or more to open pastureland. It was almost as though the years between them had dissolved. *Almost* . . .

"Katie," he called to her, "race me to the old outhouse."

"Never," she hollered back.

"Aw, come on!"

"Not on your life!"

He chuckled, letting her catch up with him. "That's my girl."

"What did you say?"

"I . . . uh, didn't mean to say that." He shrugged, a sobering expression followed. "Come back with me, Katie. Please, come back to Lancaster." He paused, his eyes searching hers. "I have no right to say this, but I still love you. With all my heart, I do."

She was out of breath from running *and* from this strange proposal. "It's . . . it's too late. I'm seeing someone else. Someone . . ." She couldn't go on. Her heart and mind struggled with differing emotions.

"Oh, Katie . . ." He reached for her hands, holding them in both of his.

She pulled away. "You and I—we've changed so much. I have a new home and new friends. I'm fancy now, just the way I've always longed to be. You're a Mennonite . . . still Plain."

"But we're *both* Christians." He argued for all the things they loved: the outdoors, their music, Lancaster County.

"I'm sorry, Dan, really I am. If there is to be anything between us, it would have to be honest friendship."

He moved to embrace her. "For all the old times," he whispered in her ear. She patted his back in response.

She agreed to let him walk her back to Lydia's, though

their long talk turned to the weather and the landscape. Safe things.

As they approached the Millers' house, he offered his business card. "If you ever want to contact me," he said, pointing out his home address and phone number, "please, feel free."

"Friends then, jah?"

He smiled at her Dutchy remark. "The Lord bless you and your new life in Christ."

"Thanks, Dan. God bless you, too." She waved and turned to go.

"I pray you'll be very happy," he called after her.

His gracious words rang in her ears as she hurried up the porch steps.

CHAPTER TWENTY-EIGHT

❖ ❖ ❖

Theodore listened as Katherine discussed with Fulton and Rosie the differences between Amish and Mennonite practices. They had been at it for more than an hour, and his lemonade needed freshening.

Excusing himself, he headed indoors, where Selig and Garrett were preparing lunch. "How many religious perspectives do you suppose there are in the world?" he commented.

"More than one can count, I'd say," Garrett spoke up as he sharpened a butcher knife.

"But you have to hand it to Katherine," Selig offered. "She's different somehow. And she plays hymns on that guitar of hers every spare minute. Quite rousing, if I may say so."

"Even the way she looks. Why, there's a radiance to her," said Garrett. "Have you noticed?"

Theodore agreed that he had. "Life's too short not to be searching for heaven. I'm all for it."

Selig and Garrett exchanged shrugs and went back to doing what they had been doing.

He went to the pantry and opened up a new bag of white

sugar. Taking two additional teaspoons, he sweetened his glass of lemonade further.

❖   ❖   ❖

When her hospice work was finished for the week, Katherine decided it was time for some fall housecleaning. She offered to help Rosie tackle the library first, knowing that a thorough cleaning would involve dusting the many books shelved there. It would be too much for one person to accomplish alone.

"Good idea," Rosie said, scurrying off to get the cleaning supplies.

They were in the midst of dusting the topmost shelves, lifting handfuls of ancient-looking classics to clean them off, when Katherine stumbled upon several small leather-bound volumes hidden behind the thicker library books. "What are these?"

Rosie stopped her feather dusting and came to investigate. "My goodness, I believe you may have found Laura's writings."

"Her journals?"

Opening one of them, Rosie grinned. "The very ones. These are your mother's personal diaries."

It was all Katherine could do to continue the cleaning project. Rosie insisted that she stop what she was doing and take the books to her sitting room immediately for private scrutiny. Yet, in spite of her maid's coaxing, Katherine refused. What she'd started, she must finish.

So it was much later in the day, after both she and Rosie were fairly winded from climbing up and down the library ladders, dusting everything in sight, that she finally had a chance to sit down with the journals. Earnestly, she located the one Laura had spoken of on her deathbed—the bright blue journal with the correct year printed inside.

Her stomach contracted into a tight ball. What things would she discover? Had Laura *really* intended for her to find and read these intimate writings?

Before ever reading the first entry, she prayed, "Lord, please guide me to what you want me to know about my birth mother."

Then, getting herself situated in a comfortable chair, she opened to January, the first day of the new year—six months before she was born, the year Laura was only seventeen.

January 1

> *Today, Mother and Daddy and I took another long drive to the country in the snow. It's nice to have off another few days for the holidays before returning to high school. So far, no one outside my family but my boyfriend knows I'm going to have a baby. He's acting horribly strange about it, though.*
>
> *Mother says not to worry. She and Daddy will take good care of me . . . and the baby. (At least they aren't forcing me to go away to an unwed mothers' home like one of the senior girls had to last year.)*
>
> *I'm gaining weight, and sometimes I feel queasy first thing in the morning. Mother says all this is normal.*
>
> *I miss my shape . . . but I love the baby inside me.*

❖   ❖   ❖

Katherine read each page through March, poring over every word. She stopped at one point and took the diary outside, propping herself against the trunk of a tree.

April 1

> *I'm as large as a blimp—at least I feel like it. Daddy's worried because I want to drop out of school until the baby is born. He thinks I'll miss out scholastically and won't get*

to attend a good college after next year.

I cry a lot these days. Can't seem to get on an even keel with my emotions.

Mother dotes on me constantly. It's amazing what she goes through to make sure I'm comfortable. I hope (if I keep my baby) I might be as dear a mother as she is to me.

❖ ❖ ❖

April 7

A tutor from the school district comes three times a week. It's so much better than having to put up with the cruel comments at school. Especially from boys.

❖ ❖ ❖

Katherine looked up when Fulton came outside with a tray of lemonade and cookies.

"Thank you," she said and went back to her reading.

April 15

My doctor wanted to do an ultrasound so we'll know if I can deliver my baby naturally. There is a tiny little girl growing inside me.

Mother and I looked through a book of names tonight. My favorite—the most beautiful of all—is Katherine.

❖ ❖ ❖

May 5

I cried every day this whole week. I feel exhausted and dreadfully hopeless. Mother says I'm having panic attacks. Daddy wonders if I need psychological counseling.

I'm heartsick! My first and only boyfriend never loved me. Never! Why did I believe him?

I can't sleep at night. I can only cry for what I've lost. Little Katherine may never know that her father abandoned me when I needed him most.

Katherine allowed her tears to fall unchecked. What despair—the tremendous pain—her birth mother had gone through, to give life to her.

By the end of the May writings, she felt fatigued and filled with sadness for young Laura's plight.

Rosie peered out the upstairs window. "Oh, I do hope she's going to be all right, out there all by herself."

Fulton joined her at the window. "Miss Katherine appears to be weeping."

"Yes, and I doubt she'll feel much like dining with Justin tonight."

"Perhaps a lavish dinner with the artist may be just the thing to cheer our Katherine," her husband remarked.

Stepping away from the window, she hugged Fulton. "Well, aren't *you* the optimist?"

He stuck out his stomach, nearly popping the buttons on his butler's vest. "I'll take that as a compliment, my dear."

"Thank you, indeed." And she turned back to the window, praying that Katherine would learn the precious things that Laura had so wanted her to discover.

❖   ❖   ❖

June 1

I've been making an infant gown for Katherine. It's the prettiest satin fabric, all rosy and sweet.

Daddy isn't putting pressure on me to make a decision, but his eyes fill with concern every time I look his way. Mother, on the other hand, I think is hoping that I keep my baby. She's left big hints about being ready for a grandchild.

Either way, I want my little girl to be happy. I think I'm leaning toward raising her myself. But I'm not so sure about bringing another child into this mansion. Would it be the best thing for her? The servants will spoil her terribly, and she'll never know what it means to work for what she wants.

Sometimes, I secretly wish we were of moderate means . . . or even poor. The books I read about poor people make me wonder if they aren't happier.

Little Katherine kicks me hardest in the early morning. I wonder if that means anything.

❖ ❖ ❖

June 4

Mother wants to take me on a trip to Pennsylvania. She has the go-ahead from the doctor. I know what she's thinking. The trip will be a distraction for me. I don't blame her for worrying. I've been through the wringer in more ways than one.

She promises that I'll love Lancaster County. I almost feel like I've visited there before, maybe because Mother loves it so much. We'll see what I think of the Plain people she keeps describing.

Getting away from here might not be such a bad idea. I want to take Katherine's baby gown along. The hem stitching is all that's left to do. Won't my darling baby look beautiful?

❖ ❖ ❖

June 6

Yesterday I gave birth to Katherine, the most darling baby I've ever seen. But I gave her up, and my stomach felt so sick later, and my head ached for hours. The doctor gave me a sedative so I could sleep.

I don't know if it's possible for me to write everything about the day without sobbing my way through, but I must try. I never want to forget the way I felt or how I made my important decision about my baby—so I'll hurry to get it down on paper while the memories are fresh.

Our chauffeur drove around the back roads in Lancaster on such a pretty day. Even Mother said it was a perfect day to spend in Amish country.

Now I know why she wanted me to come here. It was so peaceful and charming, like pictures out of an old classic. I started to relax the minute we got off the busy highway. Little gray buggies with horses pulling them were everywhere, and farmers with straw hats—even young boys and girls—worked the fields.

When I saw the first covered bridge, I couldn't believe it. It was enchanting to me—so foreign to what I knew, yet so inviting.

The more we rode around, the more I fell in love with Amish country. Strange as it is, I even wondered (and mentioned it to Mother) what it would be like to grow up Plain. Such a different world from my own. The farmhouses and the barns with their tall silos made me want to look inside. Why was I so curious about this simple life? Why, when I had everything a wealthy family could ever offer?

I hid my tears while I watched a group of barefoot Amish girls work in the garden. They were picking strawberries and making a game of it. (Something I know nothing about.)

I think I cried because I didn't want my baby to grow up the way I had, an only child. No brothers or sisters to play with. (And, worse, little Katherine would have no father.)

Something beautiful was calling to me. I felt like I had come home—to a place I'd longed for my whole life. And if this was how I felt while carrying my baby—so close to being born—maybe there was a very special reason why Mother had brought me here.

She stopped reading, the realization of Laura's decision encompassing her thoughts, her heart.

The sky was bluer than she'd remembered seeing it since last summer, and a hint of fall was in the air. A flock of birds flew overhead, their flapping wings reminded her of the duck who'd stubbornly tagged along after her that July day as she and Mary were about to revisit their island.

Leaning her head against the tree trunk, she opened the journal again and finished reading the June entries.

My heart nearly broke when I heard Katherine's first wails. The doctor placed her in my arms and we cried together. I kissed her soft head and wondered if I'd ever love another human being as much as I loved tiny Katherine at that moment.

Minutes later, there were noises in the hallway. People rushing about. A nurse was telling one of the doctors that there'd been a stillbirth. A young Amish couple. . . .

I must have known then in my heart why we had come to Lancaster. My baby was going to grow up here. I wanted her to fill the empty arms of a broken-hearted woman. I wanted her to run barefoot in the meadow, catch fireflies, learn to make quilts, and pick strawberries in the hot sun. I wanted my dear Katherine to work and play hard, to have all the simple things I'd missed out on. Most of all, I wanted her to be loved by a complete family. And I wanted her to grow up Plain.

Gazing heavenward, Katherine wept silently. A gentle breeze blew a handful of leaves off the tree, a sure sign of fall.

After a time, she dried her eyes and rose, hurrying into the house. Justin would be arriving in only a few hours, and she suspected that the evening had been well-planned, possibly a special occasion. She'd caught him whispering to Rosie in the entryway a few nights ago when he'd escorted her home from yet another fancy outing.

Quickly she bathed and dressed, then swept her hair into an elegant twist, securing it with another one of Laura's gem-studded combs. Tonight she would tell her darling of the beautiful journal she'd found. Because Justin had been extremely fond of Laura, she knew he would appreciate, too, the cherished words.

The apple green dress she chose was the most exquisite in her wardrobe, and yet it boasted simple, clean lines—less dazzling than other gowns she owned. And it was satin. Even as a teen, her birth mother had also loved the feel and sound of satin.

Katherine stood in the drawing room, not wanting to wrinkle the tea-length dress. Waiting for the doorbell, she placed a light stole around her shoulders to ward off the evening chill.

"You look truly lovely tonight," Rosie commented, an inquisitive smile on her round face.

"Do enjoy yourself, Katherine," said Fulton, standing in readiness near the door.

She thanked them both cordially. Then merrily, yet modestly, she smiled back at herself in the wall mirror across the room. Standing there, she grasped the effect her image represented. Yes, everything young Katie Lapp had ever dreamed of had come to her, to the mistress of Mayfield Manor, in the most extraordinary fashion.

Only one desire remained yet to be fulfilled.

❖ ❖ ❖

Candlelit and elegant, the stately dining room was as intimate and lovely as any setting Katherine had ever visualized. Justin was attentive, as always, and she felt at ease sharing the revealing phrases from Laura's year as an unwed mother.

"She loved you dearly," he said, reaching across the table for her hand. "Just as I do, Katherine." His sincere smile warmed her heart.

Waiting, longing to hear his words of commitment, she spooned up a bite of the fruit-flavored sorbet.

Eyes shining, he reached into his suit coat pocket. "This is for you, Katherine." He presented her with a small square box.

With trembling fingers, she opened the lid. A brilliant diamond solitaire! "Oh, Justin, it's . . . exquisite!" She could scarcely speak for the emotion.

"May I?" He placed it gently on her finger.

Staring down in amazement, she blinked back the tears. "I . . . I don't think I've ever seen such a ring."

"You'll wear it every day for the rest of your life, my dear," he said, his eyes shining.

Something beautiful was calling me. . . .

She held her hand out in front of her, admiring the engagement ring. Ach, what a large gem. It must have cost him a fortune.

I secretly wish we were of moderate means . . . even poor.

"My goodness, you're going to spoil me," she found herself saying. "I never dreamed I'd own such a wonderful piece of jewelry."

"Every time you look at it, Katherine, I hope you'll be reminded of my love, darling."

I wanted you to run barefoot in the meadow . . . to be loved by a complete family.

They went about their dining, enjoying the next course, served up on fine china, the edge of the platter rimmed in gold. She supposed she should feel elated just now, thrilled beyond belief. Every aspect of the evening was lovely: the tantalizing setting, her handsome suitor, and the engagement ring.

But the longer she stared at the diamond, the less it suited her. Not that it wasn't the prettiest thing she'd ever imagined. Oddly enough, she was thinking of Rebecca's hand. Never had Mamma worn even the simplest wedding band. Yet lifelong vows had remained as strong as her love for Samuel Lapp and for each of her four children—the boys and Katherine, too.

Her chest felt ever so heavy. Excusing herself, she fairly ran to the ladies' room. Great sobs wracked her body, and she had to sit down at the dressing table, her head buried in her hands.

Laura's whispered words as she lay dying had made all the difference. Now Katherine understood completely.

Lest she embarrass herself, she removed several tissues from the receptacle, wiping the mascara smudges from her cheeks. She dabbed at her face and applied fresh lipstick, her thoughts racing back to the things she'd most enjoyed while living here in the Finger Lakes. Ironically, they included her Amish friends—the Esler girls and their mother—the many quilting sessions at the estate, bread baking with Garrett and Selig, and entertaining and treating the hospice patients with music and Mississippi Mud.

Yet she had desperately longed to abandon her background, wanting to experience the fancy English world. The realization bewildered her, and over and over she murmured as she repaired her face, "I was meant to be Plain."

Then, bowing her head, she began to pray. "Dear Lord Jesus, I believe you placed me in Samuel Lapp's home for a reason. You had your hand on my life, always protecting me for the day when you would reveal the truth of the gospel . . . waiting for me to come to you with open arms, to accept your love. Please forgive me for coveting the world and its extravagance. This I pray in Jesus' name. Amen."

As difficult as it would be, she had to pull herself together and return to the romantic setting. Justin would worry, and he should not be kept waiting.

CHAPTER TWENTY-NINE

❖ ❖ ❖

She set out early to accomplish a full day of errands and appointments, starting with a visit to Mr. Cranston, her attorney, as well as a stop at the bank and a visit with Mrs. Esler, Rachel, and Ruth.

By nightfall she had summoned her entire domestic staff. The meeting was held in the library—cordial for some, tearful for others. Rosie seemed resigned to the announcement, though Theodore's eyes were cast down as Katherine's plans were revealed.

The next day Theodore drove her to the hospice. "I can't say that I agree with what you wish to do, though I suspected the day might come."

She listened, feeling sympathetic toward the old gentleman. "I'll always remember you, Theodore," she said. "You've been like a grandfather to me, you know?"

That brought a smile, and in the rearview mirror, she could see it spill across his dear face.

Natalie seemed pleased to see her, especially on an unscheduled day. "What a nice surprise," she said, inviting Katherine into her office.

They exchanged pleasantries, even chatting about various patients, some who had passed away since her last visit.

"What brings you today?" the nurse asked, sitting at her desk.

"I've decided to make some major changes in my life."

"Oh?" Natalie's face was sober.

"For the longest time now, I've had an idea stirring around in the back of my head," she began, her heart pumping with the excitement. "I've taken the initial steps and have discussed the plan with my attorney, so there won't be a holdup on the legal end of things."

Natalie leaned forward, eyes intent on her.

"On behalf of this hospice, I would like to make a proposition. . . ."

❖ ❖ ❖

The bed linens and a few items of clothing were the only things left to be packed. Dan had kept at it for two days straight, accepting offers of help from Owen and Eve, though he hesitated to have them quite so involved in the moving process, since Owen was losing his business partner because of Dan's decision to relocate.

Moving back to Lancaster as a grown man—a businessman accustomed to a large clientele in the Newark area—would be risky, to be sure. But he longed for his roots, was eager to get home again. Though the Old Order relationships would be strained for many years to come, he desired to fellowship with his Amish relatives on some level, guarded as it would always be. Perhaps it was the error of his ways—the manner in which he had abandoned them for so long. In some subconscious way, returning home might partially remedy that, might atone for his five-year misdeed.

It was late in the afternoon when he paused to pour himself a tall glass of water. Thinking about what he could fix for a light supper, he stood at the living room window, staring out.

A long black limousine crept slowly down the street, coming to a stop at the curb in front of his house. He peered out curiously, the darkened windows hampering his view of the people inside. Some very important folk had taken a wrong turn and had ended up in this quiet middle-class neighborhood.

Taking a deep breath, Katherine glanced down at the business card in her hand. "I think this must be the house."

Theodore turned and nodded. "If you don't mind, I'd like to wait . . . just to be certain."

She thought it a good suggestion. Gathering her bag and her guitar, she waited for him to come around and help her out of the car. She'd learned over the months not to argue with the portly gentleman. And he was definitely that: a gentleman of the highest order.

He surprised her by giving her a courtly kiss on the cheek. "I'll miss you, Katherine," he said. "All of us at the manor will."

She threw her arms around him. "I'll miss you, too, Theodore. But we'll see each other again. I promise!"

A slender, auburn-haired woman emerged from the limousine wearing a long, flowing simple dress. Her hair fell softly over her shoulders, and she stood with the poise of a princess.

Dan gave a furtive glance, attempting to determine who this pretty young woman might be. Watching as she embraced the dignified-looking chauffeur, he was astonished when she turned to walk up the sidewalk. "Goodness' sakes, it's Katie!"

Briskly, he smoothed his hair, fumbling with his shirttail, pushing it down into his jeans, striving to look presentable amidst his packing and boxes. His Katie girl was coming to his doorstep. What could it mean?

Breathing fast, he checked the window again.

Katherine's heart was in her throat. Trembling, she reached for the doorbell, wishing she'd taken time to brush her hair.

But the door swung wide, almost before she was truly ready for the moment. There stood Dan, his eyes fixed on her, same as the day he'd come upon her at Weaver's Creek.

"Katie?"

She felt awkward, at a loss for words, quite nearly aching. "Still friends?"

His eyes searched hers and held their gaze. "The dearest friend ever." Then he stepped aside, opening the door. "Please, will you come inside?"

She could see that he was packing as she set down her guitar. "I hope I'm not interrupting. I wouldn't have come if—"

"I'm *glad* you came."

She looked into the face of the boy she had loved, a grown man with tender blue eyes, disheveled blond hair, and a tentative, heartbreaking smile. She felt the beat of her own heart. Trying to smile for him, her mouth quivered uncontrollably. "Can you . . . forgive me, Daniel?"

"Forgive *you?*" A frown lit on his brow.

"For rejecting you, for—"

"Oh, Katie." His hand reached up to caress her face. It was as if he was reaching back through the long years, through the pain-filled past—to her. "I *love* you, darling. There's nothing to forgive." And he took her in his arms.

Yielding to his strong embrace, she felt his heart pounding, fast as her own. "Take me home with you," she whispered. "Take your Katie girl home to Hickory Hollow."

The past and present faded with his kisses, and her heart sang, responding with joy.

EPILOGUE

◆　◆　◆

My struggle with the Old Order prayer veiling has come to a blissful end. Reverently, I now wear the formal Mennonite covering in obedience to God and to my husband. Such a blessing and delight it is to follow my dear Lord Jesus in this simple act of faith.

Daniel took me as his bride, before God and the many witnesses—mostly Mennonites—who assembled at the Hickory Hollow meetinghouse. I had no idea until much later, after most everyone had gone home, that Mamma had been present for the wedding service, too.

I had returned to the church sanctuary to locate an extra bulletin for our wedding scrapbook. High in the balcony Rebecca stood, looking as radiant as any bride's mother should. "Stay right there," I called to her, rushing around to the stairs.

We kissed and hugged like the long-lost friends we were.

"Katie," she said, touching my white dress, "you're as perty as a picture."

"I can't believe you came, but I'm ever so glad you did!"

She smiled and her hazel eyes lit up like heaven, the way they always used to, back before my shunning. "I wouldn't have missed seein' ya joined with your Daniel . . . not for the world."

"Oh, Mamma, thank you." I held her close. "You don't know what this means to me."

She asked if Dan and I would come for dinner sometime soon. " 'Course you'll hafta sit at separate tables from us, but we'll scoot them close and throw a tablecloth over both of them."

"Yes, of course, we'll come. But, Mamma, following the Ordnung isn't what matters. Don't you see, being a follower of *Jesus* is what counts?"

Her eyes were misty now, and she gripped my hands in hers. "Keep on prayin' for us, Katie. Will ya?"

"I promise you that."

She asked about our honeymoon plans, and I said we were headed up to Canada. "But we'll be stopping off in Canandaigua on the way home. Dan and I are planning a hymn concert of two guitars at the Mayfield Hospice."

Rebecca looked puzzled, then the light dawned. "What did you *do*, Katie—give away your birth mother's estate?"

I wanted her to know. "Not to boast, Mam, but I offered Laura's mansion to the hospice, and they accepted. The Taylors—Rosie and Fulton—have decided to live there, working as full-time volunteers, and last I heard, Selig and Garrett were thinking of staying on as cooks."

"Ach, what a blessing you are." Her hands were clasped close to her heart as if she were about to pray.

"My search is over, Mamma. All the scraps and pieces of my life are a God-ordered design . . . like one of your beautiful quilts. I was looking for fancy things and found a personal relationship with the Lord Jesus. I was yearning for my roots and found a portion of heaven on earth." I patted the small white Bible I'd carried under my wedding roses. "It's all right here, Mamma. I just didn't know it."

"Jah," she said, grinning. "You're soundin' like a wise woman to me."

Thinking of Ella Mae, I said, "I believe that spot was filled years ago."

Mam's eyes brimmed with tears. "I gave my first Tellin' yesterday. The first story in a gut long time."

"And it won't be your last." I hugged her to me, then looked her full in the face. "Mamma, I'm ever so thankful the Lord chose *you* to raise me . . . to be my mother."

She smiled so sweetly I thought my heart would break anew.

❖   ❖   ❖

When the time came to set up housekeeping in our new home, I selected a place of honor for both the corner cupboard and the cedar chest Dat made back when Daniel was first courting me. How pretty they both look, and what a joy to have them as a reminder of God's goodness.

Yesterday, I sorted through my handmade linens and came across the blue Amish dress I'd sewn nearly a year ago. Rather than discard it, I wrapped it in tissue paper, along with the rose-colored baby gown. Together, the two articles of clothing tell a wonderful-good story, truth be known.

So, the Lord willing, I'll grow very old with Dan by my side. He'll serenade me on his guitar while I sow straight rows of tomatoes and a few rutabagas. I'll sing and play for him, too, after his long days of blueprint making. Above all, we'll share the love of Jesus in song wherever He leads us. And should the Lord bless us with children and grandchildren, they'll hear our story and probably beg for more.

ACKNOWLEDGMENTS

❖   ❖   ❖

I wish to thank the National Stroke Foundation, the National Multiple Sclerosis Society Volunteer/Internship Program, and the Hospice of the Comforter in Colorado Springs, Colorado. I am grateful also for the friendship and medical research assistance of Kathy Torley, as well as Harriet Mason, retired hospice charge nurse, who shared the joys and sorrows and her daily routine.

Without the support of my prayer partners and dear reader-friends, this book might still be in outline form. Blessings and deep appreciation to each of you!

As always, it is a delight to work with my editors, Barb Lilland, Carol Johnson, Anne Severance, and the entire BHP editorial team. Thanks to my incredible husband, Dave, for ceaseless encouragement and vital involvement in the creative process, as well as my parents and children who helped pray (and cooked!) through the tedious times of juggling writing, parenting, and life in general. Above all, I thank my Lord Jesus, who inspires me and directs my work.